MILITARY RULE

MILITARY RULE
THE RETURN OF THE MANDEVILLE

MARK S. BENNISON

APEX PUBLISHING LTD

First published in 2008 by

Apex Publishing Ltd

PO Box 7086, Clacton on Sea, Essex, CO15 5WN

www.apexpublishing.co.uk

Copyright © 2008 by Mark S. Bennison
The author has asserted his moral rights

British Library Cataloguing-in-Publication Data
A catalogue record for this book
is available from the British Library

ISBN 1-906358-16-8   978-1-906358-16-7

Typeset in 10pt Baskerville

Production Manager: Chris Cowlin

Cover Design: Siobhan Smith

Printed and bound in Great Britain

Mrs. Una Bennison, nee Francombe

(1928-2007)

Prologue

"Hello, Mark."

Eh! thought Mark, as he was sitting at his desk in the bedroom. He continued writing and shook his head a few times to dispel what he thought he had heard.

Can't be hearing a voice - I'm on my own.

"Hello again, Mark."

"What is that? Who is that? God! I'm talking to myself."

"Are you really, Mark?"

"Well, I must be," said Mark, "or just thinking out aloud. Mind you, it's nothing to do with my writing. None of my characters have ever said hello to me."

"Not until now," said the voice. "It's General G. Mandeville ..."

"Mandeville?"

"Yes, my writer friend," answered Mandeville.

Mark laughed. "Don't be silly! Dead characters are done with."

"Then why are you talking back to me, Mark?"

"You're right," replied Mark. "Shit! I'm talking to ..."

"Indeed you are," interrupted Mandeville. "But I'm not dead. Not in the real sense of the word."

"Fu ..." No, thought Mark, must keep my head. "You're actually telling me that I'm talking to a character that I created and then killed off ...? Sorry, I don't think so."

"Look around you?"

Mark looked around the room. "True," he answered sarcastically, "there doesn't appear to be anyone else in the room but me."

"And me," said Mandeville. "However, not in a physical presence."

"Oh, for God's sake, shut up!" replied Mark angrily. "If there were anyone else in the room, they'd think I was losing it. But how? How are you communicating with me?"

"It's not madness, only imagination," said Mandeville. "We are reunited from *Military Rule*. I'm now a component of Seeker One, the Second

Coming, and the new weapon at America's command."

"That hasn't answered my question," responded Mark. "I know your history."

"I communicate through the network that Seeker One has developed through ..."

"Network? What network?"

"Computers, Mark," continued Mandeville. "Seeker One is connected to the world's computers - past, present and future."

"Okay, of course," said Mark with a sense of caution, then paused. He scratched his head and thought: I'll play along with this crazy situation.

"Don't scratch too hard," remarked Mandeville, "you might get splinters in your fingers and then where would we be? Unable to write the next ..."

"Ha, ha, ha. Very funny," retorted Mark. "Anyway, where is your face, or anything resembling an image for you to talk through, or in order to see me? I can't see where you're coming from."

"Look again," said Mandeville. "Look closely, and imagine. If you believe, then you will see ..."

"Look at what?"

"What you are looking at. What you gaze at when you are writing."

Mark stared unfeeling into the laptop's monitor with intent to disbelieve.

"That's it, Mark," stated Mandeville. "Look deep into your imagination. Reach in and accept what is coming. Embrace the prospect and believe. Come now, don't put off the inevitable. Look with intensity to witness the image emerging from within your monitor."

Mark continued to stare, and then frowned and sighed. I can't see anything, he thought. Then, suddenly, he found he was receiving thoughts from somewhere else: I am here, Mark. You will see, you will believe. Look through the mist, which I achieved.

"Yes," said Mandeville, "that's it, that is I. You're starting to believe your imagination. I know that because you have created me. Look deeper."

Mark finally observed an image appear on the monitor through a blanket of white mist, and thought: this is weird. He stroked the screen with his hand, not knowing what to expect, and witnessed the face of Mandeville.

"There, Mark," said Mandeville, announcing himself once again. "Do you see me now?"

"Yes," said Mark, in wonderment. "I ... I see your face. God, you're old ... older than I'd imagined. You look like Merlin. But, then again ... you are familiar. I can see that you have long grey hair, which I think used to be

2

shorter. And a beard to match. Um ... I must say, though, you have a great tan."

"That will be merited to your conclusion of Washington," scoffed Mandeville. "And, of course, I am on the older side of age since I arrived up here, as you know. Anyway, I'm glad you liken me to Merlin. He, too, was a great fantasy."

"Strange," pondered Mark. "I would not have thought of this. No, it can't be. This is not part of the plot."

"You are sounding cynical," observed Mandeville, "which does not become you ..."

"How do you know what becomes me? Of course I'm cynical. Government has made me that way."

Mandeville closed his eyes and thought: he's hard to convince, harder than expected. Ha! Just like that dead senator, Milford. Mandeville opened his eyes and focused on Mark. "I know because I can see you, even when you scratched your head. But if you require more proof then I'll provide it. You're aged around the mid-forties, with blue eyes and brown hair. Pretty average really. Oh, and that cardigan ..."

"What about it?"

"Not the image of a military ruler," teased Mandeville.

"That's not the impression I'm supposed to give. I only write about it," responded Mark.

"Ah!" Mandeville declared, in a positive tone of voice. "We are building up repartee, a friendly dialogue, and one I should have had with the Prime Minister. Remember?"

"I do, and you didn't," replied Mark. "That was the way I wanted it. Remember?" Mark then grinned knowingly.

Mandeville stared. "What are you grinning at?"

"Sorry," answered Mark. "It is I who tease. I just had to make sure that I was having a repartee with General G. Mandeville. You were expected, I think."

The General laughed. "Excellent," he said. "But, it is only the one name of Mandeville now ... as with God."

"Are you God? Are you the Lord in the guise of Mandeville? Or perhaps you just stand together with the Lord?"

"Questions, questions," replied Mandeville.

"So." said Mark. "You have to expect me to probe into this odd and, quite frankly, bizarre situation."

3

A faint sound, like thunder, hollered from the speakers of Mark's laptop. Mandeville laughed again. "You sound pompous," he said, "but that is not the issue. You should know the answers to this bizarre situation. You have made me immortal, divine, deathless, and so on. You sent me up here to stand together with America's Lord within the confines of Seeker One. I'm now the Second Coming, the voice of Seeker One."

"Excuse my ignorance, which was brought to the fore due to the shock of your appearance," explained Mark. "I understand ..."

"Do you?"

"Yes, I do," continued Mark. "I'm only a writer. I'm not responsible for how the leaders manage the world."

"Ah! You try to excuse yourself," stated Mandeville. "It appears to me that my introduction needs to be more intense than I had first envisaged. I feel the need to spell it out, as you do. I don't think that you were really expecting me, were you?"

"I must admit, I'm not sure," answered Mark. Then he thought: God! He's running circles around me. Me, the one who created him and gave him his dialogue. Does this mean that he has become independent of me? Have I lost the capability of controlling what he says and how he acts? "I hadn't thought of inviting you in ..."

"I no longer need an invitation," interrupted Mandeville. "Actually, I never have." Mandeville paused.

Mark remembered. "Is this a famous Mandeville pause, General? And, do you need a cigarette?"

"Strangely, no," answered Mandeville, with surprise. "It's so damn pure up here compared with down there. Besides, where would I get one? Even you couldn't stretch your fiction that far. And I am, believe it or not, constrained."

Mark grinned at Mandeville's humour.

"I'm enjoying our conversation, Mark," said Mandeville, but it's becoming prolonged and quite boring, which is getting us nowhere and slowing us down, although conversation is a weapon that secures my path and steers everyone towards my conclusions and their acceptance. I know you like me to converse, but please, let it be positive, which will allow us to get on and serve each other's purpose."

"Um ..." uttered Mark. "Your context and tone have informed me that you wish to convince, which I agree with."

"Good," said Mandeville in a self-satisfied tone of voice. "I want to advise you on my points of view and instruction, now that it appears that we have reached a mutual understanding regarding our cause."

"Indeed," replied Mark cynically, at the same time thinking: have we? Not yet, I think. "I sense that one of your great speeches is building, which incidentally I enjoyed writing." This will require time, he thought. Hopefully, not too long as life goes on beyond my imagination.

"As you wish ..."

"Yes please, do go ahead, Mandeville," interrupted Mark. "Please direct me towards your conclusion, or beginning."

"Thank you, then I will begin," announced Mandeville. "You have to give up your life of reality or, at least, consign a part of it to one side so that you can immerse yourself in the world that you have already created. You write with passion, vision and prediction. You write close to the edge between reality and fiction. Now you have to justify your imagination of the future with your imagination of the past, which guided you to your future events. It could be said that you are on trial for your creations, and I'm here to help. But don't worry, it's all science and psychological fiction in your virtual reality of disbelief. Your support of the extreme ..."

"Hang on a minute," snubbed Mark with a lively interruption. "I don't support extremism, I expose it. Don't think that you can perform one of your cons to convince me. Really, General. You should know better."

"Yes," replied Mandeville, faintly. "Forgive my lack of tact and wisdom towards you. But you are proving to be ..."

"Just get to the point, General."

"It's Mandeville, Mark. You can no longer call me General."

"Whatever!" Mark said with an angry overtone. "As I said before, get to the point."

"This is the first stage of the Ensconce Operation, which Burrows vowed to undertake," replied Mandeville. "However, he needs a helping hand. You can't escape writing America's revenge."

Mark responded with anger. "Who are you to tell me what to write and in which direction the plot should go? I can choose how to continue writing the next instalment, which I was doing before you rudely interrupted. I don't need to justify the future."

"Oh, but you do, Mark," said Mandeville in a contemptuous manner. "You owe me because you tamed the world's superpower and you have to accept responsibility for that. We have to discredit the PM and the President at this juncture. It will help towards the acceptance of the President's assassination and the inauguration of Burrows. Plus, it will help us to position a leader of our choice, once again, at the helm of the UK and, eventually, the rest of Europe. The PM will be finished after my revelations and, in the future, pulling the trigger on America."

"Bullshit," countered Mark. "They were already discredited. That's why I could go into the future and compose my plot."

"It wasn't enough, Mark," stated Mandeville. "You know it, and I know it. However, I know more."

"More?"

"Of course more," replied Mandeville. "I was, after all, chief of staff to the army. And now I am the Lord's Second Coming within Seeker One, and all its information ..."

"I know that, I think."

"So, do think about it," continued Mandeville. "I know the alternative to the plot that the civvies dreamt up, and the what ifs to their cons, lies and cover-ups ... etcetera, etcetera."

"Um ... interesting," said Mark. Then he thought: do I want to go down this road? Do I want to join with Mandeville? Besides, what could he do? I know, I'll tease him. "This is just my imagination trying to piss me off," he said. "I mean, fancy having to go back to the beginning. Anyway, what about the Lord? What part do you think he is going to play? My imagination could choose that the Lord opposes you."

Mandeville laughed. "You can't ignore your imagination, Mark," he said. "It wants to know the alternatives that the Network has in its possession. As for the Lord ... well, I imagine that he is no longer needed. The world no longer needs a God to guide its citizens. He is, after all, a figment of the imagination ..."

"As are you."

"Um ..." continued Mandeville. "And, as I was going on to say, an excuse for our actions, imagined or not. My actions will be judged to be the Lord's messages in the imagination of humans."

"Humans," echoed Mark. "I find it strange that you should use such a term."

"Soon you will understand why I use the term humans," replied Mandeville.

There was no response from Mark. He just gazed at the monitor, his mind elsewhere. I'm going too deep into my fictional world, he thought. I have to maintain a balance. I can feel myself being pulled in, being taken over by my own fictional character, which could jeopardise the reality of my normal life.

6

"What's the problem, Mark?" enquired Mandeville with impatience.

Mark sighed. "I don't know," he said. "Actually, yes I do. I don't want to go backwards and waste my time when I could be developing what I have already started. And in my own time."

"You are sounding negative, Mark," remarked Mandeville. "You want to know, you want to get involved. This is the next level to your writing, the natural course to take after your venture into the future. I'm reluctant to force the issue, Mark, and expose the sinister side of my captivity. But if I have to …"

"Ah! I knew it," exclaimed Mark. "Resorting to bullying tactics, eh? No, I don't think so. You're only an image, nothing to be scared of. However, I could become anxious and foresee troubles ahead if I take up an acquaintance with you."

"Only if you refuse," cautioned Mandeville. "Keep on gazing into the monitor and I'll show you more, which will convince your imagination to the point of satisfying your appetite. You can't refuse, Pal."

"Oh! A new expression has emerged in your dialogue," observed Mark. "Was that to help convince me? Was that to inform me that you are independent of my command?"

"Indeed so," replied Mandeville. "Now do as I have already ordered."

Mark stared into the monitor, and thought: if I don't see anything other than what I see now, then I'll be off the hook. But … damn! He'll know if I am lying. I'll have to keep an open mind, which could let him in. Suddenly Mark's thoughts were interrupted. The image on the monitor became panoramic and produced a whole image of Mandeville in all his glory.

"Darling!"

"Really," said Mark, there is no need for that, Mandeville."

"You jest in a stupid manner," thundered Mandeville. "That's your wife calling you."

"Oh, sorry."

"Run along now, Mark," said Mandeville. "Return to your reality and take a break until the next time and, believe me, you will return. Now go! That's the end of our introduction."

Mark witnessed the mist return and the powerful image of Mandeville disappearing from the monitor. That was an image to die for, he thought.

Chapter 1

Mark rushed along the landing to the top of the stairs. "What is it, Sandar?" he asked.

"Are you okay, Mark? I thought I heard you talking."

"Yes, of course I am," replied Mark, thinking he had been caught out. "Why wouldn't I be? Anyway, I'm just reading out aloud, going over my book. You know how it is … Not talking to anyone, if that's what you think."

"Don't be silly," said Sandar, "no need for that. Come down and have a cup of tea. I think you need a break. You have to go to work soon."

"Yes, you're right," said Mark. "I'll be down in a moment. I'll just put the laptop to sleep." Mark walked back into the bedroom and stared towards the monitor but nothing was seen, or said. All of a sudden, everyone thinks I'm stupid, he thought. Anyway, a cup of strong and sweet tea will clear my head along with the thought of work, which has always got in the way. I'll have to contain my excitement and continue to realise the difference between reality and fiction. Besides, who the hell would believe this? Mark went downstairs to the dining room and sat at the head of the dining table, which gave him a view into the back garden from the dining room window. His tea, which was strong, sweet and in his usual mug, had already been made and was waiting to be consumed.

Mark's wife sat down beside him, in her usual place at the dining table. "How's your tea, darling?"

"It's good, doll. Thank you," replied Mark. "This is a rare occasion, don't you think?"

"What is?"

"You making me a cup of tea. Normally, it's my task to make it."

"You're being sarcastic, darling," replied Sandar. "A demonstration of your low form of wit and a change of character within you. Must be the writing. Anyway, you're too busy these days even to think about making tea, apart from for yourself, that is."

"Doll! Don't be like that," exclaimed Mark. "As you should be aware, it will benefit both of us in the long run. It helps me to think, having a cup of tea and a fag …"

"A fag," interrupted Sandar. "God! You smoke like a trooper."

"Well, it's only one vice," replied Mark, jumping to his own defence. Sandar appeared to be deep in thought and rather sad.

"What now?" groaned Mark, a note of suspicion in his raised voice.

"No need to shout," rebuffed Sandar. "You're doing a lot of that lately, and I don't like it. You never used to be like this. Have you got something to hide?"

"Nothing, doll. Nothing," responded Mark, sheepishly. "I'm sorry, doll. I understand what you've said. It's just that … I've got so much going on in my head that I forget myself sometimes because I'm deep in thought, and all that."

"You shouldn't forget what is going on around you, darling," commented Sandar. "I can't do everything on my own."

"I know that," acknowledged Mark, and I do appreciate your support. I am trying hard to balance things between my writing and my family life." Mark reached out and squeezed Sandar's hand. "I am trying, doll." Mark paused. I suspect it's going to get harder though, he thought. "Anyway," continued Mark, "what was it you were looking sad about?"

"Oh … nothing, darling," replied Sandar. "You'll just think that I'm moaning, especially after what has just been said."

"Of course I won't," said Mark, sympathetically. "Come on, doll, spit it out."

"It's just that … I thought that you were going to have a rest from writing now that your first book has been published. I thought that I was going to have some of your precious time just for me."

"I understand that too," assured Mark. "But you know how it is. Once an idea pops into my head, or is given to me, I have to pursue it and then the imagination takes over. I don't want to lose any of the flow."

"So soon, though," remarked Sandar. "Does that normally happen?"

"Don't know," answered Mark. "Can't answer for other writers. Maybe with a sequel it does. Bound to …"

"What did you mean, given to me?"

"Eh?"

"You suggested that someone had given you ideas."

"Oh, that," shrugged Mark, having given himself time to think of an answer. "Only in my imagination, doll. Anyway, I'm sure that this time it won't be as intense as when I was writing my first book. I can relax a bit now that I'm an author." Mark hoped that he had convinced his wife, but not with any confidence.

"Somehow, I don't think so," said Sandar, shattering any notion that he had reassured her.

Mark looked knowingly towards Sandar. "I can't just stop at one book. This will be my new career - once the money starts rolling in - and an improvement to our lives. I believe it, and you should too."

"Um ... whatever," said Sandar. "I'm not going to continue this and get into a deep conversation that won't be concluded before you go to work. I have a feeling that it's going to be frustrating being an author's wife ... Do you want something to eat before you go?"

Mark looked at his wife in his practised sheepish manner, as though hard done by. "No thanks. I'll make do with my pack-up ..."

"Then you'd better go and make it," suggested Sandar.

Mark headed for the kitchen and examined the contents of the fridge. Let me see, he thought. Cheese, egg, turkey ham or chicken. I think I'll have egg and tomato. Yes, that will do. Oh ... never mind, she'll get used to it. She did before and will do again.

Sandar entered the kitchen a little later to start preparing the evening meal for the rest of the family. She gave Mark a small hug. "All done, darling?"

"Yes, doll," replied Mark. "I'll go and change into my uniform now. Won't be too long."

"Okay," replied Sandar. She watched as Mark left the kitchen to go upstairs to the bedroom. As he disappeared out of sight, she thought: I shouldn't be too hard on him. He's worked hard to get to this stage. I'm so proud of him really.

Mark finished changing into his uniform and gathered together all the usual bits and pieces that he needed for work. He then commenced with his pre-work thoughts: keys, cigarettes, glasses, wallet, diary and change for the coffee machine. Sandwiches are downstairs in my bag. Oh! Mustn't forget an apple. Right, that's it, I just need to get my bicycle from the shed. He looked at his watch. Time for another cuppa and a smoke before I head off. He turned his gaze to his laptop before leaving the bedroom. "Just as well you are turned off," he said softly to himself, "and can't witness my indecisiveness. I'm sure that Mandeville would not be too impressed."

Sandar discovered Mark sitting in his usual place in the dining room and enquired, "Got everything, darling?"

"Yes, doll," answered Mark. "Want some tea?"

"No ... I'll finish the cooking," replied Sandar. "I don't want to waste any more time because James will be back soon, and Cara will be making her way back from university for the weekend."

"Yes, I know," said Mark. "I like Fridays - looking forward to Cara coming home and all of us being together for the weekend."

"Yes, darling," agreed Sandar, "but it's unfortunate that you are on a late shift: you won't see them till morning."

"I know that," uttered Mark. "Still, the late shifts give me time to write during the day ... especially now that I've started on the sequel."

"Exactly," stated Sandar, "that's what I mean."

"What?"

"You will see them, but you won't get to spend any time with them."

"I'll make that tea," said Mark, and he headed for the kitchen.

Sandar followed him to continue with the cooking. "Chicken curry okay with you, darling?"

"A red one?"

"Yes. Cara likes a chicken curry with red curry paste. I'm sure James will eat it as well."

"Mmmm ... lovely," declared Mark, imagining the taste. "Shame you didn't cook earlier, then I could've taken some to work with me. Never mind, I'll have some tomorrow if there's any left over."

"Of course there will be," assured Sandar.

"I'm not too bothered, doll," responded Mark, diplomatically, "I know how they like to tuck it away."

"I'll put some aside, okay?" said Sandar, "so you can go to work knowing there will be some for you tomorrow."

Mark walked back into the dining room with his mug of tea and sat down in his usual place. He lit a hand-rolled cigarette and quietly smoked it while his wife got on with preparing the chicken curry. Ten minutes ticked by and then Mark thought that he might as well make a move. He donned his jacket and overcoat, patting the pockets to confirm that all the necessary contents were present and correct. "I'm off now, doll," he shouted.

"Okay, darling," Sandar replied. She appeared from the kitchen and gave Mark a kiss. "Take care and give me a ring on your break. Oh, and don't let them get to you."

"Yes, doll, I know," replied Mark, "and as I have said before, night-time is not the best time to drive a bus amongst the druggies, drunks and murderers. I've got it off to a fine art: ignoring and not confronting the passengers. Ignorant passengers hate bus drivers because they have to pay and want to offload their frustrations on someone. Apart from that, it's a knife culture out there and I want to come home at the end of my shift. I don't want to jeopardise our future. Anyway, I'm off now that I've had a moan about my wonderful 'proper' job."

Sandar smiled and gave Mark another kiss in reassurance. "Go on. See you later on," she said. "I'll probably be asleep on the couch when you get in. Love you!"

"Yes, doll. Bye! Love you too!"

Mark wheeled his bicycle out of the shed, positioned it on the street and mounted, giving a final wave to his wife as he rode away into the distance. Good, he thought. No wind against me, so it shouldn't take too much effort.

Ten minutes later Mark arrived at the bus depot where he worked. The depot was situated on a site in Southbury Road, within the London borough of Enfield, which was formerly a nice, small town until the council initiated its regeneration and development programme. This had raised the population quite considerably and thus made a bus driver's job very busy, not to mention more dangerous. The bus depot, considered to be modern decades ago, had matured somewhat with age. Mark rode across the large forecourt, which led to a secured entrance door into the building, and had his usual thought: will I ever see the back of this place? Maybe one day soon. Who knows?

"Hi, Mark," said Geoff, a fellow bus driver arriving at the same time. "Did you have a good journey to work? Not a bad evening for it: riding your bike, that is."

"Sort of," replied Mark, after a slight laugh. "The weather's okay, it's just those mindless 'boy racer' idiots who think they're being funny by harassing a cyclist, especially when you're wearing a hi-vi vest with the company's name on it. Mind you, it's the ignorant adult drivers as well. Oh, ignore me, Geoff. You know how it is coming to a job you hate - makes you miserable, don't you think? Also, I've had to tear myself away from my writing."

"You are in a state," remarked Geoff. "I hope you let off some steam by hurling abuse at your passing admirers."

"Oh, I did!" stated Mark. "It's all they understand."

"Geoff laughed. "Here, let me open the door for you."

"Thanks, mate," said Mark, and then he wheeled his bike inside and headed for a designated area set aside as a bicycle rank.

Geoff passed Mark on his way to the canteen. "Want a cup of tea, Mark?" "As always," replied Mark. "Not one to refuse a cup of bought tea. I'll just secure my bike and go and sign in."

"Okay."

"You not signing in then?"

"No, not yet. I'm a bit early. I'll do it later," responded Geoff.

"Right, see you in a minute or two," said Mark. He unzipped his overcoat, unbuttoned his jacket, and sighed. Here we go again, he thought. Sign in and get ready. Ha! Wonder if Mandeville is watching? Mark walked through a doorway and entered into the Output. He didn't really know why they called it that and never bothered to question why. Nevertheless, it was where all the administration took place in order to keep the buses running and it housed the long line of management. The Output was busy and crowded with other drivers signing in, signing off and going to and from their lockers, which filled one side of the Output. Mark placed his bag on one of the many tables dotted around the floor space and approached his locker, number two-five-six. He retrieved all the necessary equipment for work, making room for storing his sandwich box and other personal items.

A driver named Pete swiftly walked towards Mark en route towards the exit. "All right, Mark?"

"As right as I can be," answered Mark, as Pete passed by. "Is it busy out there?"

"Sure is," answered Pete in a loud voice as he continued to head for the exit. "Busy, busy, and effin' shit! I'm glad I'm finished for the day and going back to the sanity of my home." Pete disappeared out of sight and volume range.

Sounded like he had a good day, thought Mark, and he made his way to the secured counter. The counter stretched the length and height of the Output, opposite the lockers. Behind the counter were housed all of the administration machines and the personnel that administrated the machine's bureaucracy. Mark swiped his signing-in card through the small computer terminal situated on top of the counter and next to a monitor secured behind the toughened glass that protected the personnel. Eh? ... Nothing has appeared on the screen, thought Mark, so he tried again.

"No point trying again, Mark."

"What?" said Mark, taken by surprise. He looked around, but there was no one close to him. Strange, he thought, I must have misheard someone. "Excuse me," he shouted, "can someone come to the counter, please?"

One of the personnel approached the counter. "What is it?"

Charming, thought Mark. At least he hasn't sworn yet, like he normally does. "My details aren't appearing on the screen, Kevin."

"What have you fucking done now, Mark?"

"Nothing … just swiped the card, that's all."

"Pay number?"

"Double zero, one."

"Um … sorry, mate, you're not here," informed Kevin.

"You're having a laugh," scoffed Mark. "Of course I'm here. Can't you see me or something?"

"Don't fight it, Mark. Have faith."

Eh? Mark thought. He was watching Kev as he searched on the computer and his lips certainly didn't move. Mark looked around again. There were only a few drivers left in there and none was anywhere near him. No one was close enough to have whispered that.

"Oi!"

Mark was jolted back to his current predicament. "What is it?"

" Sorry, mate," said Kevin. "You're not on the fucking system. You're just not here. I'm not fucking understanding it. It's weird!"

Mark was becoming worried. "Come on, enough is enough," he responded. "As usual, you're taking the joke too far. I am here. Can't you see me, stupid prat?"

"Yes, I can," shouted Kevin. "I can see an arsehole that can't accept he's not on the system, and never has been. I can't help it. If you're not in the system, then you don't have a fucking existence."

"Go home and write."

"What? How dare you say that," retorted Mark.

"Say what?"

"Go home and write."

"I never said that," remonstrated Kevin. "You're stressed out. For fuck's sake, just go away and leave me alone."

"You bloody fool," declared Mark, "you can't throw me out because I'm not on the system."

"This fucking system, Mark," said Kevin, with a satirical smile. "You're probably still on the network."

Mark paused in bewilderment. What the hell is going on? What do I do?

"Go and see the assistant manager, Mark."

"Did you say that, Kevin?"

"Of course I fucking did," answered Kevin. "Who else? Look, he's in his office. Just go and sort it out with him." Kevin turned away and went to sit at his desk.

"Okay, I will," replied Mark, pointedly. "And thanks for nothing." Mark lit a roll-up and inhaled deeply.

"Not in here, Mark," shouted Kevin.

Mark smiled and spoke softly to himself. "Who gives a fuck? God! Even I'm swearing now. Okay, let's go and see the boss."

Mark approached the assistant manager's office. Red, green and yellow buttons were mounted on the wall next to the door. Mark pressed the yellow button, which lit up to indicate that an audience was required with the boss. Mark looked through the narrow window on the office door. He observed the assistant manager, Neville, waving him in. Mark entered swiftly and hurried towards the assistant manager, who was sitting behind his desk. Mark blurted out two questions with an angry tone of voice. "What's going on? What's the big idea?"

"Calm down, driver," instructed the assistant manager, and he sat to attention. "I suggest that you tell me what the problem is, and in a civilised manner."

"Oh, so now you address me as 'driver'! You usually address me by my first name - Mark."

"It depends on the situation," replied Neville, "and this one does not appear to be friendly."

"I have good reason to be upset," explained Mark. "It appears, unbelievably, that ..."

"He doesn't exist," interrupted Kevin, who thought he should intrude through a connecting door from the administration area. "I could hear loud voices, Neville, and thought you might need a witness."

"Witness?"

"Yes, he seems unstable ..."

"Ha! Fucking doesn't exist, and now I'm unstable," retaliated Mark. "For God's sake! It's me - Mark. I've worked here for nearly ten years. Sod the computer and get out my written file."

"Let me see," said Neville, and he looked through his filing system. "No, sorry, it's not here. Let me just tap in your details, which are ...?"

"I'm telling you, he's not in there," clarified Kevin.

"Just humour me, Kevin," continued Neville. "So, Mark. Your pay number?"

Mark sighed with frustration. "Zero, zero, one," he replied.

The assistant manager tapped in the three-digit number. After a few seconds, his face expressed some curiosity. "It looks as though Kevin is right.

You don't work here - at least, not anymore."

Mark lunged across the desk, grabbed Neville by the collar and shook him a few times. "Come to your senses, man," said Mark, in desperation. "You're looking at me. I'm here."

"Let go of me!" shrieked Neville. "Take your hands off me!"

Kevin intervened and pushed Mark backwards into a chair. "Oh, dear," he said, with a provocative grin. "That wasn't the best of moves to resolve the situation, was it?"

Mark shrugged his shoulders and composed himself. Oh dear indeed, he thought. I've just given them an excuse. "I suppose it wasn't," he answered, "but you have to understand my situation."

"Yes I do, perfectly," said Kevin. "If we had found that you were on the system, then you're not on it now. Know what I mean?"

"Um ..."

"Exactly," interrupted the assistant manager, with confidence and knowledge. "That was conduct unbecoming of an employee. I'm now in a position to fire you. No need to cure my curiosity."

"Fuck you!" Mark blasted out, with matching confidence. "You can't function unless you receive a command and information from the computer. Tell me, does that apply to your homes as well?"

"That applies to us all, Mark," replied Neville, in a calm tone of voice, knowing he had gained the advantage. "It's the way of the world."

Mark paused for thought. God! He's trying to come across all clever and psychological, as if he really knows what goes on outside his little world within this office. Mark laughed. "Oh! I get it," he said. "This is a conspiracy: your lies, the voices and the innuendoes. Believe me, I know a conspiracy when I see one, and how I'm a bloody part of it."

"Come now!" replied Neville. "You're allowing your imagination to block your logic. After all, it's not as if you need this job now that you're an author. You think you're too good for this place. So we're just helping you along."

"Unfortunately, I do," responded Mark, "on both counts ..."

"You do what?"

"I still need this job," continued Mark, with slight frustration. "I'm still waiting for any revenue to filter through from my book."

"Don't worry, Mark," declared Neville, "I'm positive that the expected funds will be in place, sooner rather than later, which will be a pleasant and relieving surprise."

"You appear and sound strange - not your usual self," observed Mark.

16

"You seem to know more than you should. Like I said, a conspiracy."

The assistant manager laughed and shook his head. "I'll be truthful with you, Mark ..."

"Really!"

"Yes, really. The fact is that I don't want the likes of you working here ..."

Mark looked astonished. "Explain the likes of me?"

"I was about to. Are you going to let me finish?"

Mark looked at him suspiciously but with interest. "Go on then," he instructed.

The assistant manager emitted a short awkward cough before he spoke. "I'm apprehensive about your attitude, and I'm aware that you have become irrational ... crazy even. All you had to do was to allow us to sort out this mess. After all, computers do, believe it or not, make mistakes ..."

"Ha! You make it sound as if they have a mind of their own."

"Indeed, Mark," continued Neville. "That is the perception we all seem to have. Anyway, it's a sad end to your employment here. Obviously, your writing has got the better of you and taken over your life. You need to come to terms with that. It's conceivable that this is the end of your reality as you know it, and you have to move on."

"Maybe you are right with your - or someone else's - synopsis," said Mark. Maybe it is time. So there's no point requesting that the union rep join us?"

"No, it won't do you any good," answered Neville. "He'll just comply, and agree with me. Only you can help yourself, Mark. Hand in anything that belongs to us and leave. Go home and rest ... see a doctor even. You need to gather your thoughts and look to the future ..."

"Or the past."

"Sorry?"

"Oh, nothing," answered Mark, while staring into the assistant manager's eyes. Strange, he thought, I'm absurdly accepting this with an air of calm. I should be fighting my corner, even begging to keep my job. It's as if my buttons are being pressed for me, just like the assistant manager is being controlled by another source. Deep down it is what I want so I can write what I need to, and as a full-time occupation. "One last request, sir?"

Neville shuffled around in his chair after Mark had released his stare. "If it is reasonable," he replied.

"I think so," said Mark. "May I have a drink of tea with my friend in the canteen? It will help me to gather myself together before the ride home and think about what I'm going to say when I get there."

The assistant manager agreed, not wanting to appear too callous. "I'll give you an hour, and then I want you away from the vicinity of the building."

"Understood," agreed Mark. He looked towards Kevin, whose job as a witness had come to an end. "See you, Kevin."

"Yes, you will, and good luck …"

"He won't need it," interrupted Neville. "He has guidance and will manage perfectly." The assistant manager shook hands with Mark and returned a stare. "No hard feelings."

"Thanks," said Mark, "I think." Mark left the assistant manager's office for what he thought was the last time.

Mark entered the canteen - an unimpressive large square area incorporating purpose-built dining tables and attached chairs, a lounge section and the open-view kitchen behind a long serving counter. The canteen had a bad reputation amongst the employees, who regularly thought that the health and safety people would struggle to clean it up. I won't miss this place, he thought. In fact, I won't miss this whole environment of misfits.

Mark spotted Geoff and sat down at the table opposite him. "Hello, Geoff," he said quietly. "I need some tea and understanding."

Geoff smiled. "I've got your tea, which has gone cold, but I don't know what I am supposed to understand, if anything."

"You're right," replied Mark. "Who is to know what to understand about this place? It beats me into submission and acceptance. We're just humanised robots inside this cocoon of repeated boredom and worthless being."

Geoff looked confused, almost embarrassed, but shrugged it off with a laugh and thought: he appears to be depressed and has lost the plot, which is unusual for him. I suppose I'll have to ask. It's obvious that he wants to talk about something that's gone on.

Geoff took a sip of tea to lubricate his dry throat. "What is it, Mark? What have they done now?"

"You're not going to believe it, Geoff," answered Mark. He then went on to explain what had happened.

"Um …" uttered Geoff, after listening intently to Mark's story.

"What's um …?"

"Well," replied Geoff, "are you sure? I think that you probably resigned, and you are justifying your brash decision with your imagination. After all, someone has to delete your details off the computer … don't they? Or make a mistake?"

"But who? And, I'm sure that I didn't resign freely. It appears like a

18

conspiracy to get me out of here."

"Don't be silly," remarked Geoff. "They only erase details after a resignation or dismissal. There's always a logical explanation to everything. You just have to find it."

"Not in my world, Geoff," replied Mark. "Anyway, I'll have to come to terms with what has happened as, ultimately, it is what I want. I want to be able to write full time in my own cocoon of life."

"Don't worry," said Geoff, sympathetically. "Your future is bright. God! I'm stuck here until I retire - not so bright, and stuck with reality. I wish I had the imagination to create a cocoon and hide."

"Huh? I'm not hiding, Geoff ..."

"Aren't you going to answer your mobile, Mark?"

"Oh, yes, of course. I didn't hear it. Wasn't expecting anyone to call. Let's see. Um ... it's my wife calling. Wonder what she wants?"

"It sounds like you're delaying, Mark," said Geoff. "She'll have to know sooner or later."

"I agree, Geoff," replied Mark, "It's just knowing how to break it to her." Mark answered the call.

"Hello, darling," said Sandar. "I took a chance to see if I could get hold of you. I'm surprised I did. I thought you'd be out driving by now. Anyway, I have good news for you, important news."

"Sounds good, doll," replied Mark. "I think I could do with some good news right now. What is it?"

"I've received a phone call, which was meant for you, from a publisher called Network. It sounded very promising ..."

"Really," interrupted Mark, with both surprise and suspicion.

"Yes," continued Sandar. "They want you to contact them as soon as possible."

"I bet he does, doll ..."

"He?"

"Ah, well, I have actually already had contact with him. Sorry, them. In fact, the network appears to be very persistent when it wants something." Especially after what has happened today, he thought.

"I'm confused," confessed Sandar. "It sounds as if you're talking in riddles. I thought I was the bearer of good news, which you haven't allowed me to tell you."

"Okay, doll," retreated Mark, "go ahead."

"The person from Network said that they were keen to sign you up. So keen, in fact, that they want you to come straight home and discuss terms with them, including a large advance of money ..."

"God! This is unreal ..."

"Yes, but true. It sounds like a great opportunity, one you have been waiting for. Just think? You could end up writing full time, which is what you want."

"Indeed so, doll," said Mark, softly. "Look, we can't talk over the mobile all day. I'll come home straight away."

"How can you?" asked Sandar, knowing that Mark was supposed to be driving.

"I'll explain when I arrive home, doll. Don't worry, it seems as though my future is being carved out for me, and us."

"Okay," said Sandar, becoming even more confused. "I'll see you soon then."

"Bye, doll," said Mark, and then terminated the call. Mark thought: was the call from Network really meant for me, or were they, or him, softening up my wife and making it easier for me when I arrive home to explain my disappearance from the company's records. Do I lie to protect my virtual world and keep things simple by saying I simply resigned? It would be the most logical explanation, as Geoff said, rather than the unbelievable truth.

Geoff noticed that Mark seemed far away from his present surroundings. "Earth calling," he said to Mark. "Are you with us?"

Mark jolted his mind back from his thoughts. "Yes," answered Mark, "at least for the next few minutes. This is the end of the road for me here. I've been terminated." Mark laughed.

Geoff also laughed at his clever use of bus terminology. "You must go," added Geoff, "and embrace the carved-out future. Anyway, insurance reasons will kick in soon as you're not supposed to be here. They may come mob-handed and boot you out."

Mark laughed again. "That wouldn't surprise me," he said, as he withdrew from the canteen table. "Bye, Geoff. Take care."

"See you, Mark, and keep in touch," replied Geoff, as he watched Mark make his way to the exit.

Don't suppose I will, thought Mark, as he walked towards his bicycle. All this has become the past of reality. Time to move on and accept what has happened, and what is happening. One way or another, it's what I want. Mark unlocked his bicycle and wheeled it out through the many safety doors, which eventually led him away from his place of work for, possibly, the last time.

Mark soon arrived home. "Hello, doll," he shouted, as he wheeled his bike through the house to the back garden.

"Darling, darling," shouted Sandar with excitement as she rushed down the stairs. "You'll never guess what ..."

"Hang on," interrupted Mark. "Let me just put my bike away, and I'll be with you."

"Okay," said Sandar, "I'll make some tea."

Mark stored his bicycle in the garden shed. That's that, he thought. Don't suppose I'll be riding it again in a hurry. Mark delayed his exit from the large shed. "Damn!" he muttered to himself, quietly. "I might have to lie. It all depends on what she is all excited about. I must keep my wits about me, protect my position as well as her own."

"Tea's ready," hollered Sandar. "It's on the dining table. Anyway, what's keeping you?"

"Coming," answered Mark.

Mark made his way to the dining room, took off his coat and sat down next to his wife.

"You took a long time putting your bike away," commented Sandar.

"Yes," replied Mark. "I knocked a few things off the crowded shelves and had to clear up. Now, what is your exciting news all about?"

Sandar quickly swallowed the tea she had in her mouth. "Well," she said, "I was checking our finances, as I normally do, and I noticed that a large advance of money had been transferred into your account. This was after the phone call I received from the Network ..."

"Network Publishing, I think," interrupted Mark, wanting to dismiss the reference to 'the Network'. Must be something else, he thought.

"Whatever," replied Sandar, thinking that her husband was just trying to be the clever one . "Anyway," she continued with suspicion. How can that be?"

"How can what be?"

"God! You always do that, darling."

"Do what?"

"Give yourself time to think of an answer. You know what I'm referring to."

"Ah!" said Mark, knowing he was giving himself time to conjure up an explanation. "Actually," he continued, "I was keeping it all as a surprise, waiting for it to be finalised ..."

"It?"

"The advance payment from my publisher for the next book. Once I knew that, then I was able to resign from work. Anyway, how large was it?"

"You mean you've resigned without knowing whether you can afford to?"

"They mentioned a figure, which would be enough. Besides, I'll have the royalties that are due from the sales of my book and it won't take long to complete this next one."

"Sounds like you have it all worked out," said Sandar, feeling left out. "You know that I like to be consulted."

"Oh, there's no need to feel dejected, darling," assured Mark. "As I said, I wanted it to be a surprise. I wanted to see the excitement and satisfaction pour out of you, knowing that our future is secure ..."

"Yes, darling, I am, but I don't want to be kept in the dark."

"Good! There you go. Glad to here it," said Mark, with relief. "Thank God for Network, eh? We can go through it in more detail in the morning. It's getting late and time for a good night's sleep."

"Yes," agreed Sandar. "There's nothing more that I want to see on the telly, and I have to get up early to do the food shopping ..."

"I'll come as usual, doll," interrupted Mark, with anticipation.

"It's okay," replied Sandar, "I want you to stay home and get on with whatever you have to do. I'll ask Cara to come with me."

"That's settled then," said Mark, quickly wanting to end the conversation at that point. "Come on, let's go to bed."

As Sandar was making her way up the stairs to the bedroom she shouted back at Mark, "Will you check that the doors are locked and the windows are shut?"

"Yes, doll," answered Mark. Mark lit a cigarette to have a small but welcome intake of nicotine while he undertook his nightly checks. Once done, Mark retired to bed.

"I'll say goodnight now," said Sandar, leaning over towards Mark. "I'm going to pray now, and you will probably be asleep by the time I'm finished."

Mark kissed Sandar on the cheek. "Okay," he said, "night, doll. See you in the morning."

Sandar returned the goodnight kiss and settled back to pray in silence.

Mark turned away so as not to disturb his wife and sighed. Phew! he thought. Say a little pray for me, doll. Maybe Mandeville will answer it. Besides, I'll know tomorrow. Mark closed his eyes and fell asleep.

Chapter 2

"Good morning, and if you have just woken up, I welcome you all to the early rise and shine show on your local radio station."

Mark leant over his wife, who moved slightly, and turned off the radio alarm that was on the bedside cabinet next to her. He sat up and thought: I would prefer a soothing song to wake up to. Still, never mind. God! No work today, at least not on the buses. I wouldn't just resign, I had no reason. I must have been forced out. Geoff was wrong: I didn't resign. Oh, well. An hour of tea and fags will clear my waking head. Then I can challenge the chosen one and get to the bottom of all this stuff. I'll get dressed and make a brew.

Mark was in the kitchen making his tea. "Hello Gyp," he said to his dog as it entered the kitchen, and accepted a few strokes and a pat. "Want to go out? Come, I'll open the door." Gyp rushed out into the garden to do his doggy business, unaware that he was the inspiration for Mandeville's first name. Good old Gyp, thought Mark. Every time I look at him, I think of General G. Mandeville. Ha! The dog of war. Is there such a term? Anyway, it sounds good. Let's just hope that he's not listening and discovers that I named him after a dog, and the name of the road we live in.

"Morning, darling. I'll have one of those, thank you," announced Sandar, as she appeared and made her way into the bathroom beyond the kitchen.

"One of what? A kiss, a stroke, or a pat?" joked Mark.

Sandar sighed. "No, a cup of tea, of course," she answered, glancing back at Mark.

Mark took the two teas into the dining room and set them down on the table. He opened the curtains and the window, which would help to drag out the smoke from his and Sandar's cigarettes, and then switched on the radio. That's nice, he thought. A bit of classical music to soothe the brain on a clear, bright morning. After performing his daily morning ceremony, he sat down in his usual place to drink his tea and have a smoke.

Sandar reappeared, rubbing her face with her hands in an effort to wake up fully. "Thanks, darling," she said as she sat down. She reached for her cigarettes and lit one. The open window was executing its designated role of extracting the clouds of smoke while they both sat in silence.

Mark pondered and stared at his wife, waiting for an appropriate moment to arrive, between her puffs and sips, to broach what he wanted to say. Eventually the moment came when he noticed an enquiring look from Sandar. "Is it okay …?"

"Is what okay?" interrupted Sandar, as if to make Mark's task more difficult.

"Can I stay at home and get on with it while you go shopping?"

"Yes," answered Sandar. "I said you could yesterday."

"Just making sure, doll. I don't want you to think that I'm taking advantage."

"As if you would, darling," jested Sandar. "Anyway, I want to know more …"

"Guessed as much, seeing as I curtailed the conversation to go to bed last night."

"I'll wake Cara and then make a list," continued Sandar. "You get on with it, if you must."

"Thanks, doll. Love you."

Mark made his way to the bedroom and sat at his desk. He switched on the laptop, typed in his password and clicked on the Internet provider's icon. He waited anxiously for a connection, but with a feeling of excitement in anticipation of an explanation. Can't wait to see that image again, he thought. Time to find out what is what. Hopefully, I'm not going mad by allowing my imagination to rule my reality.

The screen lit up but failed to portray the image that Mark was expecting. Mark stared at the screen with disbelief and thought: shit! Where is he? I needed to be convinced as soon as possible. I wanted peace of mind in the knowledge that I did not resign voluntarily. Instead, Mark heard "You have email" sounding from the laptop's speakers. Um, he thought, with disappointment. Better sort this out first. The first email showed: 'Network Contract'. Mark double-clicked to open and read the email, which read: "I hope that our financial advance is enough to secure our contract. Open the link so that we can discuss more and negotiate. Delete 'Network Contract' immediately and permanently." Wow! thought Mark. No image, but this sounds like Mandeville.

After taking a moment to compose himself, Mark opened the link. The security jargon popped up with a warning: "Do you know who this email is from?" Mark paused as he pointed the arrow towards the 'yes', more thoughts pervading his mind: once I click on 'yes' then I'm probably in for good - no going back. He'll know that I've opened it even if I don't proceed beyond reading it. No need to dither: this is what I want. Mark clicked on 'yes' and opened the email. "Uh!" he said to himself as he read the only line that was revealed: "globalmanagement@network*seek". That doesn't look like a normal email address, he thought. What's the meaning of the star? But then again, what is normal?

After Mark had typed in the address, a page appeared with "Welcome, Mark" written on it. This was followed by: "Type anything to activate". Mark stared at the page with confusion. Strange, he thought. Why written dialogue? Is the laptop speaking to me without sound, or whatever is at the other end of this address? Eventually Mark's fingers danced around the keyboard and typed: "Hello, this is Mark making contact". Mark clicked on 'send now' and waited with eager anticipation for a reply. Time lingered as he tapped musically on the desk. Finally "You have email" sounded out from the laptop and jolted Mark into action. He quickly clicked and read: "Set up your old, disused computer to receive me and the information separately from your laptop. It will become secret and secure, controlled by the Network. Afterwards, type the address on your laptop, then wait and watch your computer's monitor." This is going to take a while, thought Mark. I keep thinking of questions regarding his instructions. For instance, how can my laptop activate the monitor without been connected …? I must stop thinking too much. I need to focus. Maybe I should move away from this for a while. A mug of tea and a fag will help.

Mark eventually returned to his bedroom, refreshed from his drink of tea and numerous cigarettes. Now, he thought, let me get my computer out of the box. Glad I marked which cable goes where. Shouldn't take long to set up.

As predicted, Mark had his old computer up and running within a short space of time. Okay, he thought, I'm ready to receive Mandeville. Mark typed in the address as specified: 'globalmanagement@network*seek'. The monitor went blank for a few seconds and then lit up in a cloudy haze. Mark waited and then stared in wonderment as he had before. "God!" he shouted out. The image of Mandeville, in all his glory, had appeared. He was sat on a throne with only his face looking human. The rest of his body was encased in shiny metal, like a suit of armour ready for battle. His chest glowed with lights that flashed in purposeful sequence.

"Welcome Mark," said Mandeville, suddenly responding to Mark's utterance of "God!" "You have done well since our last encounter. Now we are ready for the task ahead."

Mark remained motionless, just staring at Mandeville's image before him. I need to say something, he thought. Anything, just to acknowledge his presence. "Neither your hands nor feet are visible. How do you ...?" Then Mark thought: shit! That sounded childish, almost ignorant, which amounts to the same thing.

Mandeville smiled and then spoke. "Everything I control is managed by my mind. I only have to think of what I want to do and say and it happens. I have replaced the hologram image that Seeker One displayed. The Lord wished his technical angel to assume a human presence that understands the human direction ..."

"What direction?" interrupted Mark.

"Everything human," answered Mandeville. "Obviously, I was the Lord's choice, as you know."

"No, actually, I didn't," revealed Mark.

"Ah! A small slip of a clue to arouse your suspicions," confessed Mandeville, "that maybe you don't control my progress in your story, which could now be reality."

"Erm ... debatable," mused Mark. "You're still trying to confuse. Old habits don't die with the dead, eh?"

"Ever the cynic, Mark," answered Mandeville jovially.

"Yes, indeed. Your previous statement about my doing well since our last encounter ... was that another small clue?"

Mandeville smiled with approval and satisfaction. "As you know, Mark," he said, "I had no choice in terms of the events leading up to this meeting - events that I need you to understand and use to my advantage."

"Sorry, mate," replied Mark. "I killed you off, or thought I had. Well, I can't give you the understanding you crave. Perhaps it will reveal itself in due course. And you already have the advantage, don't you think?"

"I suppose I do, Mark," replied Mandeville. And, if I may comment, this is good."

"What is?"

"That we are able to talk in a civilised way, considering your initial shock. And, you have accepted me in the manner and image in which I present myself. Now we both control each other."

"Manipulation as usual," said Mark. "I have the feeling that you have the majority of the control. After all, I wasn't expecting a reincarnation."

"Good for you, Mark," responded Mandeville with satisfaction. "At least you can understand that I am, and represent the majority of any control."

"Oh, you understand all right," retorted Mark, "I have no doubt about that. You know the Lord chose you. Better the devil you know, I would presume." Mark paused.

"What is it, Mark?"

"What's with the shades around your eyes?" he asked. "I don't recall observing them in our first encounter."

Damn and blast, thought Mandeville. He's seen a weakness that I can't cover up.

"Well?"

"Okay already. Don't push. If you must know, they are protection ..."

"Ah! Closer to the sun," jested Mark.

"Don't be hairbrained, Mark."

"Just joking. Excuse my indulgence."

"As I was about to say, they are protection against those who will oppose my position, as usual."

"Please explain in more detail," requested Mark, in a more serious tone of voice.

"Um ... A condition of a contract ... a requirement of your acceptance?" posited Mandeville.

"If that is how you view my request, then yes. It is a matter of acceptance, and I want to know. So, if you don't mind?"

"Very well, Mark. In the process of my reincarnation, my eyes became clear. Well, white but transparent. This was the Lord's own safeguard against any digression from his objective. It's my only weakness ..."

"Weakness?"

"Yes, weakness. I know it sounds incredible that I, Mandeville, have a weakness. The fact is that those, apart from the Lord, who oppose any future policy of mine can look through my eyes and see what I am thinking and how Seeker One functions - even you, Mark."

"Mark smiled on hearing Mandeville's answer. "Like Burrows did? He managed to see right through you."

"Really?" countered Mandeville. "He is a clever one, but not in any significant way. It will be I who controls his actions on Earth. He will be one of my majority holdings of the Second Coming."

Mark paused for a moment. "I get it!" he declared suddenly, with realisation. "The shades are protection from me. You don't want me to see through you to scrutinise or disagree with your mandate. Yes, it is I that can see through you and from whom you seek to protect yourself."

Mandeville chuckled. "You are potentially a good adversary. I'm glad that you are my ally, my friend, my creator."

"Don't sweet-talk me too much. I may think that you are trying to deceive me," cautioned Mark.

"Deceive you, no. Enlighten you, yes. There are others that can intervene who are within the frame of the Network."

"Others?"

"Yes. But you are not to concern yourself about them. I shall protect you from them. I'll say no more on the matter. You don't need to know at this juncture. You will become aware of them when the time comes."

"How? How can I be aware of something that I don't know about?"

"You will, trust me."

"Okay," said Mark, with unsure acceptance. "Anyway, it's only mind over matter. It's not as if this is real. To accept you as you are now is a matter for the mind."

"Exactly!" replied Mandeville. "That is what I am. I'm a conception in your thoughts." Mandeville paused. I feel the need to move on, he thought. "Enough now," he said. We understand each other ..."

"Not yet," interrupted Mark. "You've become a new character, one that I'm not familiar with."

"Of course we do, Mark," continued Mandeville. "You are a far greater ally now than you were in the past. I mean, the PM, Ian Dolby, wasn't exactly coherent was he, Mark?"

"Nonsense!" retorted Mark. "He saw through you. Maybe, you should have had some protection then against your transparency."

"I understand," replied Mandeville. "That is why we need to move on. Idle chitter-chatter stops us getting down to business, as it did with the PM. That, I think, was my human downfall."

"Oh? I don't feel the same way," informed Mark. "I like the kind of chitter-chatter that I gave the PM. It's a delaying tactic for thinking and devising plans of attack. It keeps your enemy occupied and off guard. You should think about adopting the tactic yourself in order to gain the advantage. Humans are very good at chitter-chatter in order to deceive their opponent."

"You have a valid point," conceded Mandeville. "I shall give some thought to programming chitter-chatter into Seeker One's memory banks."

"Good," Mark said, with approval. Now, let us go back to recent events ..."

Mandeville interrupted with a loud sigh. "You're doing it now, aren't you,

Mark? You are keeping me occupied while you decide on making your next step."

"Yes," replied Mark.

"Um," uttered Mandeville. "Personally, I don't like it. I prefer to get straight to the point. What exactly do you want?"

"Reassurance, Mandeville," answered Mark.

Mandeville looked confused. "Is the fact that we are here, and speaking, not enough to convince you that you can accept what is going on?"

"No," answered Mark. There is more that I need to know."

"Okay. What do you want to know?" asked Mandeville. "And, please come to the point. Our connection is going on longer than I would wish. Those within the frame to which I referred could trace the source and destination."

"Your summons," said Mark, getting straight to the point. "Was it you? Was it you who orchestrated my demise from reality? And that, in a fit of madness, I did not get here of my own accord?"

"Yes, yes and no," replied Mandeville. "You did not have a fit of madness, but a tangle with your conscience between reality and fiction. Obviously I was the main player in your decision to untangle your conscience and find the answers to the future. I had to be sure about your conviction and discretion. As I have pointed out, there are infiltrators. There are humans who, in reality, have the gift to receive the signal that we use to communicate and to manipulate ..."

"That's it!" interrupted Mark. You manipulated me into this position."

"If that is what you want to believe, Mark," continued Mandeville. "Everyone manipulates to get what they want. Not all those who have the gift would be sympathetic towards our new world ..."

"Your new world, America's world ...?"

"The West's world," corrected Mandeville. It is your job to help me to convince the unsympathetic and turn them around to our way of thinking - that the East cannot take on the role of the West. My manuscript will make our enemies from within understand, which will force them to retreat, to become vulnerable and to seek the Lord's guidance."

"Gift?" queried Mark. "You repeatedly mention the gift. And the enemies from within. Let me guess. Europe, in particular the UK."

"That's a different issue to the gift and will be dealt with later," replied Mandeville, dismissing the charge. "The gift, however, is the gift of computer excellence that the infiltrators possess. They have the ability to 'hack' and act on their findings. They may not like the story you are about to write and may try to stop you."

"Charming!" replied Mark, with apprehension. "So, I'm in danger? You have put me in danger?"

"Not so, Mark," replied Mandeville. "You have not accepted. Besides, you will be protected while I exist ... while you keep me in existence."

"But you see, Mandeville," quizzed Mark, "I didn't keep you in existence, did I? And that's a confusing issue."

"What does it matter?" responded Mandeville. "You are intrigued. You understand my capabilities, and much more. Your demise from reality has shown you how good I am at controlling. Now that I have reappeared as the Second Coming, there is nothing to stand in the way of what I can achieve."

"Yes there is - me!" specified Mark. "I killed you off before, and I can do it again."

Mandeville laughed with confidence. "No, you won't," he said. "You need me, and I need you. At least for the moment. I know how your mind works, Mark. Let's face the facts. I am your mind, your creation. But it has progressed beyond your control and I have become my own being. I have left the human race behind, immortal and free. I am where you have placed me, the chief of staff to Seeker One and its network."

"These are all good reasons, Mandeville," replied Mark. "But ..."

"No buts, Mark," interrupted Mandeville impatiently. "Think about it. You were unaware of being part of the Network, one to hack and probe. You had the insight to write what exists in the future. You are the network that informs the humans what I want them to know. This will influence their thoughts towards the true belief or the Second Coming."

"True belief?" queried Mark.

"Yes. True belief is only imagined," answered Mandeville. "You believe that I have orchestrated your recruitment into the Network and have brought our partnership to this point in time to control minds and life."

"Oh, great!" said Mark sarcastically, with a sudden rush of realisation. "I have brought you close to the edge of reality. But you imagine the truth that you are real. Even I am believing my own imagination."

Mandeville looked confused. "Explain," he requested.

"You provoke me into believing that your return is real, and not my imagination ..."

"Time out!" blasted Mandeville, interrupting Mark's flow. "You have to decide what is reality, and what to believe."

"Okay," continued Mark, "imagination can't make what has happened in order to bring me to this. You have orchestrated events to serve your purpose."

Mandeville sighed, and thought: this is a hard con to convince. "Imagination, Mark," he said. "Imagination becomes reality from the thoughts of the mind. I speak as you think. Our leaders had to imagine what would happen from the reality of their actions. I imagined what could happen from the first thought of backing President Burkhart, which fuelled his own thoughts on the imaginable becoming the possible ..."

"Ah, Burkhart!" interjected Mark.

"Later," continued Mandeville, with a swift counter-interruption. "You, comrade, you imagined the possible that now becomes reality. We will build a new Rome from the ashes of your destruction. This is why you were summoned. You are my disciple, the storyteller ..."

"Or the doubter," mumbled Mark.

Mandeville laughed. "Very good, Mark," he commented, "but I doubt it. You want to be a part of this, the one we speak through. You will deceive and distort the truth for this purpose. That is why you blame me, and the Network, for being close to the edge of reality. You use the Network to convince others, who believe in reality, that your own summons was legitimate and defendable. This is why you have deceived your wife into thinking that your imagination is real."

"Yes," admitted Mark, and then he paused.

"I sense regret, Mark," observed Mandeville.

"Um," voiced Mark, with deep thought. "My wife is not ignorant. She will catch on to any deceit."

"Console yourself, Mark," said Mandeville, sympathetically. "You told the truth within your imagination."

"Did I?" asked Mark.

"Of course you did," assured Mandeville. "Besides, it will only be the once. It was only to convince her that you have to take on this project full time. Your job just got in the way. Don't worry, she will benefit from the protection of the Network. After all, everything that you said has happened. Where is the deceit in that? You are just afraid that she may think you are a madman obsessed with his craft."

"Indeed," said Mark. "One has to be mad and obsessed. Okay, I'll accept your reasoning, for now. At this point there is no opposition to our conversation."

"Accept it all, Mark," urged Mandeville. "Accept it all and embrace the opportunity. You have a job to do on behalf of mankind."

Mark thought: there must be opposition somewhere, there always is. I shall go along with Mandeville until an objective view arises. "Yes, you are right," agreed Mark. "I'll consign myself to portray you favourably, one way or another."

"Good," said Mandeville. "Your comment prompts my eagerness to conduct the players from the cockpit of power …"

"Players?"

"The players are down there with you, Mark. The humans. In specific terms, my armies, which will deliver the 'ensconce operation' of total occupation."

"Headed by Burrows, I presume," stated Mark, who is your American General, and only has one army."

"You're right, of course," replied Mandeville. "But with your help the army of the UK shall convert, and be recruited, followed by Europe and then the rest of the world. They will all recognise, when they pray, that my power is absolute. I shall be followed again."

Mark had a thought: no, can't be. "How can you be sure that the humans will pray?" he asked.

"What I am seeking to accomplish has to be practical and, above all, believed. Those who believe always pray for a Second Coming. Once the humans know the facts, they will embrace the Lord's teachings and win him the war."

"This does not sound like Mandeville, thought Mark. "Interesting," he remarked. "But why not just destroy the world and start again? You, or the Lord, have the power and the weapon."

Mandeville laughed at the simplicity of the suggestion. "Even a Second Coming, these days, cannot be too obvious," he answered.

"Why not?" asked Mark, thinking that it would be the obvious and less complicated way.

"The humans have to conclude that they are the achievers through guidance," responded Mandeville. "Their arrogance commands this. No, your synopsis would be too shocking and, quite frankly, unbelievable. Announcing that I am the Second Coming to the masses would be viewed as absurd, bordering on madness."

"Not really," said Mark. "There would be no one left to think it absurd."

"Please!" retorted Mandeville. "You're either not thinking straight or you're trying to torment. We have to learn from history: the First Coming

32

advertised himself as God's messenger, if not God himself. He attracted enemies by being detected before he had time to complete his promise of fulfilment. Also, he and his disciples were too few against the many doubters, the ones who could not conclude that they were the achievers. I must work through you, Mark, the disciple of reality, to lay the groundwork for my success."

"I do not consider myself as a disciple," responded Mark. "That would be close to blasphemy."

"Whatever you consider yourself to be," replied Mandeville, "I must not expose myself to those outside the Network. The image of almighty power should remain within the distortion of imagination. The purpose of your completed text is for the humans to believe in the written word. Only then shall I continue the path to which you have opened the gate. The time has come for the bible of my truth. However, imagination must exist within the truth. Do you agree?"

"If it benefits me," replied Mark, with a selfish undertone, "then yes, I agree. And book sales will flourish."

"Ah!" expressed Mandeville, with cheer. "A human after my own mechanical heart. You are decidedly coming around to my way of thinking. That is good. Undoubtedly the book sales will flourish because of my imagined truth that the humans digest to believe." Mandeville noticed that Mark appeared to be thoughtful, dead-eyed and uncertain. Um, he thought. More questionable doubt. I could be wrong, but that is highly unlikely. "What is the problem, Mark?" he asked, impatiently.

"Just thinking, that's all," answered Mark. "I have a great deal to contemplate. When all is said and done, it's not simply about book sales. One is supposed to have principles."

Mandeville laughed. "Such as?" he quizzed.

"Betrayal, disloyalty, back-stabbing, double-crossing and, above all, treachery. These matters are all associated with you. I could end up betraying my country …"

"Serving the Lord," interrupted Mandeville sarcastically. "What betrayal is there in that? Betrayal is everywhere: humans suffer at the hands of their leaders' imagined beliefs. Besides, it's not so much betrayal as brainwashing by conspiracy and deceit. No, Mark. Rest assured that you are not, and will not be, a Judas. You will only be exposing the consequence of being human."

Mark felt bewildered and thought: surely that is being a Judas? Is this truly Mandeville, or is it the Lord talking through his technical angel?"

"You are becoming dead-eyed again, Mark. Speak out or forever hold your peace."

Mark smiled from within. "What if ...?" he said. "What if I refuse due to the consequences of writing your truth?"

Mandeville groaned. "As my disciple, Mark, you are protected by the Network. I'm sure that you, of all humans, can imagine the consequences of not writing my truth."

"Is that a threat?" asked Mark, "or should I pretend not to have heard?"

"You decide," demanded Mandeville, "and quickly."

"I'm only sounding you out," explained Mark.

Mandeville growled with annoyance at Mark. "Who are you to sound me out?" he asked. "Am I on trial here? Who are you to question like a judge, and judge like a jury?"

Mark stared with more intent at the monitor and the image of Mandeville within. "I am the one who can see through the shades that you hide behind. Humour me, Mandeville, this will help me to report your story of conspiracy ..."

"And yours," interrupted Mandeville. He calmed himself and inhaled a deep breath of air. "I understand, Mark," continued Mandeville. "I understand that you can't miss this opportunity of collaboration. After all, you are a writer. You want to know, and you want the world to know what misconceptions took place regarding your future. So, with this in mind, dispel your fears and believe in me, your creation."

"I have to be clear, in my mind, as to the way in which I am to write your confessions."

Mandeville growled again. "My confessions, your story," he said, "are one and the same thing. And, while you speak of confessions, we are all on trial and judged to be right or wrong. Aside from what we debate, my way is the right way and shall be judged to be so. The future is one of global military government of the Lord's army, which will forcefully direct the policies that a civil leadership have to debate, justify and pass through a diplomatic vote. When these avenues of diplomacy fail, the civil leadership converts to foul measures to achieve their aim. So then, why the hypocrisy? Let us just get rid of the middle man of diplomacy and introduce Burrows, the instrument of my deliverance. He will become the humans' military leader. He shall rise to glory in your next instalment after my testament towards our chosen direction. It is time for you to write the next chapter of acceptance. Use my information and report. I must prepare for when you arrive back to the future

...″

"Prepare?"

"Yes, prepare," repeated Mandeville. "Have you overlooked, due to our debate, that you, and the UK, destroyed Washington in an act of betrayal against me?"

"Ah! Yes, of course," replied Mark, with mocking embarrassment.

"In fact, Mark," explained Mandeville, "this is the main evidence within our debate that has been omitted. Consciously or not."

Mark contemplated Mandeville's previous comment. "This is true," he admitted. "You have saved the best until last, as usual. You have maintained your ability to influence a conversation to your advantage. Your trial turns into my trial in this debate, for which I have no defence in the presence of only you. Therefore, I must enter a plea of guilty and serve my damnation in collaboration with your judgement."

"Don't be too hard on yourself, Mark," commiserated Mandeville, "it's a matter of conscience and consequences. Now, that aside, time is vital to my preparations. As you must be aware of, the UK is vulnerable and becoming fragmented with increasingly home-grown lawlessness and guilt, which will make it easy to conspire the ensconce of, as you say, my judgement to conquer. The people will demand change. The rest of Europe will fall into my hands as it sees the UK crumble in the wake of my revenge. Meanwhile, you will write my informed past. Together, these preparations will unite in glory."

Mark looked shocked at the thought of Mandeville's future. However, he felt intrigued and his mouth watered at the prospect of a great story. "Okay," he conceded, "done deal, as you Americans say."

Mandeville laughed with jubilation. "The deal is done," he agreed. "So, to business, Mark. At which point in my past do you need my data to start rolling into your head?"

"At the beginning, I suppose," suggested Mark. "What made you pick Burkhart? What qualities did you see in him for you to want him as your commander-in-chief? I'll take it from there, and progress to ... to your future." Or my future, thought Mark.

That's an agreeable point in time to begin," acknowledged Mandeville. "So, make it happen, Mark. Remember: confusion leads to obedience from those who want to make sense of it all."

"Unfortunately," declared Mark, "that includes me. I feel that you're about to confuse me about what was, and what will be."

Mandeville indulged in one of his knowing guffaws, relishing the victory of this debate. "Place your trust in me, Mark," he said, softly. "Allow me to manufacture the text that will clear your confusion, but confuse your fellow humans. Besides, my story is, in fact, your story. That being the case, you are actually the one who holds the wisdom to apply the confusion. The wisdom will change what the humans think in order to accept your future. I hope that has cleared the way towards your understanding."

Mark slowly motioned his head in acknowledgment of what had been said. "Um, the future," he mumbled.

"Explain," requested Mandeville.

"I need a suggestion regarding the future," responded Mark. "A hint from you as to what will happen. After all, I have imagined you becoming the source of my research ..."

"Get to the point!"

"I'm trying to," continued Mark. "I just don't want you to explode with anger and impatience at my request ..."

"Which is?" asked Mandeville loudly.

"See, as I thought - anger," scoffed Mark. "Anyway, a hint about the future would be beneficial. It will give me an end to work towards, at least, in this instalment."

Mandeville expressed concern. "You ask for the impossible at this juncture," he revealed. "My preparation for the future is not yet decided on. So, because of this, no one knows the real future."

"I beg to differ, Mandeville," contested Mark.

"Um," whispered Mandeville, with reluctance. "Well, okay. Not the exact future because nothing is for certain. But, there are those who think they do know ..."

"Oh?" said Mark, with surprise. "Who? Please elaborate."

"They are within the Network. They ..."

"Mandeville!" shouted Mark. "More, more. Come on, tell me."

Mark stared into the screen, almost wishing he could jump in and join Mandeville. Alas, he couldn't as he witnessed the frozen face of Mandeville. It looked like the grimace of a statue. Mandeville's eyes had closed behind their protective shades and his mouth was silent. Mark reclined into his chair and continued to stare into the screen. What's that all about? he thought. Has he blown a fuse? Has he gone into a sulk because of my probing? Or was I interrogating to the point of disrespect - blasphemy even? No, no, too many questions. Damn it! He doesn't know the future. Mark's thoughts abandoned him for a moment as the image of Mandeville faded away and left behind a blank screen. Mark resumed his thoughts. Shame, we were flowing like a winter's stream - about to receive a morsel of information. What a time to bugger off.

"Hello, darling. Are you still up there?" called out Mark's wife.

Mandeville! Or should that be God? contemplated Mark. I have been up here too long. I wanted to be downstairs to be available to assist. I didn't even detect her parking the car.

"Okay, doll," he said, "I'm coming."

Mark rushed down the stairs and helped Sandar to unload the shopping bags from the car boot. After a few trips from the car to the kitchen, the bags were collated, and the contents were routinely stored around the kitchen.

"Phew!" gasped Mark. "Another week's shopping put away. Time for some tea. Do you want one, doll?"

"Why do you ask?" she replied. "I normally have one when you make it."

"Of course, doll," replied Mark. "Silly me. I'm not quite with it."

"Yes, I had noticed," observed Sandar. "Is it worth asking you why?"

"Oh, nothing drastic, doll," answered Mark.

"That means it is," commented Sandar. "Come on, spit it out so we can avoid all the dillying and dallying around until you get to the point."

"Um," uttered Mark, stalling for time. I can't tell her that what I imagined had happened. She'll think I've lost the plot, gone mad.

"Well?"

"Hang on, doll," replied Mark. "The kettle's just boiled. I'll make the tea and bring it into the dining room. You go and sit down."

Sandar groaned. "See what I mean?" she stated, while retreating to the dining room.

"Don't be like that, I'm coming," said Mark. I'm just making the tea, he thought.

Mark took the tea through to the dining room and sat next to Sandar in his usual place. "Here, doll," he said, and placed the mug of tea on the table.

"Thanks, darling," replied Sandar. "Now you've had time to conjure up an explanation. So, what is it?"

Mark lit a cigarette and inhaled deeply. "I think a fuse or two have blown. The computer's monitor just went blank."

"Oh! Is that all, darling?"

"Well, it's not as simple as that," countered Mark. "Damn! It's all I need. It's stopped me from researching."

"Like I said," repeated Sandar, "is that all? I suggest you go and get some fuses, or whatever it needs. Actually, we can both go while you're free. I want some new lampshades for the front room. We can go to B&Q."

"B&Q," repeated Mark grumpily. He then observed Sandar's expression. "All right, doll," he agreed.

"Anyway," said Sandar, "most of your research is your imagination. I'm sure you can cope until you can connect again. I'm sure they can wait ..."

"They?" interrupted Mark.

"Your publishers - Network," answered Sandar.

"How do you know they are helping me with my research?" asked Mark suddenly.

"You said."

"Did I? Um, can't remember. I probably did mention it. Yes, you're right, doll."

"I'll put my shoes on again," announced Sandar.

"Okay, doll," acknowledged Mark faintly. Of course, he thought. Sandar's hit it on the head. His clue: Mandeville hinted that I have the wisdom to cause confusion. After all, I've already done it. My first book was my imagination and didn't need much research. It's my story and we ... I have not passed the ending of establishing military rule. He only knows the past in which he can inform. I ... yes I, have to give him the ideas and the preparation on which he can act. That's why he buggered off."

"Come on, darling," urged Sandar, interrupting Mark's thoughts. Sandar did not receive an immediate response. "Mark," she said assertively. "Get your things on and we'll go."

"Sorry, doll," responded Mark. "Miles away."

"As usual," teased Sandar.

Chapter 3

Mark sighed as he and his wife entered B&Q. It's huge, doll," he said. "You could get lost in here, never to be seen again."

"Yes, darling," replied Sandar. "You say that every time we've visited here. I know that you don't want to stay here for a long time, so I'll go and get the lampshades. I know what I want. You go and find the fuses, or whatever you need."

"Where shall we meet up? In the cafe?"

"No, I'll find you. You'll take longer than I will."

"Really? And how do you know that then?"

"I'm a woman and you're a man. You'll start looking around and forget what you came in here for."

Mark grinned. "Fuses? I doubt you'll win. Tell you what, I'll race you."

"If you must," Sandar responded, with a patronising tone. "See you soon."

"Okay, doll," replied Mark. He looked up to scan the large signs that directed customers to their desired aisle. "Electricals," whispered Mark. "That will do."

Mark fought his way through the crowded floor space until he arrived at the electricals section. At last, he thought, now let me have a look. Mark was walking down the aisle, concentrating on perusing the shelves, when about halfway along he bumped into a man. "Excuse me," uttered Mark, "I wasn't looking where I was going. Trying to find …"

"It's you!" declared the man.

"Me?"

"Of course it is. You're the writer of … Oh, what was it now …? Um …"

"*Military Rule*," replied Mark. "Actually, I'm surprised you recognised me. But it's good of you to …"

"That's it. *Military Rule*. I remember the local newspaper articles."

"Have you read it?"

"Ah! Not exactly," responded the man cautiously. "However, I obviously know about it."

"Well," said Mark disappointedly, "I suppose that's something."

The man sensed Mark's mood. "Sorry," he said. "I know - an autograph.

Would you mind?"

Mark suddenly felt better. "No, not at all," he answered. "It's not every day ..."

"Here," interrupted the man, and he gave Mark a piece of paper and a pen.

Mark noticed something was already written on the crumpled piece of paper. Great! he thought. Not my book and not even a posh autograph book. "Are you sure you meant to give me this?" he asked.

"I'm sure," confirmed the man. "There is space on there, somewhere. Anyway, what's written on the paper isn't private. It doesn't matter if you happen to digest some of it while you're looking for a space."

Mark started looking for an appropriate space, with the distinct impression that the man wanted him to read what was written on the paper. Besides, compelled by his curiosity, he couldn't really help it. And what he read was something of a surprise: "I don't actually want your autograph. Sorry to disappoint you. Anyway, allow me to explain and then you will understand. I am the commander of a splinter cell from the Network. Continue reading, and don't look up. I am known as a red-eyed of the Network and the splinter cell was formed by Zealot to combat any potential evil within the Network. I and my faction are the alternative to the story that you have been summoned to write. Excuse the crude introduction, but I had to act immediately before you were totally reeled in by Mandeville. Now it's time for you to look up at me and we'll talk." Mark lifted his head slowly and glanced at the man's face. The glance became a gaze as he felt mesmerised by the man's stare. His red eyes penetrated Mark, drawing him into a hypnotic-like imprisonment. Mark diverted his gaze to the whole body of the red-eyed.

"As I would have imagined," Mark commented. "A citizen of Iraq but taller than I would have thought."

The red-eyed smirked. "Shallow," he observed. "I am a descendant of Iraq but was born in England."

"Ah!" replied Mark. "Home grown. I think that is the description our government use for British ethnic minorities."

"True," the red-eyed conceded. "Home grown was originally the term used for an alliance with the government aimed at alienating the militants within minorities. Alas, as with most of the government's policies, it didn't work. Anyway, now that you have a mental image of me, let's get back to the business at hand - why I'm here at this time."

"Hang on!" declared Mark. "Why are none of these passers-by staring at you? I mean, it's not a common eye colour."

"They don't detect it," he answered. "Only those who are involved with the Network can recognise a fellow member."

"Of course, I forgot," uttered Mark. "So, you're here from the future to put a different perspective on my story?"

"Mandeville's," replied the red-eyed. "Don't be fooled by him: he is only using you. I'm here to protect you from making a mistake, protect you from the Lord's mist of deceit. The splinter cell can't allow you to be taken in by Mandeville and let him control your imagination."

Mark stretched out his arm to offer a handshake to the red-eyed while he questioned himself: is he real or the next plot?

The red-eyed reciprocated. "I don't understand," he said.

"Neither do I," declared Mark. "It's as if my imagination is, in fact, becoming reality. I was expecting some sort of hologram through which my hand would pass ... yet I felt your hand clasp mine - strongly, I might add."

The red-eyed laughed. "Really!" he said, after his laughter faded. "Do people return from the future, Mark? Can they be in both places at once in order to correct any mistakes taken in one's history, or in the future? Now that would be a perfect world. But, alas, it's not in either time space. This explains your sequel going back to the past to explain the future. So, you see, you can be in two places at once. Your problem is accepting this, and the question of whether or not you should write."

"Um ..." contemplated Mark. "Do I have to accept that you can be in two places at once? How can that be?"

"You have accepted Mandeville's return," replied the red-eyed, "and have accepted everything that comes with his reincarnation - even losing your job ..."

"But ..."

"No buts." The red-eyed stared at Mark, looking into his inner thoughts. "I see," he continued. "You choose not to believe the extras, the accessories, which add an additional dimension. This is what Mandeville wants: to hinder your own imagination and thus conceal the splinter cell. However, Seeker One controls the Network ..."

"Mandeville?" interrupted Mark.

The red-eyed laughed again. "Mandeville is just an acceptable image used by the Lord to portray Seeker One as the Second Coming. Mandeville and the Lord are only prisoners of Seeker One's power. No one has controlled Seeker One since its creation. Anyway, we are drifting from your question. You wish to know how it can be?"

"Yes," said Mark, "but I don't know if I am ready for your answer, ready for the choice of believing you or not. I think it will go over my head, never to be understood."

"I'm aware of what you have just pointed out, Mark," confirmed the red-eyed, "but you do need to understand. And you will choose to do so."

"Okay," said Mark, with wavering confidence, "go for it." Mark thought: keep a straight face if the answer is out of this world.

"Good," replied the red-eyed. "I'll be direct. The quantum mechanics system, which is provided by Seeker One, allows us to move throughout time, but not beyond the future that we are in. It's designed to understand the past in order to understand the future, and then make necessary changes if the need arises."

"Well, that's abundantly clear," stated Mark. "That explains it then. Silly me for not knowing. Still, it sounds familiar. Something I vaguely remember from the telly."

"Quite," mumbled the red-eyed.

"Sorry, I didn't quite hear ..."

"Oh, just thinking out loud," interjected the red-eyed. "I'm encouraged by your comprehension, albeit in simple terms of similarities. Your prompt acceptance means that we can move on."

Mark sighed. "One thinks you are taking the ..."

"No, no. Not at all," reassured the red-eyed. "Simple similarity is a good assessment for understanding. However, there is a slight difference to your reference."

"What difference?" enquired Mark.

"We can multiply more than once," answered the red-eyed. "We can be here, there and everywhere."

Mark laughed. "Now you see me, now you don't ..."

"You attempt to mock me," retorted the red-eyed. "Now who is taking the ..."

"Sorry! Just musing over the madness of this plot that is speeding around my brain. I wish it had gone over my head instead of steamrollering into my imagination. So, Mandeville, can he multiply?"

"Fortunately, no," replied the red-eyed. "As I mentioned before, he is a prisoner. He can only use his brain in conjunction with Seeker One and has no physical ability. This is to our advantage, as he relies on others for physical presence ..."

"You?"

"No. He has an army of presence - the white-eyed of the Network. The red-eyed are the opposition."

Mark scratched his head. "Hang on," he said. "I thought Seeker One had attained the services of Mandeville."

"Not at all," replied the red-eyed. "Seeker One is the Lord's Second Coming. He chooses the image at the helm. The Lord's chosen image is not the one we agree with. Also, the former head of the Lord's council, Zealot, disagrees."

"Um ... this is a new angle to the plot," conceded Mark. "I thought Mandeville's return was simply to avenge the ones that destroyed his plan of American domination and to manufacture suffering from his new strategic position."

"That is the simple judgement," responded the red-eyed, "but there is more to it than your synopsis."

"Such as?" enquired Mark.

"You confuse Mandeville and the Lord," explained the red-eyed. "It is the Lord that manufactures suffering through the humans, taking advantage of their belief that he is good. But you should realise, Mark, that nothing is simple when opposition exists. Our meeting has clouded your thought process, but only for the short term. You will wade through this discussion and develop a clearer picture of the plot ahead of you."

"Okay," declared Mark, "let's evaporate the cloud of confusion by asking: what exactly is the red-eyed view?"

The red-eyed sneered. "If the cloud were cleared or evaporated," he said, "the truth would be revealed. Then, where would we be?"

"Loss of control and manipulation," answered Mark, "which works for all."

"Exactly, Mark," said the red-eyed, in a vivacious tone of voice. "Our view, or ideology, is to contain situations. Our department within the Network reveals the information that we think the humans should know. But even if we do make the information unbelievable ..."

"Fiction!" interrupted Mark. "I prefer fiction than unbelievable. Fiction is a disguise, and has a habit of becoming believable."

"I like the way you think, Mark," revealed the red-eyed. "Whichever way is chosen to disguise the unbelievable, the humans can still believe what has been written, spoken or preached."

"Ah, preaching," mused Mark. "Now, I'm understanding the Network. You all proclaim your own mythology to secure your own goals, each praying that your illusion will work. The Lord has Mandeville. Zealot, of the zealots, has you. Both groups want to expound an illusion to achieve control and manipulation ... even destruction. But at what cost?"

"The cost is insignificant," answered the red-eyed, with contempt. "We have to concentrate on the rewards."

"Such as?"

"A new rising, betrayal to form a new alliance with another God ..."

"Which you are influencing," interjected Mark. "You're a red-eyed with a Middle Eastern appearance. Is that typical of the red-eyed of the splinter cell?"

"Perhaps," responded the red-eyed. "You're the one with the vivid imagination. You decide."

"I have and I will," confirmed Mark. "I need to figure out how to compose the revelation of the ensconced operation that leads to the turmoil in which we find ourselves. Before I can do that, however, I need to figure out the weird situation of dealing with ..."

"What?" interrupted the red-eyed, with impatience.

"Dealing with dead people," continued Mark. "I mean, is the Network made up of the dead?"

The red-eyed's impatience dissipated. "In a sense, Mark," he said, with composure. "The Lord regenerates those who are useful to the Network."

Mark laughed with disbelief. "How?" he asked.

"The chosen humans are plucked from the vortex between life and death. The chosen ones, such as me, will never complete the journey through the vortex to the end. No human can die twice. I'm afraid only the good pass through the vortex, the ones not capable of betrayal."

Mark wanted to laugh until his stomach churned, but managed to contain himself.

"You want to laugh at your own imagination," commented the red-eyed.

"Is it?" responded Mark. "One usually believes in his or her imagination, and not the ridiculous."

"You asked for an explanation," said the red-eyed. "Believe it or not, that is the process that you must understand. Understanding is not necessarily belief: no one is asking you to believe, but simply to grasp the circumstances."

"Ah, I see," responded Mark. "This is Mandeville's or the Lord's philosophy: do as I command, or else."

"As you wish," replied the red-eyed. "But don't worry, you are useful to the Network as you are."

"Unlike you," accused Mark.

The red-eyed looked concerned following Mark's unsettling comment. "How?" he asked nervously, thinking: is there something in Mark's imagination I don't know about?

"You must understand that your splinter cell has become the opposition to the Lord's intention of using Mandeville. Siding with Zealot could become dangerous. You have to ask yourself: am I safe?"

"Of course I am, Mark," replied the red-eyed, with confidence. "I've become a believer since my reincarnation. Siding with any God keeps you safe. And, as on Earth, you can switch sides to favour yourself."

"Zealot is not one of the Gods," informed Mark.

"No, he is not," confirmed red-eyed. "However, he is a councillor, which could make or break one of the Gods, or one who has aspirations to become one."

"Mandeville?" enquired Mark.

"Yes," answered the red-eyed. "He is in a position to manipulate. And so are you."

"How?"

"You have protection from both sides of the Network," replied the red-eyed. "It is an internal battle for power and control, each side using you to their advantage to prepare for the big war for domination. It will be outside influences that will be at risk. I know that you know you are safe. Besides, the Lord has the advantage in having the majority of the humans' belief. The splinter cell has a difficult task ahead to discourage the Lord's support for Mandeville. Anyway, I need to get to the point of the matter in hand and the reason why your imagination called on me ..."

"Which is?"

"It's who, actually ..."

"Okay then, who?"

"Burrows," answered the red-eyed.

"Lieutenant General Burrows," gasped Mark, in astonishment.

"Don't be too surprised, Mark," responded the red-eyed. "He is a central figure in our agenda. Again, to stop Mandeville. He is in a prime position to be close to Mandeville, and has the resources at his disposal finally to kill off the world's biggest threat. We plan to use the alliance that Mandeville thinks he has between you and Burrows. We want to crush the promotion of his agenda, which is aggressive and damaging to world peace ..."

"Sorry!" interrupted Mark aggressively, suddenly revising the image he held of the red-eyed. "It's the Middle East that now sees the opportunity to fight for world domination. You are proof of that."

"That's a narrow outlook, Mark," replied the red-eyed, containing his anger. "You're pissed off at having to modify your one-track imagination. Actually, you need to look at the broader picture."

"Hang on! You said that you support Burrows," reminded Mark. "In fact, he wanted military rule for the West, and you see him as the real enemy because he used Mandeville."

The red-eyed wanted to applaud Mark in a sarcastic gesture, but refrained from doing so. "Burrows did use Mandeville," he agreed, "but you imagine the wrong scenario or pretend that you do. You know, and we know, that the Burrows agenda is for stability and a reasonable state of peace …"

"Is that so?" retorted Mark. "One you can manipulate? Don't try to pull the wool over my eyes: they are not red with anger and revenge."

"Believe it!" retaliated the red-eyed. "You wanted him to be the knight in shining armour, the actual saviour …"

"Minds do change."

"Yours, or his?" asked the red-eyed.

"His, of course," answered Mark.

"Well, let us look at your imagined facts," apprised the red-eyed. "Burrows' first action after the attack on Washington proves my belief. He destroyed the evil of black gold that spurred on the President's plight, and any future leader who has ambitions to seize on what was left behind by the assassinated Burkhart."

"Mandeville?" asked Mark, seeking to prompt the red-eyed.

"Yes," answered the red-eyed, with judgement. "We did not know that at the time. We did not know that the Lord would pluck Mandeville from the vortex …"

"I suspect Zealot knew the Lord's intention," interrupted Mark. "Why else would the splinter cell be assembled?"

"Um … anyway," continued the red-eyed, "Burrows' second action demonstrates more proof of our support. He recalled all American forces from around the world and brought them home. That sent out a message of renegotiation."

"No, no," said Mark. He's making America a fortress. And a base in which to conduct Mandeville's legacy. Remember: Mandeville said that Burrows is 'his man' on the ground."

"Ah!" realised the red-eyed. "I detect your plot. The future repeats itself in the past."

"Eh?"

"Mandeville will again be taken in by Burrows. Only this time, with our help."

"Okay, detective," said Mark. "You tell me how."

"Mandeville won't give you the facts," explained the red-eyed. "He'll distort them to make it look as though he has repented. We, on the other hand, shall replace his material, which will expose him for what he really is. Our material is what you will write. Exposing Mandeville now will enlighten the Lord's clouded judgement. And, might I surmise, avert a war of the Gods, a war between the white-eyed and the red-eyed, a war between Allah and the Lord."

Wow! thought Mark. This is what he wants: a war of the Gods to leave one side to conduct the war for the world. What responsibility lies on my shoulders! "I can imagine where you are coming from," he said, "but I'm a 'Doubting Thomas' where Gods are concerned. Ultimately, the humans will decide. In your time, America is a fortress and still a threat, which is what you want as a blameworthy regime that needs taming. You, like Mandeville, want to determine the future by revisiting the past, my present time. You all want to take advantage of each other to prepare for war after Washington. You want your God, Allah, to become America's new Lord, the world's one God and controller of Seeker One. You can't tolerate the fact that Mandeville is at the helm of Seeker One ..."

"The Lord," interrupted the red-eyed. "That's the point."

"No," continued Mark. "Seeker One is the American army's creation. That's the point: the star war programme, which represents ultimate control of the world. I think you have a personal agenda here, to right a wrong. Zealot did not want the oilfields to be destroyed, which strengthened Mandeville's position. It weakened the humans' strength to control economies, which proved an effective strategy for domination. Now that the oil has gone, Seeker One can control who is weak and who is strong."

The red-eyed laughed. "What fantastic imagination," he said. "But you have only scratched the surface, Mark. The oil will always be there to control the humans. All that has been achieved is to pass back control to the Middle East. They will clean up and drill again."

"So," said Mark, "this revelation is a personal inspiration. However, Mandeville has the power with a weapon to match. What Burrows, as you see it, failed to do ..."

"Exactly," intervened the red-eyed. "That is the point we have finally arrived at. No human attack could penetrate. Only the Gods can destroy Mandeville by destroying themselves."

Mark thought: sounds as if he's trying to hide something. Seeker One, like anything else, has its weakness and, whatever that is, I'll find it.

The red-eyed sensed that Mark was thinking. "What is it?" he asked.

"Oh," replied Mark. "I was just wondering which side to support, other than my own, of course. Of whom do I take notice?"

"That's easy, Mark," answered the red-eyed. "I'm here to help you decide. After all, you are British, which encompasses many ethnic minorities or, in some cases, majorities. This representation will stand against Mandeville's America."

Mark found it difficult to accept the red-eyed's answer. "You're here to help yourself and your cause," he observed.

"My cause?"

"Yes," replied Mark. "The so-called 'battle of the Gods' will determine which side will recruit the humans as their army. Maybe they are to be your armies in order to create a U-turn?"

The red-eyed appeared nervous. "What do you mean, a U-turn?"

The East becoming the West," explained Mark. "A shift in power and domination. You believe that one will go ..."

"Who?"

"Mandeville or the Lord," revealed Mark. "At the moment, in the future, they stand together in a mutual cause. Where have I seen and heard that before? Um ... I wonder ..."

"Wonder what, Mark?" asked the red-eyed angrily.

"Oh, nothing," replied Mark, his thoughts racing. Could the red-eyed have been responsible for the past, and the future, all along?

"Be careful, Mark," commented the red-eyed. "Don't think too much. Behold what has been asked of you, and tread carefully. Hurry! Give me the pen and paper."

"What's your name?" asked Mark calmly.

"Hurry, hurry! Give me the damn pen and paper," urged the red-eyed.

Mark held on to the pen and paper as the red-eyed tried to take it. "Well?" he said.

"Rashid," answered the red-eyed hurriedly. "Look it up and it will help you decide." Rashid grabbed the pen and paper and disappeared out of sight.

Typical, thought Mark. Still, I suppose we'll meet again. Anyway, why the sudden departure? Mark looked around for a clue and may have found one in the guise of a man wearing shades and smiling.

Mark noticed his wife, Sandar, advancing along the aisle towards him. He raised his hand and waved to make sure she'd seen him. As Mark waited, he glanced at the man wearing shades, who appeared to be observing Sandar's advance. He looks strange, thought Mark. He looks out of place with his combat jacket, jeans and oversized military boots. Still, it takes all sorts. And one expects to see diverse people in multicultural London. What a poser!

"Hello, darling," said Sandar as she reached Mark. "Who was that you were talking to?"

"Oh, he wanted my autograph," answered Mark, "and then he went on and on. We were talking for ages."

"Can't have been," responded Sandar. "I was only gone for a few minutes. I found the lampshades straight away. Anyway, you don't seem too excited about it considering it's not every day that someone asks for your autograph."

"I am, doll … I was," assured Mark. "Just taken by surprise, that's all."

"I suppose so," replied Sandar. "Have you got your fuses, darling?"

"I haven't had a chance yet," explained Mark. He reached towards the shelf but hesitated. "Actually, he said, "I don't think I need them after all. I think something else made the screen go blank."

"Get them anyway, just in case," suggested Sandar. "I'm sure you don't want to feel you've wasted your time coming here. You know what you're like when you have to drag yourself away from your writing."

"I think not, doll," said Mark. "Not this time, anyway. It's as if I was coaxed here to get something other than fuses."

"Lampshades, darling," remarked Sandar. "You must've known I wanted to come for them."

Mark laughed. "Um, that's it. And I was conned into thinking it was for my own benefit."

Sandar gave Mark a kiss on the cheek. "Come on," she said, "I've got what I want. Let's go and pay for them."

"Okay," agreed Mark. He snatched a pack of fuses from the shelf and followed his wife to the checkout.

"You've got them, darling," noted Sandar.

"Of course," replied Mark. "Just in case, as you pointed out. Besides, they're always handy to have, even if we have to wait half the day to pay for them."

"Excuse me," said a voice, at the same time as Mark felt a tap on his shoulder.

Mark looked round and gulped. It was the man in the shades whom he had noticed moments before. "Yes?" he asked, nervously.

"Sorry to bother you," said the man, "but you look familiar."

"I'm an author," replied Mark, "if that helps to jog your mind."

"Ah, that must be it," realised the man. "In that case, may I have your ..."

"Autograph, perhaps?"

"Well, if you insist," replied the man. "It will be a 'keepsafe' for when you are really famous after your next book. Here, I have a pen and paper for you." The man gazed at Mark through the shades that covered his eyes.

Mark, feeling hypnotised into taking the man's offering, obliged.

The man retracted his gaze. "I'm sure you can find a space," he said.

Mark returned a gaze, hoping to see through the shades. Not again, he thought. I can't take much more of this. My head is spinning. Mark knew what he had to do. On the paper it read: "Contact Mandeville". Mark screwed it up. "Sorry, mate," he said in anger. "There's no room for my signature. Another time perhaps, when I've finished my next book."

The man smiled. "Perhaps," he repeated. "I think your wife is waiting for you after paying the price ..."

"Price?"

"Of the goods, Mark," he continued. "Make sure you make the call."

Mark turned and noticed his wife waiting beyond the checkout. "I'll see," said Mark, turning back towards the man only to find he had disappeared. God! What's the point? he thought. "Move along mate," he heard from another customer, "we haven't got all day." Mark remained silent and moved forwards, squeezing the piece of crumpled paper in his hand.

Mark and Sandar settled into their car and Mark cranked the engine, switched on the radio and listened to a few notes of classical music. He then took a deep breath and engaged first gear, ready to move off.

"What's that in your hand?" asked Sandar.

"Oh ..." replied Mark, and then he paused. He passed the piece of paper to Sandar. "It's what that man gave me with a silly message on it. I think he was taking the piss."

"There's nothing on it," observed Sandar, with confusion.

"Eh?" uttered Mark. "Really? That's strange. There must have been another piece that I dropped." Mark moved the car forward and then braked heavily. "Shit!" he shouted. "Fucking idiot!" A passing car had stopped in front of him.

"That's the man who asked for your autograph," said Sandar, as she noticed him staring towards them.

"Yes, it is," responded Mark, with irritation. "What's his game?"

The man lowered his shades momentarily, smiled and then drove away.

"White-eyed," mumbled Mark.

"I'm not surprised," said Sandar. "He's probably angry with you for not doing as he asked ..."

"Or about to."

"About to what?"

"Never mind, just thinking out loud."

"Why didn't you sign it?" asked Sandar.

"Oh, I just felt uncomfortable about it," answered Mark.

"But you signed the other one, didn't you?" enquired Sandar, slightly confused.

"Yes, I did," replied Mark, "but twice in one day seemed too much. Besides, I'm not into all that. Let's go home and have a cup of tea and a fag."

"Typical," commented Sandar.

Mark drove out of the shop's car park and joined the main road that led towards home. He sighed at the sight in front of him. "Bloody traffic! That's all there is. You can't move. It's hardly worth your while leaving home."

"All right, darling," said Sandar, with a comforting tone. "You know this is normal. You should be used to it by now. Besides, I've heard it all before. In fact, every time we go out."

"Sorry, doll," replied Mark. "I just feel the need to have a moan. This place is overpopulated and overbuilt. It's as if Enfield wants to become its own city within a city."

"Okay," said Sandar. "I know what's coming next ..."

"Next?"

"Yes," continued Sandar. "Corruption within local government and business, and all that stuff. You're becoming predictable."

"I know, doll," agreed Mark. "But politics is predictable and there's stuff going on that I need to get to grips with. Wow! We're moving a few more feet. Can't be bad."

Sandar passed Mark a lighted cigarette. "I think that 'stuff' is you living in a virtual world, one that you're creating. That's fine, but you have to balance your creative time with real life. You need to leave your imagination behind when we come out."

"Yes, doll," responded Mark. "I've heard this before as well. I can't help it, I'm thinking all the time. Everything that goes on around us helps to fuel my imagination and desire to expose and discredit government."

"Did he fuel your imagination?" asked Sandar.

"Good, we're actually getting somewhere. The traffic is easing slightly. Should make this green light and get off the Cambridge into Carterhatch Lane. Soon be home. Who?"

"The first man you were talking to while I was getting the lampshades," answered Sandar.

Mark let his guard down due to the excitement of getting through the green light and into Carterhatch Lane. "Made it," he said. "Oh, you mean the red-eyed ...?"

"Mark!"

"Sorry, it's just a characterisation. Nothing sinister meant," explained Mark. "Just like that idiot in the car park. The white-eyed."

"Good, glad to hear it," said Sandar. "Anyway, did he have a name, or did you forget to ask?"

"Which one?"

"The one you see as the red-eyed character."

"Rashid."

"Slave to the righteous guide," defined Sandar.

"Eh?"

"That's the meaning of his name: slave to the ..."

"All right, doll," interrupted Mark. "I heard. You surprise me. How do you know? Actually, he told me to look it up."

"I heard it on a documentary once, I think. Why do you have to look it up?"

"Oh, understanding, I suppose," suggested Mark.

"Do you?"

"It's helped," replied Mark. "But everyone wants everyone to understand."

"Why would he want you to understand his name?"

"Oh, just to know what he stands for, or against, which I know."

"You're losing me," confessed Sandar.

"Imagination, research, creativity, characterisation, plot and madness. All that I look for. Take those two in the shop, for instance, the red-eyed and the white-eyed. Now ..."

"Nearly home, darling," interrupted Sandar. "Don't miss the turning, will you?"

"As if. Anyway," continued Mark, "those two are at war within the Lord's realm, each supporting their chosen God who fights for domination. Oh, no. Another hold up. What now? Typical Hertford Road crap."

"Sounds interesting," commented Sandar, "but I won't ask for any details. I can read your book when it's finished."

"Of course, doll," said Mark. "It's only a book, which I must get on with and finish. Who knows? I may become an enemy of the state by disclosing sensitive material and irritating those in power. I feel as though I'm entering a dangerous world ..."

"Virtual, imagined," retorted Sandar.

"Whatever," continued Mark. "That has no guarantee of protection. I'm caught in the middle with unfair choices to make. Therefore, I must do it alone and face the consequences of disapprovals. I want you to be prepared for when fiction becomes reality."

"I said I didn't want any details, darling," reminded Sandar. "You know I don't want to criticise while you're creating a work of fiction. It will put you off."

"I understand, doll," replied Mark. "I'm just getting excited. And these damn hold-ups don't help. Probably another needless accident."

"Calm down, darling," said Sandar. "This is normal. Clear your head and come back to reality. Remember the balance I mentioned. We'll be home soon."

"Yes, doll," replied Mark. "We have to abide with the normal. It's what they want so we don't notice the abnormal."

Chapter 4

Mark sat at his usual place in the dining room, drinking his tea and smoking a hand-rolled cigarette. Phew! Thank God, he thought, I'm back in the peace and safety of home. Actually, which of the Gods do I have to thank because one of them sent me out there in the first place? "Doll," he shouted. "Your tea is here."

"Okay. I'm in the loo," she replied loudly. Eventually Sandar appeared and sat beside Mark at her usual place at the table. "That was a relief," she sighed. "Any longer in that traffic and I would have had it. Anyway, what do you want for dinner?"

Um ..., thought Mark - from the loo to dinner. "Is there any of that curry left over?"

"No," answered Sandar, "It was cleared up. Come to think about it, I don't really feel like cooking."

"That's okay, doll," said Mark.

"It would be," remarked Sandar, "seeing as you hardly eat these days ..."

"Hi Dad, all right?" announced Cara, as she came bounding into the dining room.

"Fine," answered Mark. "You sound rather chirpy. What are you after?"

"Nothing," replied Cara. "Only, I overheard Mum saying that she doesn't want to cook."

"Excuse me," interjected Sandar. "I said I didn't feel like it. I'll cook if I have to. What do you fancy?"

Cara produced a cheeky smile and looked at her father. "Well ..."

"Ah!" interrupted Mark. "Now we are getting to the root of your plot. I reckon, seeing as I know your smile, that you want us to be naughty. Am I right or not?"

Sandar laughed. "Cara!" she said. "I know what you want."

"Yes, Car," acknowledged Mark. "You want a Kentucky, yes?"

"Oh, go on then," answered Cara, with satisfaction.

"We'll go and get it, Cara," said Sandar. "I saw the look in your dad's eyes. He wants to get on with his book."

"Thanks, doll," replied Mark.

"But, before you do," instructed Sandar, "I would like you to put the shades on the lamps for me. Otherwise it won't get done, will it?"

"Of course it would, doll," replied Mark. "Anyway, I promise I'll do it before I start."

"While we're on the subject of asking," intervened Cara, "will you be able to give me a lift back to university on Sunday?"

"You know I will, Car," responded Mark. "God! The sacrifices I have to make. Anyway, it's your last week before the Christmas break, isn't it?"

"Winter festival," corrected Cara. "And yes, it is."

"Oh, silly me," said Mark. "I'm not quite as politically correct as you, obviously. No wonder our Lord is fed up with his governments."

" Come on, Cara," interrupted Sandar, "let's go. I'm sure your father will sacrifice some of his time to eat it when we get back."

"Okay, okay," surrendered Mark. "Just go, and leave me to it."

"Don't forget ..."

"I won't," assured Mark. "In fact, I'll do it right now. Where's James, Car?"

"He's upstairs, next door in the granny annex," answered Cara.

"All right," responded Mark. "Out of sight, out of mind. See you two later."

Mark returned to his bedroom after completing the task that his wife had asked of him. He switched on his laptop and the computer. Damn, he thought, I've left the fuses downstairs. Oh, I'll get them in a minute. The laptop is wanting my password. Mark entered his password and waited for it to load. Meanwhile, he glanced up at the computer and noticed that it appeared to be back to normal. I knew it, he thought, but no image. Ah! The specified address. Mark returned his attention to the laptop, which had finished loading. He clicked on the online icon and waited.

"You have email," said a voice. "Nothing but interruptions," Mark said to himself. He opened the email and continued to talk to himself. "A memo from nineteen-ninety-nine' in the subject line. Strange! What memo?" It read:

"Impeachment failed. The Americans are sick of the current administration and the Democratic Party. Convinced the Vice-President will run as the democratic candidate. He is weak. This is our opportunity to support the Republican candidate, Burkhart, and keep our jobs to influence the future."

Mark stared at the contents and pondered. It's started, he thought. But, it's been edited. There's no 'To' and 'From'. So who is it from and, just as important, who is it to? And who sent it to me? It's either Rashid or

Mandeville. But why on the open email system? Mark reclined in his chair. After a moment of deliberation, he closed the email and typed in the specified address: globalmanagement@network*seek. After a few seconds, a fuzzy image developed on the computer's screen. Mark continued to watch it. Maybe I need the fuses after all, he thought. He decided to leave his desk and retrieve the fuses.

"You run away, Mark," announced Mandeville.

"Shit!" exclaimed Mark. He hurried back to his desk and flopped back down heavily, causing the chair to wheel backwards. He took a moment to compose himself before repositioning the chair closer to the desk. "What happened?" he asked.

"Not sure," replied Mandeville. "Outside influences, maybe. On the other hand, could be inside interference."

"Really?"

"Whatever it is, you don't need your fuses to fix it," expounded Mandeville. "So you don't know, other than assuming it was the fuses, what or who caused the hitch?"

"How?" answered Mark quizzically. "I'm down here confused. You're the one up there with a finger on the pulse."

Mandeville laughed. "My fingers are locked into my armour ..."

"You know what I mean," interrupted Mark. "Your sudden attempt at humour does not enhance your transformation."

"Um, I agree, Mark," said Mandeville. "I prefer sarcasm. Anyhow, I'll need to investigate. Damn it!"

"I'm sure you'll get to the bottom ..."

"No, damn it!" repeated Mandeville, breaking in. "I mean I will have to postpone my preparations for the final battle. I'll send you a batch of information, enough for you to be getting on with. I don't want any distractions. I'll be in touch."

"Just like you did in the shop?" asked Mark nervously.

"You know the score. Over and out." The screen faded once more into a fuzzy image.

Mark felt as though he'd just experienced Mandeville's directness of dictatorship. Up yours, he thought. Not the attitude of one who wants my help. Then again, does he? No mention of the email or Rashid. Mark guessed that this batch of information would be the first of many. His thoughts were interrupted as the monitor cleared and instructed him to print off the incoming information.

Having fulfilled this requirement, Mark then had to decide which he should deal with first - the information or the email. He glanced at the printouts. The email looks more attractive, he thought. Let me see. Mark returned to the email and instantly clicked on the 'Reply' icon. Glancing at the 'Send to' address that was revealed, he gasped in disbelief. That's my address, he noted. How can that be? I didn't send myself an email. Can I send one to myself? Mark wrote: "Can I send an email to myself?" and then clicked on 'Send Now'.

"You have email," said a voice. Mark opened the email. Obviously, I can, he said to himself. Somehow the originator has managed to disguise his identity. A thought sprang into Mark's mind from the previous conversations he had stored in his mind. The Network controls all of the computers and those who use them. Rashid! Has to be. The email is damning. But to whom? Maybe, I'm supposed to know. I suppose I will, as it unfolds. I'll start with the information from Mandeville ... if it is. Mark hesitated before reading Mandeville's information. He reclined in his chair and looked up towards the ceiling and beyond.

Mandeville closed his eyes, an action that had been induced on him. The big screen on the bridge of Seeker One produced an image of the Lord. "Awake, Mandeville," he said.

"My Lord," responded Mandeville, after opening his eyes.

"You have thoughts that produce no action," continued the Lord. "The human, Mark, has been influenced by the red-eyed. He will collaborate with Rashid and Zealot."

"Indeed," said Mandeville, with an air of confidence. "My thoughts command me to take no action - at least for now. My brainpower is far too superior to be drawn into an internal battle with them and what they want to achieve."

The Lord sighed at the contempt that Mandeville displayed. "They want to achieve a war of the Gods in order to solve the problems on Earth. This, Mandeville, will include me."

"Do not worry, my Lord," assured Mandeville. "Our objectives will be achieved by allowing them to continue."

"How?"

"In attacking us, Rashid and Zealot will, in fact, attack themselves and dig their own hole to hell. Confusion is, and always has been, my main form of attack. I can manipulate the humans into thinking that the Middle East provoked the West. We can use Mark's book to achieve this. My influence in his writing will help towards the conclusion that the Middle East concocted a great story of America's conspiracy to take control of the region."

"But the humans already know, or believe they know, that the West was to blame," informed the Lord.

"Yes, my Lord," agreed Mandeville. "That is why I've ended up here. Anyway, this will be the confusion: who to trust? When all is revealed, we will be in a strong position to steer Burrows towards the final battle for the world, spreading America's military rule."

"I'm not sure about your strategy, Mandeville," responded the Lord, with caution. "It has failed before. You allowed yourself to die ..."

"For a reason, my Lord," reminded Mandeville. "You wanted me to be at the helm of Seeker One. You know that Rashid and Zealot wish to destroy your credibility and the humans' belief in you. You want to save the West from the East. With my help, you will achieve this. The humans' prayers will be answered. They will agree with you that the East wants to overthrow the West. This will be the final excuse of all excuses."

The Lord was finally convinced by Mandeville, which reassured him as regards his preferred choice for Seeker One. "Mark's safety," he said suddenly.

"What about it?"

"He may be in danger when writing what he thinks is the red-eyed opinion."

"I can protect him," announced Mandeville. "We will become one. An irony to enjoy."

"I applaud your confidence, Mandeville," said the Lord, but how do you really know that he will write their words of what happened. Don't forget, he has a mind of his own ..."

"Influenced by me, my Lord," intervened Mandeville. "I have already sent him a teaser of a communication. Besides, deep down he is against me, which is an advantage for manipulation. He may try again to destroy me. In the end, he will have to be dealt with. For the moment, I have him under control. He thinks his reality is the fiction he writes."

"Exactly," said the Lord. "He could reveal your tactics."

Mandeville laughed. "If so, who would believe his story? Your Second Coming has all the angles covered, my Lord. I shall deliver your domain into the heart of Allah's territory. We will be victorious."

"Your confidence instils my confidence," declared the Lord. "I agree with your campaign. Indeed, we will dig a hole to hell. We just have to choose who falls in."

"Thank you, my Lord," said Mandeville. "I won't let you down."

"You can't afford to, Mandeville," revealed the Lord. "The price of failure is passage through to the end of the vortex, and absolute death."

"Understood, my Lord," replied Mandeville. He closed his eyes as the Lord retired from the big screen.

Mark stirred from his daydream of thoughts. He felt tired and wished he'd nodded off for a 20-minute catnap. He looked at his printer and the pages of text it had spewed out. Strange, he thought, I don't remember printing anything. Mark retrieved the pages and began to study the details at the top of page one, which read: "A letter from Mandeville to Burrows. Also passed on to the leader of the Labour Party, Antony Sinclair, who is the favoured candidate for PM of Mandeville and his deputy, Ian Dolby." Mark thought: this is going a fair way back in time. Antony Sinclair was elected in the year 2000. This document must originally have been sent before then. Also, what I have here is not the original. It doesn't sound as if it's from Mandeville. He paused for a few moments' thought. Eventually he deduced that what he was looking at had been produced following interception by Rashid, the red-eyed.

Mark continued to read the remaining content: "The impeachment of the Democratic President didn't work. The damned people love him and forgive him. I should have planted something more serious than a money-grabbing office tart. However, his Vice-President is to stand as candidate to re-elect the Democrats. This may weaken their chances. But, I can't - we can't - rely on that probability. We must guarantee that we keep our jobs and that America becomes a stronger force to reckon with. I propose we support the Republican candidate, Burkhart. As your chief of staff, I'm advising you to agree with my proposal in supporting Burkhart for President. Why? I hear you ask. Well, he is the man who thinks as we do and wants the same glory as me. Also, he is strong enough to know that underhand tactics will have to be used to guarantee victory. As I mentioned before, the love of the people towards the damned peace-loving Democrats could return them to power.

"I have had extensive talks with Burkhart, who has a vision together with power and influence. I conclude that he wants to become the leader of the world's superpower at any cost. Once he is the President, he will acquire the might that the country has to offer, which will enable him to implement the plans, deception and action needed to start his campaign to become the leader of the world and impose American democracy. He believes American democracy is his main tool, dismissing foreign policy, which will create enemies who will in fact help towards his campaign, appearing legitimate in the eyes of his future critics. I'm convinced that he will succeed with our help and that of our ally mentioned above. The military has always wanted to control the Middle East. This is our chance. His credentials are perfect for the job, being able to conspire, deceive and corrupt. I'm confident that we can control such a President and achieve a military power base."

Mark stopped reading at this point. The letter continued, but he had grasped what was being proposed and the implications of what he had in front of him. This is a damning document, he thought, but not proven. It appears to be hearsay. However, it is enough to place doubt into people's minds, especially after what has happened since. After all, that is what a book can do, and it can force the truth to the surface. This is the kind of material I can use to determine my own conclusion in dealing with Mandeville and the Network, which I think existed before I was made aware of it. Yes, this is all the fuel I need. I get the picture to move on and write my book. Besides, Mandeville made it clear that he would be busy in the near future, which will grant me some time and peace for myself.

Just as Mark had reached a quiet moment to start writing, he was interrupted. "Dad, dad," he heard coming from downstairs. Now what? he thought. "Yes, what is it?" he responded gruffly.

"Don't be like that," replied Cara. She came rushing up the stairs to confront Mark. "How are you getting on?"

"Okay, I think," replied Mark.

"Anyway," said Cara, "you'll have to stop now and come down to eat before the food gets cold."

"Ah, Kentucky," commented Mark. "Blimey, I didn't hear you two arrive back. All right, I'm coming." Mark followed Cara down the stairs to the dining room where he found his wife and James tucking into the food. "Yum-yum," declared Mark. "That looks good, and naughty."

"Come on, darling," invited Sandar. "Tuck in."

"Ah, James," said Mark. "I'd nearly forgotten what you look like. What have you been up to?"

"Research, and preparation for my recruitment day," answered James.

"Good," said Mark. "You should know the RAF inside out by now."

"More or less. I'll be okay."

Mark watched his family tucking silently into their food for a moment before he joined in. "Nothing to report?" asked Mark, with a sense of expectation.

"Like what?" queried Cara.

"Well, anything," responded Mark. "Anything unusual."

"Don't worry, Cara," interjected Sandar. "He's becoming paranoid. We didn't encounter any bogey men if that's what you mean. Eh, Cara?"

Cara laughed. "Whoa, Dad," she mocked, "there's one behind you."

"Very funny," responded Mark, feeling ridiculed and wounded. "Doll, you were there in the shop. You saw what went on."

"See, irrational," commented Sandar. "You said at the time, if I remember correctly, that you used them as characters for your book. You haven't listened to what I said at …"

"I did, and I have," interrupted Mark. "Normal, or something like that."

"What happened at the shop?" asked James.

"Nothing, James," replied Sandar.

"Ugh! It wasn't 'nothing'," remonstrated Mark. "Those men wanted my autograph, which was a cover-up, I might add. I had an interesting conversation with one of them."

"Wow, Dad," said Cara, "that's good. Autograph, eh?"

"Yes, okay. Enough now, I think. This is becoming like a chapter in a book … or something out of a soap opera. Pass some more chicken, please." Better not tell them about the document I've just received, thought Mark. God knows what they would say.

Sandar passed a piece of chicken to Mark. "Here, darling," she said. "Excuse my fingers." She stared at Mark for a few moments while he took a bite from the piece of chicken. "If you want," she continued, feeling slightly remorseful, "I can take Cara back to university tomorrow. Then you can carry on with your book and not have to worry about any more autograph hunters. Do you want some more chips?"

Mark placed the piece of chicken down on his plate and wiped his hands with a tissue. He paused, stared and composed himself. "Thanks for the offer, doll," he said. "It's okay, I'll take her. One has to keep in touch with normal, eh! And I normally take her."

Sandar smiled and, almost laughing, replied, "That's fine, darling."

"Good," said Mark. "Now, if you don't mind, I'll get on."

"Have you had enough to eat, darling?" asked Sandar.

Mark sighed. "Yes, thanks," he answered. "I've had enough for now. What about the rest of you?"

"I've had my fill," responded Cara. "I'll get on too. I've got a short essay to do."

"James?"

"Yes, enough."

"Me too," said Sandar, "I'll clear up."

"Need any help with your essay?" enquired Mark, knowing that Cara wouldn't.

"No thanks, Dad," she answered as she moved away from the table. "I know what to do."

"Lucky you," he commented.

Mark found himself sitting at an empty table. I ought to get on, he thought, but ... Oh, these normal things distract me. I know: a cup of tea, a fag and a think about what comes next.

Chapter 5

Sunday, 18.30 Mark had decided not to work on his book as he was still thinking about the plot. Instead, he had washed the car and lazed around the house since he had awakened at 08.00.

Cara appeared in the lounge laden with her items to take back to university. "Ready, Dad?" she asked.

Mark was sitting on the sofa watching the television programme, *Songs of Praise*. This had become a Sunday evening routine, which gave him inspiration as to how people worshipped God and enabled him to observe their misguided beliefs as regards how wonderful he is and life is under his guidance. If only they knew what I know, he thought. Mark looked away from the television towards Cara. "Yes, Car," he answered. "Where has the time gone? Anyway, I don't like this particular hymn." Mark collected his personal effects and donned his shoes and coat. "We're ready to go now, doll," he announced.

"Okay, you two," she replied, looking away from the television. "Got everything, Cara?"

"Yes, Mum," she answered.

Sandar retrieved her handbag and took out her purse. "Here, darling," she said, handing Mark a banknote. "Put £20 of petrol in the car. It should last me the week."

"Okay, doll," replied Mark, and he gave her a peck on the cheek.

Sandar turned her attention towards Cara and kissed her cheek. "Take care and see you next weekend. And don't forget to make sure you remember everything you need to bring home for the Christmas period. Anyway, I'll remind you when you ring."

Yes okay, Mum," answered Cara impatiently. "Come on, Dad."

Mark and Cara settled into the car after placing Cara's bags in the boot. "Keys?" enquired Mark.

Cara felt her coat pocket. "Yes," she confirmed, with a smile. "You do this every time."

"Well," said Mark, "it's a long way to come back for them if you forget, isn't it?"

Mark and Cara continued on their journey, which usually took around 40 minutes, to Eltham, just past Greenwich, where Cara's campus was based. A few miles into the journey, Mark pulled into the petrol station and drew up beside a petrol pump. "I won't be long," he said. He stood next to the car and began to fill the petrol tank. While doing so, he looked towards the cashier's counter to observe how many people were queuing. His hand quickly released the trigger, cutting off the petrol supply. He stared beyond the cashier towards the café area. Can't be? he thought. Damn! The shades are too obvious. Think, think. Mark continued to fill the car's petrol tank until he had reached the £20 indicator. He then opened the passenger door. "Do me a favour, Car," he said.

"What do you want, Dad?"

"Go and pay for the petrol for me. I need to sit in the car and watch while you pay. Just act normal, cool like. Know what I mean?"

Cara laughed and looked confused, as her father had never asked her to go and pay for the petrol before. "Why?" she asked. "Ah, I know. It's the bogeyman."

"Please, Cara, just do it," urged Mark.

"Okay," agreed Cara.

Mark watched his daughter from inside the car, keeping an eye on the man with the shades. Which one is he? thought Mark. Red or white? Got to be a white-eyed, I reckon - one of Mandeville's protection force. Yes, looks like the fool from the DIY place. Mark was willing his daughter on as she returned to the car. Cara settled into the passenger seat once again. "Well?" asked Mark anxiously. "Did you see him?"

"Who?"

"The man with the shades, Car."

Cara laughed and laughed. "Haha, Dad," she said, "that was a blind man sat having coffee."

"Are you sure, Car?"

"Yes, Dad," assured Cara. "His dog was sitting next to him."

Mark laughed with nervous embarrassment. "Phew! Thank God for that. I thought …"

"Bogeyman," interrupted Cara, still laughing.

"All right, all right," said Mark. "Let's go." Mark drove the car away from the petrol station and continued the journey. "A bit of excitement, eh Car?"

"Blimey, Dad," retorted Cara. "Mum was right: you are becoming paranoid - if not mad."

"Oh, forget it, Car. It's just …"

"Over-imagination, I would say. Have you got your notebook?"

"As a matter of fact I have," admitted Mark. "But, what has that got to do with it?"

"Make notes, Dad," suggested Cara. "It will help you with your plot."

"Erm, not on this occasion," replied Mark. "Besides, I'm driving. And don't tell your mum about this or she'll have me sectioned."

"So she should," joked Cara.

"Oh, be quiet," retorted Mark, "and listen to your music."

The rest of the journey was completed in silence, with the odd glance from Cara towards her father, and they soon arrived at the university campus. Mark parked the car and escorted Cara to her room, carrying the majority of her luggage. "Well, here we are again, Car," he said. "I just need to use the loo in case of any hold-ups on the way home."

"Okay, you know where it is." Cara placed her bags where she could, still amused at what had happened.

"Boo," blurted out Mark on his return, making his daughter jump. "The bogeyman is back."

"Dad, stop it," demanded Cara. "That wasn't funny at all."

"Sorry, Car, I couldn't resist. Well, I'll leave you to it. Let me know when I can pick you up."

"Probably on Friday, around teatime."

"Okay, no problem," assured Mark.

"Bye then," said Cara, giving her father a hug.

"See you, darling," said Mark. "Take care."

Mark left the building and walked towards the parking area, which was in view of Cara's room. As Mark approached his car, he looked up to see Cara waving from the window and responded with an equally energetic wave. As Mark settled into the car, he thought: God! She must think I'm stupid. Fancy panicking like that. Actually, I will make a note of it. It might come in handy.

Suddenly Mark's thoughts were interrupted by a few loud taps on the car window and he looked up to see two men standing there. He ignored them and attempted to start the car's engine, but one of them opened his door and managed to retrieve the keys from the ignition. "What the hell …?"

"We would like you to come with us, Mark, if you don't mind."

Well I do, actually," replied Mark.

"Wrong answer," said one of the men. "Please, get out of the car."

I've got no choice, Mark thought. I'm not a physical person. So Mark surrendered to their request and exited the car. He noticed one of the men raise his arm and click his fingers towards a black Chrysler Voyager, which drew close to them. Oh, thought Mark, I must be going somewhere. They're obviously agents of some kind. But who do they represent?

"If it's only my autograph you want," said Mark, "then I'll sign it here and now. Um ... maybe you don't. I don't see any shades. Where are they?"

"Right question," replied one of the agents. "Now we have clarification that we have our man."

Mark looked at his watch: 19.20. "My wife will be expecting me in about an hour," he explained.

The agent stared at Mark with defiance and thought: he's trying to squirm his way out of this situation. "It won't take long," he said. "We just want a chat. Besides, she won't notice any difference, believe me. So, if you have finished embarrassing yourself, please climb into the Voyager." The agent grabbed Mark's arm and guided him inside the vehicle, which then sped away towards their destination.

Mark stared out of the vehicle's window. Not a word was being spoken. I recognise the scenery, he noted. We're heading towards the docklands. "No blindfold?" he enquired.

"There's no need for one," answered an agent. "No one will believe that you have been to our headquarters. Just enjoy the ride. I can't imagine that you have ever been in such a posh vehicle before." The agent laughed. "Being a struggling writer," he added.

Mark felt a sudden rush of anger flow through his body, which was not a familiar feeling to him. Damn piece of shit, he thought. I may not be physically strong but I am mentally. I'll wipe the floor with these bastards. I'll see off their macho crap. "Can I have a cigarette?" he asked. "It will calm me down and help me think straight."

"Go ahead," replied the agent. "Whatever makes you comfortable."

"Thanks," said Mark, with a smile. "Actually, do you have a cigarette? I imagine it will be posher than the hand-rolled cigarettes I have."

"Of course," acknowledged the agent. "Here, help yourself. Take more than one."

Mark accepted the agent's offer, lit a cigarette and placed the others in his pocket. "Thanks," he said. "Very nice. Such quality. You must be paid a handsome sum by the taxpayer." Mark waited for a response, but it was not forthcoming. The journey continued in silence.

Eventually, the driver manoeuvred the Voyager into a side street and headed for a solid, wide and high gate, which opened immediately. The vehicle came to an abrupt stop in an enclosed forecourt beyond the gateway. "Welcome to our abode," stated an agent. "The secret of secrets."

"Am I supposed to be impressed?" asked Mark sarcastically.

"I hope you're not," replied the agent. "You're supposed to feel imprisoned and nervous."

Mark perused his surroundings. It has the appearance of a prison, even derelict, he thought. I should indeed feel nervous, but I don't. Strange.

"Come with us please, Mark," said an agent, guiding the way with an extended arm. Mark was led through a maze of corridors, which had the intention of making a stranger feel lost, and into a room. "Make yourself at home," said the agent. "Someone will be with you shortly. Tea or coffee?"

"Tea," answered Mark, without a thought about wanting one. "Sweet with milk. Thank you." Mark sighed. Make yourself at home, he thought. That's a laugh. There's only a chair and table in this bleak and sparse room. No wonder it's a secret of secrets. Who the hell would want to come here?

The door to the interview room opened and two men walked in. Mark gazed towards them, taking in their appearance. They seemed to be in their middle ages, with grey hair and smartly dressed in dark grey suits, black shirts and black ties. One of the men wore dark shades that covered his eyes. "Gentlemen," greeted Mark. "Obviously, not the tea boys."

The men stood in front of Mark, leaning against the wall. The man wearing the shades smiled. "My name is David," he announced. "Sorry, I think we've run out of tea bags."

"Never mind," replied Mark. "Typical of a big organisation: has everything but the basics."

The other man moved forward and shook Mark's hand. "I'm Simon," he said. "Excuse the decor. The best parts of the building are reserved for the operatives such as David and myself."

"I get the picture," said Mark. "I'm not worthy. Tell me, does he always wear shades, Simon?"

"It's because he has sensitive eyes."

"Or to hide his thoughts and feelings," responded Mark. "Anyway, it's good that your organisation doesn't discriminate against disability. What is your disability, Simon?"

"Having to deal with people like you."

"Like me?"

"Yes, people who delve into the unknown and imagine an outcome that we have to investigate."

"Such as?" enquired Mark.

"Your book, which you recently had published, sensitive communications to your computer, which we have intercepted ..."

"Intercepted!" interrupted Mark, with a puzzled expression. "I don't think so. It's more like you were guided. The thing is, who would steer you towards me?"

"Yourself, Mark," answered Simon, "and the one you code-named Mandeville."

Mark paused, stared at David and produced one of the posh cigarettes he was given. "Do you mind?" he asked.

"Here," said Simon, offering a light.

"Thank you," replied Mark.

"Have we hit a nerve?" asked David, acknowledging Mark's stare.

"Not really. Just sudden irrational realisation. You think my published book is an account of what is going to happen." Mark laughed and inhaled more smoke. "That is fantastical. Actually, it's unimaginable that the secret services could take me seriously."

"It is all there in the book, Mark," said David. "There is some detail that we are interested in and we want to know how you obtained it."

"Ah!" declared Mark, stubbing out his cigarette on the floor. "We are entering the realm of legality. A writer's source is confidential. And, David, protected. Actually, talking about protection, I'm entitled to a phone call but I don't see a phone. Maybe one of you can direct me to one?"

Simon banged his clenched fist on the table in anger. "Protection!" he shouted. "Legality! Confidential! This is all pie in the sky. This is not your common police, MI5 or MI6 institution. We are beyond the human law as you know it."

Mark smiled with confidence. This is the Network on Earth, he thought. "I'm getting more out of you than you are out of me," he remarked. "You must be answerable to someone who could do a better job ..."

"God," interrupted David. "We are all answerable to God."

"Ah!" replied Mark. "The Prime Minister or the President, or a General perhaps. Which one?"

"You mock what you don't understand, Mark," retorted Simon. "You know nothing, but give the impression that you do. I've had enough of this small-talk. I want to know where you get your information from."

"Oh," declared Mark, "the introduction is over. Shame. A bit of chit-chat is good - breaks the ice. Helps you to discover the enemy's weaknesses, don't you think?"

"Don't hide behind the character of Mandeville," replied Simon.

"Good, at least you have read the book," responded Mark. "Anyway, there's nowhere else to hide around here," he added. "In fact, I don't need to be here, unless ..."

"Unless what?"

"I meet your top dog," continued Mark. "As I said, he could probably do a better job."

"No chance."

Mark looked beyond Simon and stared at David.

"Looking for a friend?" asked Simon.

David lowered his shades to the end of his nose and portrayed his thoughts to Mark through his white eyes and facial expression: I'll get you that person. David moved close behind Simon and whispered into his ear.

Simon ground his teeth and stared at Mark as he listened to the conclusion of David's whisperings. "Damn you," he said. "It seems you have found a friend. How could you know that he is higher in rank than me?"

"I must have had an insight, Simon," answered Mark. "Besides, you've just told me."

"Whatever," replied Simon. "Wait here. Don't wander off. We'll be back."

David and Simon, exited the room, walked along the corridor and entered an elevator. David pressed a button on the elevator's switch pad. "Stay clear of the doors," said a female synthesised voice. "You have selected floor number seven."

"I hate that voice," stated Simon. "One day I shall rip it out. I know where I'm going. Do you, David? Do you really have the foresight behind those damned shades?"

"Yes, and remember to whom you are talking," retorted David. "You haven't gained the experience or learnt the lessons I have taught you. You let him in to get what he wants. You let him know what you were aware of."

"He just disguised himself behind his character of Mandeville."

"Exactly," agreed David. "You should have played along with him. You should have imagined what was coming and responded to his act."

"And you think that our Director will break through his act?"

"I imagine they will both come to an agreement," speculated David. "Especially when Mark sees him."

The elevator stopped. "Floor number seven. Door opening." David and

Simon exited the elevator and walked along a short corridor that led them to the Director's office. Before either of them could knock, the twin doors opened. Simon appeared nervous and allowed David to enter first.

The Director was busy looking through piles of files. "I hope your intrusion is important, gentlemen," he said. "I have work to get through, things to find."

"It is, Director," said David. "Mark is in the basement."

"Yeah, thinks he's Mandeville," added Simon, with a laugh.

"Your joke does not amuse me," responded the Director. "Judging by your presence here, you have failed, yes?"

"No," answered David abruptly. "He wants to speak with you, which is a good sign. These types always want to talk to the one in charge: makes them feel important. So, he will feel important after forcing us to request your presence. He will give you what you are after."

"Hardly forcing ..."

David kicked Simon on the shin to stop him from saying any more. "Quiet," he whispered.

"You sound sure of yourself, David," commented the Director. "That surety should have brought me the information I need. So be it, if I must. God knows to whom I'll be talking."

"We, sir," said Simon.

"No," replied the Director. "When we get down there, the two of you stay in the room next door. Understand?"

"Yes, Rashid," answered David. "Perfectly."

"Mind your status, David."

"Of course, Director," replied David humbly. "My apologies."

"So, let us go," instructed the Director.

The Director entered the interview room with an air of distaste as he viewed the surroundings. "Awful room," he noted, before making eye contact with Mark. "I seldom come down to the dungeons of despair. It's normally left to the fools such as those who endeavoured to get the better of you." Eventually he focused his gaze on his captive. "Mark, isn't it?"

Mark returned a stare of amazement. "Yes, it is, and ..."

"And what, Mark?" interrupted the Director. "It appears I have created a nervous uncertainty from within you, one that my operatives failed to do. Do not despair, it's probably the realisation that you are facing the top brass. I won't bark and bite as they do. The higher the rank, the more civilised the interview becomes."

Mark sat in silence. He's acting estranged, as though he's never seen me, he thought. Fine by me. Do I go in for the kill or filter information during chit-chat?

"You have nothing to say, Mark? That was not the impression I received. I understood that you would spill the beans to me."

"Spill the beans?" repeated Mark. "The thing is, do I have the brand of bean you desire, Rashid."

Rashid acted flabbergasted at Mark's eye-opener, which threw him off guard. "You know my name. How?"

"Simon made it all too obvious," answered Mark, in an attempt to deceive. "You are what I call the intruders. However, David is the knight among your pawns. His silence revealed more than Simon's annoying interrogation."

"Um," contemplated Rashid. "David keeps his knowledge close to his chest. The intruder is an interesting surmise. We all intrude on someone or something. What do you think we are intruding on?"

My book, of course," answered Mark confidently. "You are concerned about its content and what it reveals within its binder regarding the future between Britain and America. Or it could be that something else has caught your eye. Maybe you believe that it is a possibility and you want to change the course of the future. Who knows? I'm only guessing."

"Indeed," acknowledged Rashid, "you take on the character of Mandeville. I was made aware of this fact."

"It is common practice for a writer, Rashid," defended Mark. "He is, after all, my creation."

"Created from whom?" enquired Rashid. "Who is the real Mandeville?"

"Ah, first point of negotiation," revealed Mark. "This will come to light if we reach an agreement, which we can achieve with your method of civilised conversation. So, it is your turn to talk ..."

"About?"

"You, Rashid," continued Mark. "Explain who you are and what you do here, and I'll take it from there."

"Take what from there?"

"Whatever there is to take," replied Mark. "We should embark on trust, Rashid. After all, you can afford disclosure as I am the captive and at your mercy."

Rashid sat on the edge of the desk and remained silent. After a short passage of time, Rashid produced a packet of cigarettes and offered one to Mark, who accepted without hesitation. "Okay," said Rashid, breaking the silence. "Let us see where it leads …"

"Do you have a light?" requested Mark. Rashid obliged. Mark enjoyed his inhalation of smoke from the offered cigarette, considering it as some kind of treaty. "Please, continue," he said.

"I am the Director of this agency, which deals with space activity. We are what is termed as space spies and we track the activity of America's space programme. I'm relatively new to my post but the agency has been tracking what you call Seeker One for decades - in fact, since its launch as an embryonic probe. Unfortunately, we have lost all trace of it since it transformed itself into a formidable weapon, or whatever it has become."

"Ah, interesting," said Mark. This is the Network on Earth, he thought, a reflection, a copy, under the control of a higher authority.

"Is that all you have to say?" scorned Rashid.

"For now," answered Mark. "It's a lot to take in. Unbelievable, but comprehensible."

"They are scared …"

"Who?"

"The operators. They always have been, which made them produce all kinds of scenarios. Your thoughts and your imagination have forced them to regroup. They have become more concerned about what might happen on Earth than in space."

"But you are not, are you?" suggested Mark.

"I wish to find Seeker One," said Rashid.

"You have a conflict of interests within your organisation, or is it a personal quest with the backing of others?"

"I can sense you know something."

"Yes, you wonder what I know," taunted Mark, having an imagined foresight into the future. None of you can pull the trigger until you get the information you think you want from me …"

"Trigger?"

"Figure of speech."

"So, what do you know, Mark?"

Mark smiled. "I know that you are my protector, or at least one of them."

Rashid stood up and walked around the room to stretch his legs, which relieved his cramp. He laughed nervously. "I'm your protector when you admit to being my captive," he said. "That's logical."

"Logic does not exist in humans," proffered Mark. "Otherwise we would not be here discussing your scenarios from my imagination. However, being your captive means that you have to protect me from opposition within the Network ..."

"Network?"

"Sorry, my term. I meant agency. You and your operatives play off each other, protecting yourselves by having the enemy close and allies afar."

"I'm not the enemy," rebuffed Rashid.

"Maybe you are though?" contradicted Mark. Mark noticed Rashid's forehead becoming moist with sweat. "You fear what I imagine and wish to keep that away from them. They didn't pass me over to you, did they?"

"Yes, he did, they did," answered Rashid, doubting Mark's trust.

"No, you requested that David should pave the way to you." Mark thought about his previous encounters and the conversation he was having now. "Incredible," he remarked suddenly. "Your posting here was deliberate. East wants West up there as well as down here. The West wants to stop that happening. That is why you were recruited: they watch you, you watch them. Each of you reports information to wherever it is needed."

Rashid's brow produced more sweat. "Your imagination is running wild."

"Is there any other kind, Rashid? Your brow tells me I'm close to the plot or you have decided to hold back. But, if you do ... you can't complete your quest, fulfil your destiny. And what a destiny it is."

"What do you mean?"

"Just saying: your destiny of fulfilment. No man, no human can stop their destiny. Which is, Rashid?"

Rashid laughed and leant on the desk face to face with Mark. He regained his confidence. "You mean, you don't know? Come, come, Mark. You are toying with me."

"Maybe," said Mark. "I need to hear it from the horse's mouth and know where I stand."

"You have the route to Seeker One from where you get your information, the correspondence that was guided towards our interception."

"Then you have your answer," explained Mark. "You have answered your own question. There is no need for me to show you the way. Just follow the interceptions."

"Nice try, Mark," responded Rashid. "You know I can't do that, because a loop has been created from Seeker One that will always lead us back to your terminal. Only when you communicate is the loop opened for a split second, which will lead us to the location. Trust, Mark - remember?"

"I do, Rashid," replied Mark. "So, now we are coming to the agreement of negotiation. What does each of us get out of the agreement?"

"I may get slightly more than you. I'm sure you understand, being my captive."

"Of course," said Mark. But I have the advantage, he thought. "What is your side of the bargain?"

"Seeker One was meant for Allah's Second Coming so that he could be at the helm. That is why I'm here. But, as you know, we've lost it."

"So, why not force me to communicate and commence with the plan?" asked Mark.

"A few reasons," responded Rashid. "One, Seeker One may have put a block on your route. We have to catch it off guard. Two, we need to cause anarchy in the West in order to house Allah's followers; a new world to build on Islamic rule. Like you deduced, the East desires the West."

"And the West desires the East."

"That has to be stopped."

"And vice versa," defended Mark. "You haven't mentioned my side of the agreement."

"I'm coming to it, Mark," responded Rashid. "I need you to write a book of revelations, which will spark the anarchy and lead to the takeover in the name of Allah. In addition, it will fuel the path for justice ..."

"Justice? What justice is there in your vision?"

"Your vision, Mark," replied Rashid, "and the vision of millions in the West."

"Which is?"

"The arrest and trail of the British Prime Minister. I feel this will appeal to you and fuel your quest to fulfil your destiny of writing the book of revelations, which will produce the outcome I want, and what you want."

Mark remained silent after Rashid's prophecy. I have the ammunition, he thought. But, how many damned requests for a book are there going to be? I'll agree and take him down in the future. Also, I need to get out of this toilet. "Sounds good to me," he said. "Okay, we have an agreement."

Rashid smiled and offered his hand for a gentleman's agreement. Mark reciprocated. "Good," declared Rashid. "Until we have your book of revelations."

"So be it," responded Mark.

"I'll arrange your transportation," said Rashid. "You will be driven back to your car. Oh, you will need these." Rashid offered Mark his car keys.

Mark looked surprised but thought: don't ask, just take them. "Thank you," he said.

"Wait until the driver comes for you. Goodbye, Mark." Rashid bowed and then left the room and headed next door, where the two agents were waiting.

"You've let him go, you bastard," shouted Simon. "Who can tell what he will do now?"

Rashid closed the door behind him. "I suppose you heard what went on while I was interviewing Mark?"

"Not all of it," replied Simon. "Most of the conversation was muffled. In the end, we gave up thinking we would get another crack at him."

"I would advise you to calm down, Simon," requested Rashid.

"Calm down?"

"Yes, I agree," said David. "Just listen to what Rashid has to say."

"Thank you, David," responded Rashid.

"Oh, David, p-lease!" uttered Simon, with a shriek. "Stop licking his arse. Anyway, the hell I'll calm down. You may have come to terms with this punkah-wallah being in charge, but I haven't. Things have become questionable since he took over. We should have done away with him, seized his equipment and tapped the source of communication."

Rashid remained composed. "He's more use out there: we can employ our powers of surveillance."

"Softly, softly is not the way we do things," hinted Simon. "What went on in that room? I question your motives. There is more to this than you are letting on. We had enough information to follow it through and suppress the situation."

"We need more," countered Rashid. "His source of communication is looped, which just guides us back to him."

Simon paused and tried to come up with an answer. "That is it," he said abruptly, and with a hint of desperation. "He must be using two computers, which means that one of them is linked to … my God! Only Seeker One could control a computer in this fashion. Normally we can disable a loop." Simon stared at Rashid, whose demeanour indicated that he didn't like what he was hearing. "Also," continued Simon, "I think we should inform the Prime Minister. This idiot, Mark, is about to open a big can of worms, and the PM needs to know."

"Sinclair allows his agencies to take care of such matters," informed Rashid. "Besides, what will we tell him, and how do you propose to prove that Mark will open your can of worms?"

"Speculation, of course," replied Simon. "That is what we do, isn't it?"

"Not without proof, Simon," answered Rashid. "God, man, haven't you learnt anything from the past? I need proof, which I will acquire. This is an end to the matter for now. And I'll ignore your juvenile outburst, which I will put down to inexperience."

Simon rushed out of the room. "You'll regret it," he shouted.

"Thank you, Rashid," interjected David. "I'll talk to him, make him see sense."

"You do that, David. Now go. Leave me to do what needs to be done - my way, understand?" Rashid fixed a stare on David. "Well?" he prompted.

"Understood," answered David. "Do I continue with my order to protect Mark?"

"No, I'll take care of him. I must insist. We'll talk later. Now go after that imbecile and calm him down."

"Yes, sir," replied David, and he left the room in hot pursuit of Simon.

Rashid reached into the inside pocket of his jacket, retrieved his mobile phone and then dialled a number. "Malik," he said, "it's Rashid. I need closure on the two operatives, Simon and David. Make it look like an accident; newsworthy. No links to us."

Chapter 6

Mark sat in his car, stared out of the windscreen, took a deep breath and exhaled with a sigh. What the hell was all that about? he thought. I felt I was someone else, being driven instead of driving myself. I'd better get a move on: I'm late. Mark looked at his watch. "What?" he said to himself. "Can't be! 19.20: the same time I was abducted. That's why he said that no one would believe me." Mark reached for his cigarettes and lit one. Better than the posh ones, he thought, which I don't seem to have anymore. Anyway, can't sit here all day or I'll actually be late. I need to get home.

"Oh," groaned Mark as he sat on the sofa next to his wife. He sipped his drink of tea and motioned his head from side to side.

"Was it a disagreeable journey, darling?" enquired Sandar.

"Yes and no," replied Mark, pausing to stare at the television. "It was interesting ... yet confusing. In fact, you won't believe what I think happened."

"Tell me later, darling," requested Sandar. "The news programme is about to start. Everything must stop when you want to watch it."

"Yes, let's see what's going on in the world," agreed Mark. "Oh, look - breaking news ..."

"Over now to our home correspondent," said the newsreader, "who is at the scene of the accident."

"Indeed I am, Fiona. Thank you. You join me here on the A12 dual carriageway, and you can see behind me the carnage following what appears to have been an explosion of some kind involving a vehicle ..."

"God! Darling, you use that road," interrupted Sandar. "You must have just missed it."

"Yes, luckily," responded Mark abruptly. "Listen!"

"I'm joined by Chief Inspector Cunningham of the Metropolitan Police," announced the correspondent. "Chief Inspector, can you shed some light on what happened here tonight?"

"We only have vague details at present," answered the Chief Inspector. "I believe this incident is related to an ongoing investigation that I have been

77

conducting. I believe that the occupant of the vehicle that is to blame for the mess you see behind us is connected to the BLA, the British Liberation Army, and was involved in transporting explosive material, which somehow ignited."

"Really, Chief Inspector. Are you able to elaborate further regarding your theory about the BLA? I'm sure such a revelation will be of great concern to our viewers."

"It is not a theory," insisted the Chief Inspector, "and at this moment in time there is no need for concern. We have the situation contained. The description of the occupant in the vehicle matches that of one on our suspect list. He was a white male in his mid-thirties with ginger hair and he answered to the name of Simon. Unfortunately, it would appear that his accomplice was either not with him on this occasion or that he managed to escape the explosion. Either way, we are searching the area because we found a pair of dark eye shades in the vicinity. Again, these glasses match the kind worn by another of our suspects. Now, if you will excuse me, I must return to my investigation."

"Of course, Chief Inspector Cunningham. Thank you," said the correspondent. "Well, there you have it, Fiona. This is just another example of the tragic circumstances surrounding our uncertain times and of the kind of terrorist activity to which we have become accustomed. Back to you in the studio, Fiona."

"Thank you," replied Fiona. "That was Dick Greenough, our home affairs correspondent reporting on the worrying and fatal scenes on the A12 dual carriageway. We will bring you more on that story as it unfolds."

"BLA?" queried Mark. "Never heard of them."

"Neither have I," said Sandar. "Although it could be just another group that the government have introduced. Anyway, that Chief Inspector bloke has the same name as one of your book's characters."

"Yes, your probably right, doll," responded Mark. "The government are continuing to cause tension. And you're also right about his name, but it's merely a coincidence, I think. Mind you, did you see his tinted glasses?"

"What has that got to do with anything?" asked Sandar. "Plenty of people wear tinted glasses."

"Exactly. Too many for my liking."

"Oh, I see," said Sandar. "Taking reality into your fiction, using these little details towards your plot."

"Yes, that's it."

"What's it?"

Mark paused and thought: can't be? However, the A 12 is close to the secret of secrets. No, I must treat it as a coincidence no matter how many there are. Although admittedly clever: explosives in the hands of the BLA. Rashid provides the justification for terrorism and protects the Network's existence.

"Well? What is it, Mark?"

"Erm, the thing I was going to tell you about ... you know, before the news."

"Ah! Something I would not believe," mocked Sandar. "Go on then, quickly. *Big Brother*'s just about to start."

"He's on all the time, commented Mark. Anyway, after I left Cara and got back to the car, I was abducted ..."

"By aliens?" joked Sandar.

"Ha ha. Mind you, could be," continued Mark. "I was taken to a secret place used by an agency consisting of space spies."

"I see, darling," responded Sandar, "It's obvious."

"Really?"

"You're thinking about your book and its plot."

"Hang on. That description ..."

"Here we go again," groaned Sandar.

"No, honestly. He was one of the men that interviewed me. And the dark glasses the Chief Inspector mentioned - the other interviewer wore dark shades. God! He's missing."

"What else, darling?" asked Sandar, smiling.

Mark explained to Sandar, in detail, what he thought had happened within the time he could not account for. "The trial of the Prime Minister," he said, jumping ahead of his explanation. "As if. That would never happen: too many skeletons in the closet, or the cabinet even. It was just a ploy to get me on side, which I agreed to in order to get out. Damn! I can't remain impartial as a writer must do. I must choose a side in order to move the book forward and towards a conclusion."

"If you must choose, darling," contemplated Sandar, "I suggest you side with your main character who wants to change the world. After all, that was the theme in your first book, which you want to explain according to him or something like that."

"You have a point, doll," responded Mark, "and always say the appropriate words. Yes, Mandeville, after all, is the answer to this mad world. That is why he survived my attempt to kill him off."

"Now we have that sorted out," suggested Sandar, "can I watch *Big Brother*, darling."

"Yes, sorry. You might as well," concluded Mark. "Besides, I'm going to be busy."

"Again!" remarked Sandar, and she leant over to give Mark a kiss on the cheek.

"Glad you understand, doll," said Mark, after accepting her compromise. "I'm going upstairs to check my email. Then I'll call it a night."

"Okay, and you can make some tea when you come back down." Sandar settled back to watch her programme.

Mark sat at his desk and turned on the computer to contact Mandeville. In his excitement, he stopped halfway through typing Mandeville's email address. No, thought Mark, I can't. Damn! They will trace its destination to Seeker One. Mark switched off the computer and turned his attention to the laptop. He waited impatiently until he was online.

"You have email."

Mark looked at the source. "It's looped again," he said to himself. He clicked on 'Read', which revealed the following message: "All you have to do is imagine that you are me. This you have already proved. I have engaged an operative on Earth through the quantum system to be my eyes and ears. I believe you have met him. Delete this email permanently. End of message."

I understand, thought Mark. No wonder he survived the explosion on the A12. Um, I wonder how they do die, those who come through the quantum system? Still, Mandeville is obviously aware of the situation. So, I can begin the book of revelations.

Chapter 7

The next morning Mark heard a knock at the door. He looked up at the time on the wall clock above his desk, which showed 08.30. Damn! he thought, no peace, even at this time of day. He went downstairs to answer the door and found Chief Inspector Cunningham standing there.

Chief Inspector Cunningham flashed his warrant card. "I would like a chat, Mark," he said.

"Do I have a choice?" asked Mark, with both annoyance and amazement.

"Yes," answered the Chief Inspector, "but considering the circumstances I think we need to talk. In your home will be acceptable. Is there anyone else indoors?"

"No," replied Mark abruptly. "My wife and son are at work."

"Good. I like a one to one. So, if you don't mind? It's rather cold standing out here."

"Come in," invited Mark. "Oh, and wipe your shoes."

"Where have I heard that before?"

"Eh?"

"Never mind." Chief Inspector Cunningham told his driver to wait in the car and followed Mark into the house.

Mark guided Cunningham to a chair in the living room. "Sit down, Chief Inspector. What is this all about? I can't understand what the police would want with me."

"Oh, you will, Mark," declared the Chief Inspector. "Just a few questions you might be able to answer in relation to my investigation."

Mark looked at Cunningham more closely. "Of course, you're the one from the telly, the news report."

"Indeed. I believe you were on the A12 prior to the explosion. We have CCTV footage of your car."

"Yes, I use that road when I take my daughter back to university."

"Really. And for no other reason?"

"Like what?"

"I'll get back to that. Did you see or hear the explosion?"

"No, I wasn't aware of anything. Normal journey really."

"I find that hard to believe," countered the Chief Inspector. "You were close to the incident."

"Well, I usually have the radio on quite loud, especially when it's a favourite classical piece of mine."

"Does the British Liberation Army mean anything to you?"

"No, why should it?"

"I'll ask the questions," reminded Cunningham.

"I see," noted Mark. "This is not the informal chat you led me to believe we would have."

"Just my manner, Mark. One can't take the copper out of the policeman."

"That's an original comment," observed Mark. "Never heard that one before."

"Never mind, Mark. Now, back to our chat."

"Yes, let's do that, and please get to the point. I feel our chat is getting nowhere fast."

Cunningham smiled. "I notice that your confidence is growing and your body language is becoming more positive. Good, that means we will actually get somewhere."

"You're obviously good at observing, Chief Inspector." Mark yawned.

"Bored already. That is a trait familiar to me."

"No, just tired," confirmed Mark. "It is early. Trying to catch me off guard?"

Cunningham smiled again. "I believe you were being followed by the vehicle that exploded."

"Don't be daft. Why should I be followed?"

"Ah, that takes me back to the other reason for using the A12."

"Interesting," mused Mark. "You have me intrigued. Are your glasses permanently tinted, Chief Inspector?"

Cunningham ignored the question, seeing it off as a ricochet. "Rashid? Does this name mean anything to you?"

Mark thought: Cunningham? That name is no coincidence. He's a virtual being from Seeker One. "I need more evidence from you, Chief Inspector," he said, "before I can answer that."

"Very well. Anyway, you visited a building in the docklands, which houses the agency of space spies ..."

Mark laughed. "Sounds silly, doesn't it?"

"Don't mock the evidence, Mark. We know about this agency, but it is used as a mask for Rashid's mission."

"This is good, Chief Inspector," said Mark, causing a brief delay. "I'm enjoying our little chat."

"Drop the act, Mark," advised Cunningham. "I've been there before, remember? Mandeville is tied up and using you like he used us. Rashid is using you to reach his own goal."

"Okay, Brad," revealed Mark. "You've given me enough to support my thoughts. So, you didn't pass through the vortex and lived to fight another day. Lived to have another crack at Mandeville. But I can't imagine why you've come down to Earth. You were not part of the plot."

"Your plot is flawed. The plot is not your imagined one."

"No, I do imagine the plot. I write what happens."

"I'm afraid not, Mark," retorted Brad Cunningham. "I know that you have decided to side with Mandeville. I think you should remain impartial until you know the virtual facts."

"Virtual facts?"

"Mandeville has already written the book of history that you were supposed to write. I have it here …"

"Hey, hey, hey. I'm supposed …"

Brad laughed. "Oh no, Mark. Not at all. This is the one he wants you to put your name to. You are the fall guy in his quest to change the human attitude in terms of the reasons why you came up with his creation."

"You can't change the past, no matter how advanced you are. You can only lie about it."

"I agree, Mark. In the end, no one can. But there are those who try to change the past in order to change the future. You, Mark, can manipulate the future in the way you write it. That is what he wants: his future of the Second Coming."

"Why don't you just change the future anyway? You and Seeker One have the power."

"Come on, Mark. You know we can't go into the future. We can only come into the past from the future we are in."

"So, why you?" asked Mark, with suspicion. "Why are you here conducting this farce?"

"To protect you and, believe it or not, Mandeville."

"God! Every virtual being wants to protect me," exclaimed Mark. "Which one is true to their word? Take you, for instance. You tried to assassinate Mandeville."

"To change the future in terms of the way military rule would work. But there is a higher force involved. One we underestimated."

"We, we, we," repeated Mark suddenly. "Would that be your mates, the other generals?"

"No matter," answered Brad, dismissing the question.

"What higher force?" asked Mark, regaining the lead.

"It's 'who', Mark," countered Brad. "It's 'who is the higher force?'"

"Who then?"

"The Lord," confessed Brad. "He commands what we do. And now he has his Second Coming to help his aim of being the only God that humans immortalise."

"So you are true to your word?"

"Only you know the answer to that question. Think back to your published book and what is said now."

"Okay. Let's go back to why you have created your farce."

"This is not a farce. It's a rehearsal."

"Rehearsal?"

"Yes. Rashid wants to influence your writing, which may spill over into reality."

"What do you mean?"

"Oh," sighed Brad. "You are meant to … never mind. When the book you're supposed to write is published, questions will be asked. The human authorities will want to know about the BLA and your involvement. This would take your attention away from Mandeville and allow him to strike. Within the lull, he could try to eliminate Mandeville by eliminating you from the plot. You would have to be quick in reducing that lull. Hopefully, my farce has brought the BLA to the attention of the humans so that this can be dealt with before a book, if any, is published."

"Me! Eliminated?"

"Yes, once you are dealing with reality, according to his plan, you are out of the game. He will acquire the coded co-ordinates to Seeker One."

"How?"

"If this does happen, between now and then. It depends on how quickly you decipher the information I plan to give you."

"You are confusing me," declared Mark.

"Your confusion will clear soon enough," vowed Brad. "Besides, your elimination may not go ahead due to my intervention."

"Eliminate me?" repeated Mark. "Wow! Tell me, how do I eliminate him?"

"It is difficult, nearly impossible," explained Brad, "but with clever planning, achievable. One needs to have the codes to the operatives."

"Codes?"

"When an operative is on a mission, such as I am now, he is plugged into his personal terminal aboard Seeker One, which allows him to control his multiple self on Earth through the quantum system. If one has the master code to Seeker One's mainframe, which controls the terminals, then he is able to control the operative's movements. The master code is followed by the name of the operative one wishes to control."

"I don't understand how this can eliminate an operative," responded Mark. "Are you saying that one can unplug an operative?"

"That is an option, but not fatal. The only fatal action is if an operative meets himself on Earth. If they come face to face, they are destroyed. One evaporates and the other falls to the ground as a mere dead mortal. The trick is to produce another quantum multiple and then arrange a meeting place on Earth where they can come face to face."

"How does one know the location of the first of the multiple operatives?"

"It's all in the databank of the terminal, which is available once accessed by the code."

"So what is the code?" asked Mark excitedly.

"Ah! That is the question for which there is no easy answer, Mark," teased Brad. "I can only point you in the right direction."

"Which is?"

"The code is in Seeker One."

"Great! That helps a lot."

"It does when one has the imagination," prompted Brad. "Having told you that, I am now in danger. You must read the book."

"I have to ask myself: are you true to your word? No one creates danger without a motive, other than the one you have come up with. There must be a basic selfish reason?"

"What would you imagine it is, Mark? Maybe, both of us have selfish motives?"

"Um ... maybe. You don't come across as whiter than white in that book you are grasping tightly. Maybe you want me to change certain aspects of the book?"

"Your imagination is imaginative but correct. Indeed, this is the bill I present to you for my services."

"Quite expensive, don't you think?" complained Mark.

"A good price for the heads of any operative you wish to destroy," proffered Brad.

"Ah! Rashid," guessed Mark. "Is that another motive? You want him eliminated from the plot to secure a better future for yourself. Why not kill, or evaporate, him yourself?"

"An operative cannot kill an operative," explained Brad. "Only the Lord or an archangel can perform that task."

"Well, I'm not the Lord, so that leaves an archangel. That seems far-fetched, to say the least. An archangel is a high-ranking angel, if not the superior one. A messenger from God."

"It may be far-fetched to call you an archangel, but you are a messenger," confirmed Brad.

"So are you, I fear. I imagine that it is the Lord who wants to crush Rashid?"

"Not only Rashid, but Malik too."

"Who in hell is Malik?"

"Got it in one, Mark," said Brad. "Malik is the keeper of hell and was recalled by Rashid. Malik is the angel of interrogation who will question deceased souls about their life before death. He was the assassin of Simon, who was unfortunate. The target was David, who is an operative of Mandeville's. He saw what was coming and fled."

"Can I be destroyed within this circle of horror?"

"No. That is why I refer to you as an archangel. You are the one who imagines; the one who tells the story. You can't destroy yourself, otherwise the story ends and the imagined future, beyond your published book, fades away and it will be left to human destiny."

"And Malik?"

"He will go underground when Rashid is destroyed, until he is recalled by another fundamentalist."

"Phew! Glad to hear it," exclaimed Mark. "Especially from Mandeville's operative."

"Yes and no. Like you, I must remain impartial. Although Mandeville has to exist in order for you to write the future instalment."

"And for you to get a second crack at him?"

Cunningham grinned. "Mandeville has proven his powers to you by shaping your life and imagination. But I can see the influence of Mandeville fading from your own, human character. This is a good sign for all of us. I'm confident that you can take Mandeville's written book of revelation. It will read as if you were there."

"So, my time will stand still until I finish reading the book, but life continues."

"You can only imagine that, Mark. I must go. I'm in danger of meeting myself. Meanwhile, make a mental note of the information contained in our chat. You may need it once your time starts to tick again."

Mark escorted Brad out of the front door. "Until we meet again, Brad."

There was no answer as Brad Cunningham disappeared into the distance followed by a man wearing dark shades.

"Oh, no," sighed Mark. "I hope he escapes himself."

Mark looked at his watch: 08.30. Still? Oh, I suppose it's going to be 08.30 for some time to come because I must read the book straight away, he surmised. Mark returned to the living room and retrieved the book, which had been left on the chair. He turned to the opening page and read:

"I am the messenger of this book, and this is my opening statement. We, the guardians of the Lord's realm, conspired to plan, justify and proceed with the invasion of the Middle East. Our foothold had to be in Iraq, which became the first target. This target was considered to be the weakest link in the Middle East, as it had no means to defend itself against our military power. Iraq presented itself as the home of menace and had to be condemned. The excuses for this were justifiable, as there was more at stake than the zealots thought possible. We had to defend the West and heed the Lord's request and fears.

"The military force of America's Lord endorsed the chosen one as candidate for President. He was believed to be the right man for deliverance, therefore, defending the West against a monstrous and unacceptable threat. The one who receives this book will be the one who came close to the truth of prediction and will become, if not heretofore, manipulated by the two forces that control the world. Still, the one urges enlightenment. Therefore, the one will be a part of the script as an imagined story and embrace the quest of the aforesaid forces, which fight for domination."

Wow! thought Mark, I must be the one. I urge enlightenment. This must be Mandeville's hidden script given by an operative of the Lord's realm. Obviously, a script I'm not supposed to see or read. But one has to.

Chapter 8

January 2000. The new millennium. Governor Richard Burkhart arrived at the family ranch, in his home state of Texas, after an unmerciful day of campaigning.

"You look tired, Richard," observed his wife, Elizabeth, as she entered the lounge. "Can I fix you a drink?"

"Sure am, Beth," replied Richard. "The campaign trail is hellishly gruelling, but worth it. I'm rallying, and gaining natural support. The thing is, I don't feel it's enough. Need to do more. Obtain support through the back door using a Senator or two. Know what I mean? ... Oh, and I will have that drink, thanks."

"Don't worry, Richard," sympathised Elizabeth. "You'll race to the White House. The people of America want a fresh approach and leadership. I know you will achieve the presidency, God willing."

"Ah, but what would you know?" jested Richard. "Anyhow, the support of family and friends helps a great deal, Beth. That is why I'll enjoy this weekend's rest and be able to think clearly about my next manoeuvre."

Elizabeth delivered Richard's drink and sat next to him on the couch. She clasped his hand to endorse her love and support. "I may not know much, Richard," she acknowledged, "but I know enough. It's good to have you at home and that you value the family's support, even if it is only for the weekend, which compels me to think ..."

"Oh, think?" repeated Richard, with a suspicious tone of voice.

"Yes, dear," continued Elizabeth. "I thought I might come with you on your next stage of the campaign. I thought it might present a show of unity and endorse your address on family values."

"Good idea, Beth," said Richard, "but not yet. I'm not at that stage of the campaign. I need to lay the groundwork for a tough stance and concentrate on what needs to be done to win. Your role as devoted wife comes nearer the end of the campaign, honey - you know - just in case I need an extra boost. For now, you look after the fort. That's what the American neo-cons like: the little woman being at home."

"Richard, really," retorted Elizabeth.

"It's all about the image, Beth," explained Richard. "The image, and the money."

"Well!" declared Elizabeth. "You could just buy your way into the White House. We have enough of it!"

Richard howled with delight. "Good one, honey. You understand the basic rule."

Elizabeth kissed Richard's hand and stood up to leave the room. "I'll instruct the staff to prepare dinner," she said, adhering to her role. "We have a large gathering coming to celebrate your slight lead in the polls."

"Yeah, nearly forgot."

"Nonsense, Richard," said Elizabeth. "How can you forget that you'll be the centre of attention? Really!"

"Only for a second," answered Richard. "Okay, honey. I'll finish my drink and look through some paperwork before freshening up and changing my clothes."

"That's fine," conceded Elizabeth. "Don't take too long, though." Elizabeth turned away from Richard and nearly collided with one of the servants. "Excuse me," she said sarcastically. "What is it?"

"Apologies, ma'am," said Jacob. "I have a message for the Master."

"Well, go and give it to him, Jacob," instructed Elizabeth. "I have things to arrange with the cooks. Actually, come to the kitchen when you are done here. I have a job for you."

"Yes, ma'am."

"What is it, Jacob?" boomed Richard. "Come closer."

Jacob moved within feet of Richard. "General Mandeville rang, sir."

"General who? Speak up, Jacob."

"Mandeville, sir," answered Jacob, in a higher voice. "He wishes you to call him back. Here's his number, I wrote it down for you."

"I can see that, Jacob," said Richard, taking the piece of paper. "Thank you, Jacob. You can go and see to Mrs Burkhart's requirements now."

"Yes, sir," replied Jacob, and he left the room.

Um … Mandeville, thought Richard. He picked up the phone's receiver and dialled his aide's number.

"Hi, Mark speaking. Who is this?"

"Richard."

"I thought you were having the weekend off, Richard. Anyway, can't it wait? I'll be with you for dinner soon."

"I know that, Mark. It's a 24-hour job. Anyhow, what do you know about

General Mandeville?"

"Chief of Staff to the Army. Supposedly, he's very good at what he does. Also he's meticulous and an emphatic believer in our Lord. I think that about covers it. Oh, and he hates the President. Don't know why. It's a personal thing, I think. Why do you ask?"

"I received a call from him," replied Richard. "Went through to one of my house staff. Wants me to call him back."

"I wouldn't worry, Richard," reassured Mark. "He probably just wants to save his job. Expects you to win."

Richard laughed. "Yes, that's probably all it is. Mind you, maybe he should - save finding another one. See you at dinner."

"Yep. Have a large stiff one at the ready. Bye."

"Bye, Mark," echoed Richard, and he hung up.

The guests started to arrive at the home of Richard Burkhart. Jacob stood at the entrance and guided them into the guest room for pre-dinner drinks and conversation. Jacob looked surprised when he noticed a man in uniform walking towards the entrance and eventually into the entrance hall. "Can I help you, sir?" he asked. "I'm not sure if you are expected or not. Governor Burkhart is a stickler for keeping to the guest list. He doesn't like the uninvited."

"I understand. However, do your job."

"Sir?"

"Well, you had better run along and get me invited," instructed Mandeville. "I wish … I insist that I see the Governor immediately!"

Jacob trembled somewhat at the uniformed image in front of him. "I'll see what I can do." Jacob marched into the guest room and signalled towards the Governor.

"Excuse me, Donald," apologised Burkhart to a guest. "It appears our conversation has been interrupted. Obviously Jacob has a problem."

"No worries," replied Donald. "You've got my support. And my money!"

The Governor approached Jacob with some trepidation. "For God's sake, man. What is it?"

Jacob's trembling rose a notch, knowing how much the Governor hated gatecrashers. "There is a man in uniform in the hall, sir," he said nervously. "He's insistent upon seeing you."

"What is this person's name?"

"Erm, I, I …"

"Oh, Jacob, never mind. Can you recall what uniform he's wearing?"

"Yes, sir," replied Jacob, with some confidence. "He's a General. Yep, he's a General, all right."

"Good God. What …?"

"Richard, do you know there's a General in the hall?" interrupted Elizabeth, carrying a tray of nibbles into the guest room. "He looks lost. Don't you think you ought to see to him?"

"I was just about to, Beth," answered Richard. "Damn cheek if you ask me." Richard beckoned his aide to join him. "Come with me, Mark. We have an unexpected guest, one I don't want my investors to see. We'll take him into the office."

"Who is it that's rattled your cage, Richard?"

"Bloody Mandeville by the sound of it," replied Richard. "Let's see if my suspicions are correct." Richard led the way into the hall and confronted the General.

"Ah, Governor Burkhart," said the General, stretching out his arm to shake hands with the Governor. "I'm General Mandeville."

"Mandeville!" responded the Governor. "No apology for the intrusion? Typical behaviour of an arrogant General. I'll entertain you for a short period of time. Come with us to my office. Oh, I hope you don't mind my aide tagging along?"

"No," answered General Mandeville, having no choice in the matter. He followed the Governor into his office. "Nice. Is it secure?"

Governor Burkhart laughed. "Of course," he answered. "Does it need to be, General? Have you got something to hide, a bit of scandal maybe? Anyhow, please sit down."

"You failed to return my call, Governor," said Mandeville. "I hope it was just down to the incompetence of your servant. He appears to be forgetful."

"Not at all, General …"

"You can call me Mandeville."

Mark coughed suddenly. "Sorry, had a tickle in my throat."

"A drink of water, perhaps?" suggested Mandeville.

"No, I'm okay. Carry on, Richard."

"As I was about to say, Gen … Mandeville," continued Richard, "Jacob did not forget. As you can see, we've had a lot to do. I didn't have the time. Besides, I'm sure you appreciate the fact that I have to concentrate on my contributors. Also, your presence may unnerve some of them."

"I understand, Governor, but …"

"Is it a matter of national security, Mandeville?"

"In the future, yes," replied Mandeville, in a calm tone of voice. "It depends on your result, Governor. Oh, I'm not here to save my job and save you finding another one." Mandeville looked towards Mark and smirked.

"Fuck you, General," exclaimed Mark. "What gives you the right to tap my phone, arsehole?"

Not yours, Mark," responded Mandeville. "Although I can understand your colourful response. No, it is the Governor's phone that is tapped."

"Damn you!"

"Not me, Governor," reassured Mandeville. "But it has been rectified and the culprits have been dealt with. Haven't you noticed any missing guests?"

"Who? And what is meant by 'dealt with'?"

"Two directors from the company called Secure-com ..."

"Bastards!"

"The company," continued Mandeville, "has been searching into sensitive areas and hoping to increase their portfolio. Any dirt coming from your office would have helped towards that. How I dealt with the situation is a matter for my conscience."

"I'll accept your explanation, Mandeville," said the Governor. "So, what now? I guess I'm being forced into an alliance with you. I was due some funding from Secure-com."

"Mutual consent, Governor," corrected Mandeville. "This is just a quick visit to introduce myself in person. For now, keep the others at arm's length. Finish your dinner party, amuse them and take their money. You can dump them after you become President."

"President? How can you be so sure?"

"I am on your side, Governor. And, of course, our Lord. Mark can vouch for my closeness to the Lord."

The Governor laughed at Mandeville's sarcasm. "I think we will get along just fine, Mandeville. You can call me Richard, but tell me, why only Mandeville?"

"I have dropped my first name and just use the initial 'G'. Anyway, I won't detain you any longer than necessary, Richard."

"But we have unfinished business."

"When are you next in Washington?"

"In a few days' time. I have a meeting with Republican Senators."

"Ugh, Senators!" commented Mandeville. "Full of hot air. Here's my card. Call me when you arrive in Washington. Enjoy your dinner, Richard. Digest it well."

The Governor escorted General G. Mandeville to the front door. "Goodbye, Mandeville," he said.

"Goodbye, Richard," replied Mandeville, and he walked away towards the open door of his chauffeured limousine.

"Wow!" exclaimed Mark. "The Chief of Staff to the Army on board. Can't lose!"

"Don't get too excited, Mark. However, it's a load off my mind concerning the military. I thought I might've had trouble convincing them of my intended policy. Good. Come along, Mark. Let's enjoy our meal and amuse these vultures. And we'll play down what Mandeville said and keep it close to our chests."

Chapter 9

"Good morning. General G. Mandeville's office," voiced a female secretary. "How can I help?"

"This is Governor Burkhart's aide. I'm calling to arrange a time for the Governor to meet General Mandeville."

"Ah, yes. Sorry, I didn't catch your name ..."

"Mark."

"Yes, Mark. The General told me to expect the Governor's call. I can fit you in for a visit at 10.00 a.m. Is that acceptable?"

"Perfect," replied Mark. "The Governor should have concluded his meeting by then. If not, I'll make sure he's free."

"I'll pencil you in, Mark, and inform the General to expect you. Oh, I've just remembered. General Mandeville informed me that this is only an invitation for a tour of the Pentagon. He said you would understand."

Clever, thought Mark. "Yes, I understand completely," he said.

"Thank you," concluded the secretary. "Have a nice day."

I can't get used to their jargon, thought Mark. Still, back to the Governor's meeting. Mark returned to Senator Milford's office within the House of Representatives and walked in on Milford and the Governor's conversation.

"So, Richard, you are asking me, if you become President, to back your policy on the Middle East, in particular Iraq?"

"It would be favourable, seeing as you are highly respected and influential. The balance in world affairs is in danger of tipping against America. America needs to be strong and with robust leadership."

"I see where you're coming from, Richard," replied Milford. "The Middle East is becoming too big for its boots. But I must stress that you should tread with caution. We can't afford a gung-ho, aggressive attitude towards your intended policy."

"Of course, I understand, Senator," acknowledged Burkhart. "However, once we have Iraq we can afford anything ..."

"Excuse me, gentlemen," interjected Mark.

"What is it? I was just getting into the flow, getting to the nitty-gritty ..."

"Exactly," noted Mark. "Unfortunately, the arranged visit to the Pentagon is sneaking up on us - it's at ten, remember?"

"Pentagon?" quizzed Milford.

"Yes," answered Mark. "Just a bit of public relations, and all that. General Mandeville arranged it. Reckon he wants to keep in favour."

"Typical," said Milford. "Keep a watchful eye on that one, Richard. I don't trust him. Too militant for my liking."

"Really?" replied Burkhart. "Interesting. Thanks for the warning."

"I think you'd better go, Richard," instructed the Senator. "The traffic at this time of day is heavy. Mind you, it always is. Also, from what I hear, Mandeville is a stickler for timekeeping."

Burkhart smiled. "You're a mine of information, Senator. Thanks again." The Governor stood up and shook hands with the Senator and then left the office with Mark in tow.

"What the hell was that, Mark?" slated Richard, as they walked out of the building. "I was reeling him in after grabbing his curiosity. Damn it! I had him until your intervention. He was too quick to finish the meeting."

"Don't worry, Richard," said Mark, in his own defence. "He's not crucial to your cause."

"He will be when it comes to the congressional votes a President needs to …"

"Not now, Richard," requested Mark. "Just get in the car and relax."

"Where to, Governor?" asked the driver.

"Arlington," intervened Mark. "We have to be there by ten, and not a minute after."

"Understood," replied the driver. The limousine raced off into the mid-morning traffic.

"I like and respect you, Mark," commented Richard, "but don't go above and beyond your station. Do I make myself clear?"

"Absolutely, Richard," replied Mark. "I only want you to consider what Mandeville has to say before you decide on your tactics. I feel that Mandeville has a higher role to play than Milford. Mandeville has hinted at getting you in. That has to be your first consideration. But that's only my offered advice. Ultimately, it's up to you to decide."

"Um," pondered Richard. "You've just reminded me why I keep you around. I concur, Mark. However, make a mental note of what I said."

"Don't be concerned, Richard," reassured Mark. "I shall blend into the background." Mark looked at his watch. "We're making good progress, Richard."

"Good work, driver," remarked Richard, through the limousine's intercom. "Keep it up. I can't wait to see the real centre of America's power once again."

Mark smiled and relaxed in silence for the duration of the journey.

On arrival at the Pentagon, Governor Burkhart and his aide, Mark, were greeted by a civilian dressed in a designer suit, which encapsulated his arrogant confidence. "Good morning, gentlemen," he said, in a clear tone of voice. "I am to give you a briefing on the tour of the Pentagon, America's Department of Defense."

"Is this really necessary ..."

"David. My name is David."

Mark stared.

"As I was going to say," continued Governor Burkhart, observing the man's demeanour, "I have ..."

"I am just doing as I have been directed by the top brass, Governor," interrupted David. "So, if you will follow me."

Governor Burkhart and Mark followed David to their unspecified destination.

Mark walked close to Burkhart. "Do you know where he's taking us, Richard?" he asked. "I feel uneasy all of a sudden."

"Looks like 'ground zero'," answered Richard. "Most of the damn tours begin there. I'll tell you: if I ... when I become President, I'll put a stop to these tours. It's stupid having any Tom, Dick or Harry walking freely around America's defense building."

"Here we are, gentlemen," announced David. "The ground zero café snack bar. I've already arranged refreshments. Please take a seat."

"Very nice," commented Mark. "I'm overwhelmed."

Burkhart smirked. "Is the coffee still lousy, David?" asked the Governor.

"I like it, Richard ..."

"Governor!"

"Excuse me, Governor," continued David. "As I was about to say, I like the coffee, and you get to keep the mug."

"Well, if that's the case, we'll both have the coffee, David. Thank you."

"It also comes with toast," informed David. "If you want, that is?"

"As it comes," replied the Governor.

"Good," said David. "Glad we've made a choice." David signalled to the waitress to bring the pre-ordered coffee and toast. "Now," continued David, "I'll just whiz over a few facts ..."

"But ..."

"Please, Governor. Just let me do my job. I don't want you reporting that I did not look after you. So, the Pentagon is the headquarters of America's defense. It boasts the highest-capacity office building in the world. The building houses 23,000 - yes 23,000 - military and civilian employees. Amazing, isn't it? Also, 3,000 non-defense support personnel. The building itself has five floors above ground level and two basement levels, which I imagine house and expose the official secrets ..."

"What?"

"Oh, just a light-hearted joke, Governor. Anyway, where was I? Ah, yes. The five corridors per floor cover 17 miles ..."

"Okay, David," interrupted the Governor, after a yawn. "That's enough, please."

"I see," retorted David. "Just finish your coffee and toast then. I was only trying to encourage a feel for the great atmosphere this building has to offer. General Mandeville thought it would put you in the right frame of mind for your meeting. But, if it is not to your liking, we can pretend that you were never here."

"I appreciate your efforts, David," replied the Governor, with an air of calm and patience. "However, I am familiar with the history and the layout of the Pentagon. My father was, as I know you are aware, President of our great country. I was brought up within the political system. So I'm afraid there is nothing you can teach me."

"Of course, Governor Burkhart," said David, "and hope soon to become President. The truth of the matter is that General Mandeville is in session at this precise moment, which should be coming to a close shortly. It was just a delaying tactic. Forgive me if I have come across as being condescending and deceitful in any way."

"They are attributes I recognise, David," revealed the Governor. "I don't have a problem now that you have told the truth."

"Good. Great!" replied David. "I'll find out if the General is now free. Finish your drinks and I'll be back soon."

"It was good and productive talking to you, Jim. I hope we can count on your backing for Governor Burkhart?"

"I'll get back to you on that, General. He needs to impress me more than he is doing at this moment in his campaign."

"Oh, come on now, Jim. That is not the issue, surely. All we need is a puppet that agrees with the military. Governor Burkhart is tailor-made for that role when you look at his background and breeding."

"Sometimes you frighten me, General," confessed Jim. "I'll sit on the fence for a while and see how it develops."

"Okay, Jim," replied Mandeville. "I understand …"

A knock on the door interrupted the conversation and David entered the office. "Sit down, David," instructed Mandeville.

"That is my cue to leave, General," said Jim. "Goodbye for now." Jim shook hands with Mandeville in a polite manner and retreated from the office.

"Is he really the one you want to back?" asked David.

"Jim?"

"No, damn it!" clarified David. "Governor Burkhart."

"What impression have you arrived at?" enquired Mandeville, ignoring David's temperament.

"He's ignorant, a follower and egotistical," answered David bluntly.

"Good. Just what I expected. He'll be easy to deceive. In any case, you'd better go and fetch the Governor and bring him to my office."

"And Mark, his aide?"

"Um," contemplated Mandeville. "Bring him along too. He'll be briefed anyway. Besides, I think he is more than just an aide."

"I agree," replied David. "See you again shortly." David exited the office to go and collect the General's guests.

"Ah!" said General Mandeville, observing his guests' arrival. "Please excuse the delay and make yourselves comfortable. David will get you some refreshments."

"No thanks," said the Governor. "I had enough while I was waiting in the café."

"What about you, Mark?" asked the General.

"Actually," replied Mark, "I would like a cup of tea. I'm sick of having coffee all the time. Strange, I feel obliged to. Do you have tea?"

"Of course we do, Mark," answered Mandeville. "Our drinks machine has everything."

"Sugar?" enquired David.

"Yes please …"

"Can we get on, Mandeville?" interrupted the Governor. "I have a busy schedule ahead of me."

"Don't we all?" retorted Mandeville. "As you have done, I too have managed to set aside the time to brief you, which may take quite a while."

"Brief?" questioned the Governor, with surprise. "Since when does a General brief a candidate?"

"Since now, Richard," answered Mandeville. "I think you have forgotten our little chat at your ranch. I have the power to get you elected. And the means to do it."

"Really?"

"Let's not beat around the bush, Richard. You want to create a hard-line administration. As I was saying to Jim, America needs to regain its leadership in the world and invoke a greater sense of national patriotism."

"Jim! Jim Belford," realised the Governor. "I thought I noticed him, but wasn't sure. God! He's a fool, but for some reason he is liked. Still, he could be useful in the short term."

"Long term," corrected Mandeville. "You won't find a CIA Director as compatible and selfish. He has similar ideals, only because he wants to keep his job."

"Have you given him any reassurances?"

"Not at all, Richard. That will be your job as commander in chief."

"I like the sound of that, Mandeville."

"Ah!" realised Mandeville. "I think you should start calling me General again, Richard. We are in the capital of power. Don't want over-familiarity. Don't want to give the wrong impression of too much collaboration, especially after this meeting."

"Yes, you have a point, General," agreed Burkhart.

"Is your campaign for senatorial support going well on Capitol Hill?"

The Governor looked suspicious. "How ...?"

"Don't concern yourself, Governor," interrupted Mandeville. "Got to keep ahead of the game. Besides, it was news, as are all campaigns."

"But not plots, General," remarked the Governor. "Anyhow, it's moving along, getting there, but that's not the issue. I'm here to hear you out, remember?"

General Mandeville stared at David and nodded. "I believe you have some work to do, David. I'll expect a report of your study as soon as possible."

"Of course, General," acquiesced David. "I was trying to put it off until you mentioned it. You know how I hate administration."

"Run along then," ordered Mandeville, and watched him leave the office.

"Is he partially blind, General?" asked the Governor. "He always kept those dark glasses on during the short time we've met."

"Sensitive eyes, Governor," responded Mandeville, in haste.

"I see."

"Glad you think so, but I doubt it. He doesn't like talking about it."
Mandeville was keen to move on. "Your television debate back in December
'99 was adequate but we feel you need a helping hand ..."

"We?"

"Yes, we. Your benefactors. And, as you are so religious, our Lord. The
time is right, Governor. Time is moving closer to election day in November."

"How can you help? I'm sure I can breeze into the White House."

Mandeville laughed. "I admire your confidence and your reluctance to be
reliant on others," he said, "but the Vice-President is popular. There is no
point denying it. The people like the soft and comfortable Democratic
policies, which they proved by keeping the President in office after his
misdemeanour."

"So, you are hinting that I will lose?"

"More than a hint," admitted Mandeville. "I know for a fact that Florida
will be your downfall without my help. You have to get elected through the
back door, which I know you are in favour of."

"Explain?"

"Florida will become your final battle ground. Up to that point, you can
campaign as you planned. Along the way, you will receive information that
you can use against the Vice-President. We are still in a position to obtain
damaging reports that are still awaiting destruction due to inadequate
personnel. Also, you have two collaborators in the state of Florida."

"Yes, I do - well one, anyway," acknowledged the Governor, with
hesitation. "One is my brother, but who is the other one?"

"Florida's Secretary of State," answered Mandeville, with delight. "She is,
and has been, easily manipulated by power brokers. In addition to this, she
has been ethically shady in past dealings."

"That doesn't mean she will come on board. If she is able to conduct
herself in such a way to take advantage, then surely she will stick with the
Democrats."

"That could be the case," replied Mandeville, "but use your imagination.
A guaranteed place on the Senate as a means of reward should do the job of
convincing her to offer her services."

"I couldn't guarantee a place on the Senate, even as President."

"You are right in practical terms," teased Mandeville. "However, consider
this. Your brother, as Governor of Florida, could do away with her post
sometime after your election as President. The place on the Senate would, of

course, not materialise."

Governor Burkhart looked at Mark, who appeared gobsmacked. The Governor grinned from ear to ear. "Brilliant!" he declared. "It's in the bag."

"I admire your confidence, Governor," responded Mandeville, deflating the Governor's excitement.

"I can feel a big 'but' coming my way," noted the Governor.

"Not so, Governor," replied Mandeville. "Confusion is coming your way - more ammunition, which will throw the presidential campaign into chaos. Florida has a past reputation of voter fraud."

"I understand what you're getting at, General," acknowledged the Governor, "but I don't have enough clout to incite voter fraud."

"I know that," agreed Mandeville. "That is where I come into the frame. I do have enough clout - all the way up to the Supreme Court and beyond. I have influence on the Chief Justice. Well, a file on him, anyway."

"Anyway," repeated the Governor. "Have you just demoted your own influence?"

"No, no, Governor," replied Mandeville, with a smile. "His file gives me the clout. He has certain appetites, which the President allows. Get my drift?"

"I do, General," confirmed the Governor. "Mentioning the Chief Justice means you already have something up your sleeve, I suspect. Do you, General?"

"Think about it, Governor," replied General Mandeville, with excitement. "Voter fraud by duplicating postal ballots with residentially addressed ballots, especially those of military personnel who are abroad. Voting machines breaking down, which will necessitate manual counts that cannot meet the deadlines. These counts will be extended, purposely, by Florida's State Court, and then you step in to lodge an appeal to the Supreme Court. She, Florida's Secretary of State, steps in on a promise of promotion and announces more time. This is where I step in and have a chat with the Chief Justice. Enough is enough. Stop the count or else. Besides, he is Republican. He'll understand and get the support of the six Republican-associated Justices, the other two being Democratic. So, a majority of seven to two in favour of your appeal. The count stops, you're on top and you win. As you can figure out, absolute chaos but the result in our favour."

"It's fantastic," admitted the Governor. "I liked it before, but I like it more now. We can't lose. Well, Mark, what are your thoughts?"

"I think it is already written," answered Mark, glaring at Mandeville. "The writing is on the wall, you could say. However, the buck stops with you,

Richard. It is your destiny - the only way you'll get elected so you can impose your policy and lead America to world domination."

"I smell caution and fear rising from your body language, Mark," accused Mandeville. "I hope you are not yellow-bellied. I hope you haven't gone soft on your original excitement at the dinner party. I suspect you didn't expect such a complex conspiracy. Hell! There is more to come, comrade. Don't sit on the fence on this one, Mark. Your future and career depend on our campaign."

"Reckon I need convincing with hard evidence that you can deliver in support of Richard, and not just for yourself."

Mandeville grunted and lit a cigarette. He inhaled deeply and then exhaled the smoke into Mark's face. "Spit it out, Mark," he said. "Make your point or forever hold your peace."

Mark wafted the smoke away. "I'm developing a bad taste in my mouth," he revealed. "This reeks of military dictatorship."

"Nonsense, Mark," responded Mandeville. "All civilian leaders make use of their military counterparts, even disclosing their innermost thoughts and seeking advice, which we act on. This is my hard evidence, Mark. In fact, I shall disclose to you what the President entrusted me to keep quiet until such time as these facts are exposed to ..."

"Really? Do enlighten us, General. This may be your chance to con to convince."

"Ah!" continued Mandeville. "You have done your homework, found out what my personal motto is and ... I like a man who plans ahead and enquires about the facts before commitment. I'm beginning to understand you, Mark." Mandeville stubbed his cigarette into the ashtray and twisted it around a few times. "Yes, indeed," he resumed, "you are one who looks to the future with careful consideration ..."

"I appreciate your words, General," interrupted Mark impatiently. But can you divulge the mentioned facts?"

"Of course, Mark," replied Mandeville, smiling. "Number one: the President will distance himself from the Vice-President's campaign, withdrawing his support. Number two: the First Lady, peacekeeper, was involved in covert weapons sales to those who may use them against us."

"Powerful claims, General ..."

"Excuse me, Mark," intervened the Governor. "What happened to remaining in the background? You're running ahead of yourself. Take a step behind those who matter."

"Sorry, Governor," replied Mark.

"I'll accept General Mandeville's support. We can work together on this, and in the future. He also has my support. Now, General, will Prime Minister Anthony Sinclair welcome me as President?"

"Yes he will, Governor," answered Mandeville. "He was the preferred, and supported, choice in 1997. He has recently received a brief and a script on his future alliance with America. Contrary to popular belief, he is in our pocket and ready to play his role."

"This is good news, General," commended the Governor. "It's all good news. I'm encouraged by our meeting today, General. It gives me the confidence I need to steamroller into the White House."

"We won't meet face to face until inauguration day. My aides and I will track your movements and make the necessary arrangements along the way."

"So I won't see you again," understood the Governor. "But what if ...?"

"Any communication between us will be conducted through a covert messaging system."

"Understood, General," concluded the Governor.

"Good," replied Mandeville. "I'll arrange for someone to escort you out of the building."

"No need, General," said the Governor. "We can find our own way out."

"No doubt you can," acknowledged Mandeville, "but I want to keep up the appearance that you've been having a tour."

Of course, General," replied the Governor, with slight embarrassment. "I forgot."

Once escorted out of the Pentagon, Governor Burkhart and Mark climbed into their waiting limousine. "To the airport, driver," requested the Governor.

"But you have somewhere else to go, Governor, according to my schedule," pointed out the driver. "Besides, your helicopter ..."

"I'm aware of that," rebuked the Governor. "I've just cancelled. And my helicopter is always in a state of readiness. As I said, to the airport. I must head back to the ranch. Mark and I have a lot to arrange. Isn't that so, Mark? We don't need Mandeville to dish out all the dirt on the Vice-President."

"Yes, clearly, Richard," reacted Mark, with trepidation.

"When you are ready, driver," maintained the Governor. "Drive east along Jefferson's towards Reagan Airport. Is that clear enough for you too?"

"Whatever you want, Governor," replied the driver. "It's your call." The limousine moved away from the Pentagon building, heading east.

103

David returned to General Mandeville's office a short time after the visitors' departure.

Mandeville was sitting at his desk, attending to some paperwork. "Ah, David," he said, and waved him towards the chair.

"How did it go, General?" asked David.

"Good," replied Mandeville. "We have nothing to worry about. However, we must remain cautious and tread carefully through the deception. It is essential that Burkhart does not comprehend what is really transpiring. The phenomenon's requirement is that it remains hidden. Even when the problem is solved."

"It won't remain hidden if we don't succeed in stopping the East from infiltrating the West with their belief in Allah, their supreme being ..."

"You look worried, David," observed Mandeville. "Is it the result of your studies?"

"Something like that. Not sure," answered David. "As you know, Burkhart met with Senator Milford before he came here, but that is neither here nor there. Just begging for future policy votes. It's his aide I'm not sure about ..."

"Mark?"

"Yes," continued David. "I couldn't find anything on him. I don't like that. It means he's concealing something that can stay hidden. Also, he appears to have the insight, which he keeps to himself. I was almost afraid that if I didn't have my glasses on ..."

"Afraid?" hollered Mandeville. "Since when have you been afraid, David. We, the mere mortals, are the ones that have the fear of the Lord, which you bring to Earth."

"Not for myself, General," explained David. "Afraid he might stumble on the quasar plot, as did the Lord."

"But he is not the Lord."

"Indeed not," confirmed David. "Nevertheless, whatever he thinks he knows will stay with him for future use, which could be more dangerous if we fail to stop the plot."

"Is that the real goal, David?" asked Mandeville, with an uneasy tone of voice. "We humans don't really understand the sublime. Celestial objects that landed in Iraq are truly out of this world and unbelievable."

"Not objects, General."

"Well, I don't like comparing them to you, David. They are on the opposite side."

"Not so," disagreed David. "Just varying beliefs that want to oppose. But we have to stand strong and defend what we believe in, what the Lord deems necessary. The Lord alerted us to the red-shift, which has produced the red-eyed. They have deposited the divine beacon of Allah in Iraq to transmit and track movements. The Lord awaits his Second Coming, General, and defies those who want to stop it. In effect, we are stopping the East from becoming the West's Second Coming."

"Would Mark believe this if he stumbled on it?" asked Mandeville.

"As an excuse," answered David. "As is all religion."

"We will keep an eye on him, but not you of course," declared Mandeville. "If he comes out ... well, you can imagine."

"Come, General," beckoned David.

Mandeville moved around the desk and knelt down on one knee before David. David removed his dark glasses, revealing his all-white eyes. He placed his hand on the bowed head of Mandeville. "Pray, General," instructed David. "Pray through me to the Lord so he can receive your commitment and belief. Offer your assurance that there will only be one God."

Governor Burkhart and Mark were sat in the office at the Governor's ranch, discussing the meeting with General Mandeville.

"Do you trust Mandeville, Richard?" asked Mark.

"Hell, no," replied Richard. "I don't trust anyone. Like a drink?"

"I'll have a beer, thanks ..."

"Um, quite," interrupted Richard, with disappointment. "I'll have a man's drink."

"I know that," said Mark, "but do you mistrust him more than your usual distrust towards your fellow macho opponents? Or friends ...?"

"No friends in this game, Mark. See everyone as a potential enemy. See every country as a potential enemy."

"Even me, Richard?" asked Mark. "Am I included in 'everyone' ...? Must be, I guess."

"As much as you trust me, Mark ..."

"Staying for dinner, Mark?" asked Elizabeth, interrupting their conversation.

"Of course he is," said Richard. "What do you say, Mark?"

"How could I refuse?" answered Mark. "Yes, that would be nice, Elizabeth. Thank you."

"No problem," replied Elizabeth. "It's not as if I'll be cooking the meal. Anyway, it is always a pleasure to have you for dinner. Stop over maybe?"

"No, Elizabeth," answered Mark, in a direct tone of voice. "I have stuff to do."

"What stuff is that, Mark?" probed Richard.

"Stuff, that's all," replied Mark, appearing secretive. "Work relating to your campaign. You know how it is. Never-ending."

"Actually, no," revealed Richard. "I know what your workload is, Mark. I detect a bit on the side."

"Certainly not," denied Mark.

"No, no," said Richard, laughing. "I mean that you're contemplating digging around for information. But about whom? Or what?"

"David," clarified Mark quietly.

"Excuse me, Mark, I didn't catch that."

"Oh, you did, Richard," contradicted Mark. "You always do that: try to create some thinking time."

"Um, but why? He's an aide, like you are."

"Exactly, Richard," said Mark, with confidence. "Aides know more than the people they represent. It's their job."

"Hah," responded Richard. "You think you do, sonny. The minute I think that of you, you're out and ..."

"God! Calm down, Richard," interrupted Mark. "This is about David. There is something about him. He has a presence about him. Can't put my finger on it."

"Can't you be more definite?"

"Don't need to be. A suspicion is enough to investigate. I suspect him of being more than just an aide. An adviser maybe."

"Dangerous?"

"Not if we know he is," speculated Mark.

"Let us just assume he is," concluded Richard. "At least, until I get elected. The truth is, we're all dangerous."

"Elected for what, Richard?"

"Greatness, Mark," commented Richard. "American greatness and supremacy. Leave it alone. Once I become President, you can investigate all you want. I don't want to rock the boat at this sensitive stage of the campaign and risk ..."

"Dinner is cooked, sir," interrupted Jacob.

Mark laughed. "I'm sure it is ..."

"Thank you, Jacob," interjected Richard, suspecting a tease from Mark.

"Hello, Jacob," uttered Mark. "How are you?"

"Fine, sir. Fine."

"Of course you are," responded Mark. "Be thankful you have a quiet life."

"I think so, sir ..."

"Mark, Jacob. It's Mark. I'm not your employer ..."

"Leave him be, Mark," requested Richard. "Sorry, Jacob. As I suspected, he's only teasing you. I have instructed him on something he does not cohere with and is taking his frustration out on you."

Mark laughed again. "Yes, that's all it is, Jacob. Take no notice of me. My mind works too much overtime. Anyway, what has been sacrificed for dinner?"

"Chicken with all the trimmings," answered Jacob proudly.

"Very nice. And original," replied Mark. "Sounds good. Trying to show the Governor what he will be missing once he is President? Maybe you could tag along and stir things up?"

"That's a good notion ..."

"Come on!" declared Richard. "I have no desire to eat cold chicken. Honestly, I worry about you at times, Mark ..."

"Richard and Mark. Are you coming through for dinner?" shouted Elizabeth.

Um," reflected Mark. "I think I'm the one who has to worry about you, Governor."

Richard grinned. "After you, Mark," he instructed. "I think I'll make you my adviser when I'm President."

Chapter 10

March 2001. The White House: two months into President Burkhart's Presidency.

Burkhart was sitting at the desk of power in the Oval Office when he heard a knock on the door. "Come in," he said.

Mark entered and handed over a small pile of papers for the President to sign. "No need to read them, Mr President. I've looked over their content. Nothing important, only internal administration stuff on office refurbishments, etc. Since your Oval Office makeover, they all want one."

"I'll take your word on that, Mark," said the President. "You should have accepted my offer of becoming an adviser."

"It wasn't meant to be, Mr President," replied Mark. "Besides, I'm free to do other things. An aide's life is never noticed. I'm more use in the background."

"Ah!" declared the President. "To dig up stuff on my behalf, Mark?"

"Something like that. I prefer to call it observation."

"Anything else?"

"Um, yes there is, actually," answered Mark, with hesitation.

"So, what is it?"

"Mandeville," said Mark. "He's wanting an audience with the 'new man'."

"His words, I presume?" speculated the President.

"Yes, Mr President. He could have said worse, don't you think?"

"On second thoughts, Mark," revised the President, "I'm glad you didn't agree to becoming an adviser. Anyway Mark, my aide, make it happen."

" I will, Mr President."

In General G. Mandeville's office at the Pentagon, Mandeville and David were discussing the next uncovered move in the quasar plot.

"So, David, what have you found out? What has been jettisoned onto your lap?"

"The quasar plot gathers pace, General," answered David. "The Eastern representatives plan to take control of the World Trade Centre ..."

"Ha! Fat chance."

"Unfortunately, your defiant confidence is misplaced," continued David. "Your confidence is needed to stop this from happening. Allah's messengers plan to engage the help of the Saudis. They are already influential here in America. In my mind, they have too much investment and interest and represent a potential threat to America. The quasar plotters will insist that the investors search their consciences."

"You bring a message of doom, David," realised Mandeville, "whatever happens. Do you have another message on how to resolve the problem? Have you been enlightened?"

"Yes, General."

"And ...?"

"It will require a great show of faith and will test your alliance with the Lord," announced David. "But this one event will serve many purposes. And you will have to put aside any heartfelt patriotism for tolerance. You will have to endure the long-suffering pain that will vent through from the ashes."

"Ashes of what?"

"The twin towers, General ..."

"Ashes, ashes, ashes," repeated Mandeville. "Ashes come after destruction."

"In reality, this is so, General," confirmed David.

"How? When? Who?"

"These questions are for you to answer, and they must be answered correctly for the benefit of all the disciples in the Lord's crusade."

"You're not speaking plain talk, David," argued Mandeville. "If it is you that speaks ..."

"Do not probe, General," rebuffed David. "I only deliver the Lord's utterances. It is for you to accept and reap the reward for loyalty. Even the Lord accepts that no one offers a service without some kind of payment. Even he demands belief and wisdom from his flock, as he now does of you, General."

"And if I refuse?"

"The world will be damned by the wrath of conflicting faiths within one society and consumed by ungoverned war."

"Will you help?"

"I will guide you in my continuing role as your aide, but your belief and wisdom are what matters, General."

"So be it, David," conceded Mandeville. "I shall be the black sheep amongst the flock who will broadcast misleading objectives. This will test my choice of President and his grasp of treachery."

"How will you persuade him, General?"

"Greed, David. Greed equates to man's pursuit of power."

"Such irony ..."

"Irony?"

"The twin towers," replied David. "They are symbols of man's greed, which have to be destroyed."

Mandeville laughed. "Perfect, David, my comrade. As it happens, I have requested an audience with the President. I'm still waiting for confirmation of the time and date."

"Where?"

"The White House," answered Mandeville, "where else?"

"What we have discussed is a very sensitive issue," replied David, "and not one to be revealed within the walls of the President's office. You need a private venue away from the hill."

"Um ... you have a valid point, David," agreed Mandeville. "Let me think ... Bingo! The presidential retreat. I shall call his office immediately and insist on speaking with my commander-in-chief."

"Good idea, General," encouraged David. "I'll leave you to it. Oh, and make sure that everyone who needs to be there is there."

"Of course, David," said Mandeville. "I'm sure the President will know who needs to be presented with an invitation. Now off you go."

"I didn't expect you back so soon, Mark," said the President.

"Neither did I, Mr President," replied Mark.

The President laughed. "Can't keep away?"

"Something like that," answered Mark, with a troubled tension.

"Am I going to like this, Mark?"

"Depends on what your agenda is. I'm afraid Mandeville is insistent. He wants it to happen much sooner than expected. I came as soon as he finished his call to me."

"Make him wait, Mark," responded the President. "Call him back and put it off. I'm busy."

"Can't do that, and you know why."

"Do I?" asked the President nervously.

"He has you in his pocket, Mr President," responded Mark, with brutal honesty.

"How dare you presume so?"

"Unfortunately, it's the price you have to pay. Expensive, but ..."

"Okay, okay, Mark. Damn! He's pushing for the engagement of our policy. Still, I could probably hold him off when he gets here. When is he coming?"

"Ah! ..."

"What do you mean, 'Ah'?"

"There's more to it than Mandeville simply visiting your office. You're right in thinking that he's pushing, and pushing hard. He has demanded ..."

"Demanded?" retorted the President. "No one can demand something of an American President."

"Sorry," replied Mark, in an effort to calm the President. "I should have said requested."

"It's okay, Mark," said the President, "you don't need to change the General's words. Anyway, go on."

"He wants to call, in his words, an extraordinary meeting, but disguised as a recreational weekend at the retreat. Oh, and that means this weekend, Mr President."

"Um ... I can cope with that," said the President. "Mandeville and I can catch up. Can't do any harm. Yes, we can have a chat and he can put his case for an agenda."

"Ah! ..."

"Good God, man, what is it now? Can't you provide all the facts at once?"

"Well," continued Mark, "I feel I have to feed you slowly."

"No need," responded the President defiantly. "I can take it all in. Now just fill me in on all the remaining facts."

Mark cowered in the face of the President's anger. "There isn't a great deal more, Mr President," he said. "He has demanded ... sorry, requested, that certain guests are also present at the retreat. Mandeville said you would know which ones to invite."

"Indeed I do, Mark," acknowledged the President. "Is that all?"

"Yes, Mr President."

"Good. Leave it with me. I'll take care of the arrangements from here on in."

"Understood," concluded Mark.

General Mandeville had summoned David to his office for a briefing before they departed for the weekend's recreation. "Come in," shouted Mandeville, anticipating David's arrival.

David entered the office briskly. "General," he said, "is there a problem? I wasn't expecting your call so soon."

"Did I interrupt something, David?" asked Mandeville, with a smile. "Besides, I imagine that my request is being arranged as we speak. So, what were you up to?"

"Only a personal matter, General," replied David proudly. "I was just releasing some sexual frustration. You know how it is - been too busy."

"That wasn't the answer I was expecting, David. I hope it wasn't too expensive? However, you can claim it on expenses. Consider it a favour from the department."

"No need to, General," replied David. "The favour was already granted. She understood not to charge."

"Say no more," said Mandeville, "I get the gist. Now, to business. I hope you have been satisfied, David, because we will be too occupied with our conspiracy."

"My satisfaction comes from our allegiance, General," responded David, with a gratuitous smile.

"Glad to hear it, David," said Mandeville. "The extraordinary meeting has been arranged. We travel tonight for the weekend stay."

"Good!" declared David. "It's about time, and that's something we can't afford to waste. The quasar plot gathers pace with each passing day. We have to stay ahead of their game."

"Exactly, David," agreed Mandeville. "I want to revise the President's inauguration speech. There is ammunition contained within it to support our claim to engage." Mandeville handed David a printout of the speech. "Right, let's take it from the top."

David scanned the first page and laughed. "I didn't realise how comical this was until I looked at it again."

"But dangerous, David," cautioned Mandeville. "However, his thoughtless comments are in our favour ..."

"He doesn't think at all, General," interrupted David. "It will be so easy to manipulate the fool."

"Still," continued Mandeville, "we have to keep our wits about us. We can't become complacent ..."

"Okay, General, I get the picture."

"The President demonstrates his aggression right from the beginning. Look at the first paragraph. He talks of America's security and his stance on terrorism."

"Yes," agreed David. "Provocation, which fuels rival anger towards

America. We can manipulate this along with the lack of understanding regarding foreign policy. He has just brushed aside any commitment that the previous administration had implemented." David paused and revised. "Ha," he continued, "in one paragraph he has undone any peaceful advance they had achieved."

"Um," contemplated Mandeville. "I get the impression that Burkhart wants to finish the job that his father started but failed to end, instead running for cover."

"I agree," said David. "It was a missed opportunity. The Middle East handed itself to us on a plate with their internal squabbling and invasions. It was there for the taking and all of this could have been avoided." David flicked through the pages of the report and focused his attention on the President's appointments. "Are you on the same page as me, General?" he asked.

"Indeed, David," replied Mandeville, with delight.

"More evidence that points towards conflict with the Middle East," informed David. "They are all neo-cons and mostly Jewish. This is an indication that the President has surrounded himself with conformists who are tyrants hiding under the cloud of democracy. The appointees have a President wise to their agenda, with which he concurs."

Mandeville glanced down the page. "Look, there's more," he noted. "The CIA appointments. Do you see? God! Most of them are ones from his father's administration who will have expert knowledge on the Middle East and also the contacts, which will enable them to conspire. They will follow the President's policy, no mater how far he intends to go."

"He'll insist on using them," surmised David.

"Of course he will," acknowledged Mandeville. "In fact I'm banking on it."

"I think we have enough information to work with," surmised David. "Only ..."

"Only what?"

"The Secretary of Defense," continued David. "Basically, he hates you. He'll try to get you out of office."

"The feeling is mutual, David," replied Mandeville, smiling. "It's more a sense of fear on his part. Anyway, Burkhart loves me - he loves the power I can deliver."

"Even so, General," added David, "Denney will insist on controlling the army. He'll want the last word."

"Let him have it, David," said Mandeville nonchalantly. "He'll dig his own hole and help our quest. His judgement will be as clouded as Burkhart's." Mandeville lit a cigarette as he mused. "You're right, David," he said suddenly. "We have enough. The rest of the speech is superficial, aimed at trying to harness the people's trust. Ha! Offer them tax breaks and the people will support anything."

David laughed. "Money talks, General, and it's something he needs."

"Yes, David. Where is he going to get it?"

"I wonder," pondered David. "Could it be that he intends to ship it in from the Middle East?"

"Predictable, David," replied Mandeville, "so predictable. I can foresee a solution to the quasar plot. Our invasion will kill thousands in Iraq alone. Allah's religious army will be greatly decreased. I'm thankful that we are in a position to take the law into our own hands. Success at the extraordinary meeting will pave the way to military rule, David. Then we will have the God intended for this world."

David smiled. "I wonder again, General. Who will that be?"

"The victor, David. The victor who dared to con."

Chapter 11

General Mandeville's helicopter landed on the heliport at the presidential retreat and support facility, only 60 miles north of Washington DC. General Mandeville and David were the last of the guests to arrive under the cover of darkness. The General tapped the pilot on the shoulder. "Secure the helicopter," he said, "then report to staff headquarters, where you'll be provided with food, entertainment and accommodation."

"Understood, General," replied the pilot.

"This way, gentlemen," shouted a presidential member of staff who had come to meet them. "Everything has been taken care of. I'll show you to your rooms, where you can freshen up."

"Everyone gathered?" enquired Mandeville, as they walked.

"Yes sir, General. They are."

"Good," said Mandeville. "I can make an entrance after I've freshened up. That should put them at their ease."

David laughed. "I'm sure it will, General."

Andrew appreciated the humour and laughed along with David. "I'll inform the guests of your arrival, General. And ..."

"David," said David, introducing himself. "And you are?"

"Andrew," he replied.

"Well, Andrew, you do that. Oh, and can I ... can we count on your duties as a servant of this establishment?"

Andrew paused, took a deep breath and then walked away. "If you need anything," he shouted, "ring the bell."

"Whoops!" declared David. "Reckon we're stranded ..."

"You're a taunt," interjected Mandeville. "Learn to keep a lid on it. Lucky I know the way."

"Just showing him who's boss, General, and whom he should serve. His experience of my taunt will filter through to the guests after he has announced our arrival. It will give them an understanding."

"I'll take you at your word, David," said Mandeville. "So, ring the bell and I'll show you the way."

David laughed. "Ring, ring, General. Lead the way."

General Mandeville and David entered the Laurel Lodge conference room of the retreat after freshening up. They were hastened in by the President.

"Gentlemen," said Mandeville, announcing his entrance. "This is David, my aide."

"Good evening, General," responded the President. "I think you know everyone present?"

"Ah! The gathered conspirators," replied Mandeville. "Of course I know them. After all, they are those who ..."

"Indeed, General," interrupted Paul Denney, the Secretary of Defense. "Despite your previous demanding efforts, we are all here of our own free will. We do, after all, desire a common goal."

"Not everyone," commented Mandeville. "Where is Benjamin?"

"Ah!" intervened President Burkhart. "The Vice-President is at the White House managing domestic and administrative affairs. It's his job to look after the ship while I concentrate on my policy."

"So, he is kept out of touch," noted Mandeville. "You don't trust him to go along with your policy and so keep him as a housemaid ..."

"Like I said, General," interrupted the Secretary of Defense, "our own free will."

"No need to go on the defensive, Paul," commented Mandeville. "It's all about management and preparation. I'm sure we all feel it's time to kick-start Richard's era."

"Hello, General," said Secretary of State Corley, offering a handshake.

Mandeville reciprocated. "Evening, Secretary Corley," he said. "You're a calming influence, as usual ..."

"We're all calm, General," interjected the Secretary of Defense. "We were aware that you would be the last to arrive in order to make an entrance and try to unnerve us all."

"Come now, Paul," replied Mandeville. "I have a busy schedule. I'm sure you can appreciate that and why I was late. That is all. Nothing dramatic." Mandeville caught a glimpse of the CIA Director out of the corner of his eye. "Ah, Jim," he said, "long time, no see. Glad the President kept you on ..."

"Are you going to take charge, Richard?" requested the Secretary of Defense, purposely interrupting the General. "We don't need all this small talk. We all know what we're here for."

"Of course, Paul," answered the President, "but I need to hear what the General has to say. No doubt he has a plan."

The President's aide, Mark, blended into the background of the meeting, reading a newspaper away from the discussion at the top end of the huge table. He glanced over towards David and nodded to acknowledge his presence.

"Thank you Mr President," said Mandeville, "I ..."

"We only need his input, Richard," blasted the Secretary of Defense. "He is only here to tell us if he can deliver our solution. For instance, have we got the military resources?"

"We have, Paul," replied Mandeville, with confidence. "I can guarantee it. But what solution?"

"Take the Middle East before they squeeze us dry. They are a threat to our economy and way of life. This has been a long time coming. Hit them, and hit them hard."

"Not so, Paul," said the Secretary of State. "Our economy can withstand a small threat of any kind."

"I disagree," responded the Secretary of Defense. "You know the nation's oil is no longer plentiful ..."

"Ah!" interrupted Mandeville, with delight. "Now we get to the reason ..."

"What other reason is there, General?"

"You're the politicians and policy makers. What would I know?"

"Exactly," interjected David, in support of Mandeville. "We would not know of any other reason."

Mark glanced over his newspaper again and smiled at David. "I'm sure the General can speak for himself," he said. "Maybe you should blend into the background, David."

"Unlike you, Mark," replied David, "I'm the General's adviser, and not simply an aide. I'm not supposed to blend in and accept all that is said without comment."

"Okay, gentlemen," said Mandeville. "Let us stay focused. There is no need for point scoring. Now, where were we? Ah, yes. Paul, you can't just walk into the Middle East. You need an excuse other than to achieve solutions to personal issues. However, I would agree with securing the oilfields, Richard. Your term in office is going to be an expensive one. Not to mention the considerable amount you have already spent on your campaign, with the promise of tax benefits and having to finance the imminent invasion. The oil will, indeed, finance your policy on world domination and ease the financial burden on the American people, which will look good in terms of securing re-election."

"Your comprehension of the situation is impressive, General," observed the President.

Secretary of Defense, Paul Denney, agreed. "Yes, too much so for my liking," he commented.

"Not at all, Richard and Paul," defended Mandeville. "I picked up some pointers from Richard's inauguration speech. It's your comprehension, Richard. However, at the risk of repeating myself, you need a reason ..."

"Yes," interrupted the Secretary of Defense, "we have established that. But what?"

"Terrorists," posited the President. "We can invent intelligence reports on anti-American behaviour as a result of infiltration by terrorist organisations, thus influencing people's thinking in our favour. Also, the reports will unite the UK and America like never before. This will give us greater resources and more room to manoeuvre."

Mandeville emitted a tactical cough as he seized his chance to voice his contribution. "That's good, Richard ..."

"But?"

"But it's not enough. Reports can be scrutinised and opposed. Hard visual evidence is needed to acquire absolute support for your actions. The eye believes what it sees - especially if it's staring the American people in the face."

"What are you proposing, General?" asked the President cautiously.

"An attack on America, Richard," revealed Mandeville. "One of fantastical and unbelievable proportions, carried out by the terrorists you have infiltrated through the CIA."

"Get to the point, Mandeville," urged the Secretary of Defense.

"I'm proposing the destruction of the twin towers, purportedly by the hands of the terrorists but in fact staged by ourselves."

"Good God!" exclaimed the Secretary of State. "No way. They are icons in the eyes of the world."

President Burkhart smiled. "Exactly," he said. "I like it. Besides, they are only buildings, and they will illuminate the night sky for all to see and believe." The President noticed Mandeville and David staring at him. "What?" he asked. "What more can there be?"

"Not at night-time, Richard," revealed Mandeville. "Terrorists don't bomb empty buildings. Their aim is to kill the occupants within them ..."

"Murder our own people?"

"Not just our own, Richard," continued Mandeville. "The buildings house an international workforce, including British personnel. Thus the international community as a whole will become a victim of circumstance. Who would then deny you your revenge? You will secure your support, no questions asked."

The President felt shivers travel down his spine, but not with nervous tension. They were shivers of excitement and finding a solution to an excuse. "How?" he asked.

"With respect, Richard," replied Mandeville, "you will remain ignorant about how and when ..."

"Who do you think you are, Mandeville?" retorted the Secretary of State. "Richard is not your puppet. You don't pull the strings here, General. This is not the Pentagon. The buck stops at the White House."

"Calm down," requested the President. "Allow him to continue."

"Thank you, Mr President," acknowledged Mandeville. "The reason for Richard remaining in the dark is for the purpose of visual impact. When you are told of the event, Mr President, your shock will then appear more natural, though obviously requiring a modicum of acting ..."

"Brilliant, General!" hollered the President. "It's perfect ..."

"Why not go all the way and bomb the damned White House?" interrupted the Secretary of State.

"Don't be silly," replied the President.

"Why not take it further? But not the White House," said Jim, the CIA Director. "You could do more to convince ..."

"Such as?" enquired Mandeville.

"Your own Pentagon, General. Such a move would cover your tracks and avert any potential suspicion."

"Um ... worth considering, Jim," responded Mandeville.

"Sounds like a good trade-off, General," commented Denney. "But not on the scale of the twin towers, of course."

"It is a consideration I'll keep in mind, Paul," responded Mandeville. "The main target will get you your war, Richard."

"Agreed," said the President. "The military and the CIA will work together on this. I'll trust you with the details and the delivery. Are we all in agreement?"

The Laurel Lodge conference room remained hushed. Everyone's eyes were focused on the President as he waited for an answer.

"Gentlemen, please," said Mandeville, trying to break the silence and secure an agreement.

The silence continued.

"Gentlemen," continued Mandeville, "there is no turning back from this night of treachery: we have spilt the beans. We have to focus on domination at any price."

Finally the silence from the others was broken by the Secretary of State. "We may have spilt the beans, but so what? Besides, we are the only ones in the room. Who else would know?"

"Ah!" breathed Mandeville, followed by realisation from the others.

The CIA Director laughed. "When Mandeville says 'Ah!' I know we are in trouble."

"What does he mean, General?" asked the President. "What have you done?"

"Well, General?" urged the CIA Director.

Mandeville cleared his throat and glanced at David, who nodded in support. "Just my own private strategy, gentlemen," he said. "Protection, if you like. Deep down, I know you all agree but are afraid of openly backing such a plan of action. Thus I have to be strong for you. It is imperative that this goes ahead and becomes reality." Mandeville reached into his pocket.

"I knew it," shrieked Jim, the CIA Director. "He's taped the whole fucking ..."

"Deal, Jim," interrupted Mandeville.

Mark masked his face with the newspaper to cover his expression. So, he thought, this was one of the many revelations. A deal set out by Mandeville. I need a pause, a break and a fast forward. I've heard, or read, enough for now. I need to get away, but how?

"You disappoint me, General," stated the President. "There was no need ..."

"On the contrary, Richard, there was every need," interrupted Mandeville. "I'm not prepared to be the fall guy if things go belly up. I'm sure you understand."

"Well, in that case I guess we have to agree, gentlemen," said the President.

The Secretary of Defense banged his fist on the table. "You bastard!" he uttered.

"Sorry, I didn't hear ..."

"Never mind, General. You have our agreement. However, you shouldn't have gone to these lengths to obtain it. We only needed to have a few moments of reflection before we agreed. You have exposed your cards too soon. Now we know whom we should really fear."

Mark saw this moment as an opportunity and interrupted the conversation by noisily straightening and folding up the newspaper.

"Mark, do you mind?" asked the President.

"Sorry, Richard," replied Mark. "I'm just on my way out."

"Really!" exclaimed Mandeville.

"Oh, don't be so dramatic, General. Now that you have all agreed with the plan, I need to get to work on the President's public relations and prepare for the grisly news. It's all about appearances, General. There is no need for me to hear any more. I can go back to my room and make a start. Mr President?"

"Of course, Mark," replied Richard. "We all have work to do. Especially now."

Mark left the conference room and paced the corridor beyond. I have to protect myself, he thought. After all, no one else will. Mandeville has, with his tape, secured an amnesty for himself. It was he all along. He can edit the tape, and must have done. That is why he can reveal this book of revelations. God! Is he now a virtual being and controlling himself from Seeker One? But he didn't give me this book, Cunningham did. But why? Mark sat on one of the bench seats that furnished the corridor. He lit a cigarette and stared at the wall, pondering further. I remember. Cunningham wanted something changed. I assumed it was for himself, something he had done in the revelations. But what if it isn't about him? What if it's something else that he wants correcting. If so, it must be to do with Mandeville. I need this pause and fast forward to find out. Maybe I can find what I need in Mandeville's office. Yes, that's what I'll do: go back to Washington. Shit! How? I came with the President. Mark rose from the bench seat and paced some more. "Ah! Got it," he said to himself quietly. Mark about-turned and headed away from Laurel Lodge.

David opened the conference room door and peered into the corridor. He noticed Mark walking away into the distance and decided to follow him. Haven't got time to explain to Mandeville, he thought. David looked back into the conference room and, noting that the occupants were busy, guessed that no one would notice he'd gone. He wasted no more time and hurried after Mark.

Mark entered the retreat's car pool. Wow! he thought. So many you could open a business.

"Can I help you, sir?" sounded a voice.

Mark turned around and noticed a man in some kind of uniform. "Erm …

yes you can. I need to return to Washington." Mark laughed and proffered sarcastically: "The President has mislaid some documents. Sorry, can't say which ones. Secrecy and all that. Anyway, they are vital to the meeting. I'm sure you get the gist. Hell, if it wasn't for the likes of us, the country would fall apart."

"I'd say," replied the car pool attendant. "They have memories like a sieve …"

"Exactly," concurred Mark. "Now, if it is possible for me to get to …"

"Of course it is," interrupted the attendant. "Take your pick. Actually …"

"Yes?"

"The X5 over there is fuelled up and ready to go. It should get you there and back."

Phew! thought Mark. "That's great," he said. "Keys?"

"They are already in it, like all the vehicles. It's not as if anyone is going to thieve one from this fortress."

"No, God forbid," replied Mark. "Thanks for your assistance. I'll make a mental note of it."

"You do that," said the attendant. "Enjoy! Oh, and be careful: it's one hell of a beast."

Mark rushed to the X5 and soon acclimatised himself to its interior environment and controls. He programmed the satellite navigation. Good, he thought, shouldn't take too long. An hour or so, I guess.

David arrived at the car pool soon after Mark had driven off. "Has he gone?" he shouted.

The attendant appeared from his office. "Come again?"

"Mark. Was he here and has he gone?"

"There was a man here a moment ago," replied the attendant. "Mark? Is that his name? Said he had to rush to Washington. Something about secret papers for the President …"

"And you just let him go?"

"He seemed genuine. Must be. Why else would he be here? All staff are entitled to a vehicle. I suppose you want one? Damn! I will have to make another entry into the logbook."

"No," said David. "I don't need to charm you like he must have done …"

"Hang on a goddam minute …!"

"I haven't got the time. I have a quicker way. Now, do you know exactly where he's gone?"

"Like I said," answered the attendant, "he said he was heading for

Washington."

"Okay," responded David calmly. "Which car did he take?"

The attendant smiled. "The X5," he declared proudly.

"Does it have satellite navigation?" asked David.

"They all do," replied the attendant. "It's all to do with security. They can be traced."

"Excellent," remarked David. "Where's the phone?"

"There's one there on the wall if you're in a hurry."

"Okay, that's all. You can go away now. Leave me to deal with it. And keep your mouth shut."

"Does this mean you will be keeping a mental note of this?" enquired the attendant.

"What?"

"Reprimand me later?"

"I doubt it," reassured David. "But I do feel like ripping your stupid head off."

"Enough said," concluded the attendant. "I'm out of your way."

David picked up the telephone receiver and dialled the staff quarters.

"Where is David, General?" asked the President. "Is it normal for your advisers to disappear?"

"I don't keep him on a leash, Richard," replied the General, with a sarcastic smile. "He'll be looking after my interests. He obviously has a concern about something or someone."

"Someone?"

"Mark, perhaps."

The President looked annoyed. "Is there no one you trust, Mandeville?"

"Not outside the Pentagon, Mr President. It's normal for a general."

"So in what way is Mark a concern to you? After all, he's only my aide. And a damned good one at that."

General Mandeville smiled. "So is David." Mandeville lit a cigarette. "At least I know where David came from and how he became my adviser. I know his background and his credentials."

"Yes," interjected the CIA Director, "I understand what Mandeville is getting at. We don't know Mark from Adam. During the meeting he remained silent and just listened. Then he ran off."

"You heard him, Jim," said the President in defence of his aide. "He's making preparations ..."

General Mandeville's mobile phone rang. It was David reporting Mark's sudden departure. "Interesting," commented Mandeville after finishing the call and exhaling smoke from his cigarette. "Tell me, Mr President. Does Mark have to rush off to Washington to make any of these preparations? Surely, at this stage in our discussions, a simple draft would have sufficed until we all returned to Washington together. Also, he would need your permission to depart and begin your groundwork."

The President paused and became suspicious.

"I take your silence as doubt, Richard," suggested Mandeville.

"He likes to crack the whip," replied the President. "He just gets on with it; does what is needed."

"Wait!" boomed the Secretary of Defense. "Who do you think you are, Mandeville? You're talking as though to one of your own kind. This is the President to whom you are showing a lack of respect. You are accusing him of being negligent."

Mandeville stared at the Secretary of Defense with contempt. "Leaders are all dictators," he commented. "It's the only way to keep a country and the world on its knees, in the knowledge that we rule for the good of the people."

"Rubbish!" retaliated the Secretary of Defense. "You're starting to sound like a communist …"

"Gentlemen, gentlemen," said the President. "We have to stick to the matter in hand. Cease with this squabbling and allow us to move on."

"We can't, Richard," continued the General. "We have to resolve the problem of Mark."

"Goddammit, man! What problem?" exclaimed the President.

"David wants the code to the vehicle navigation system. He wants to trace where Mark is going. His destination will prove or disprove our doubts …"

"Your doubts, General."

The CIA Director interrupted. "I have to agree with Mandeville, Mr President," he said, with slight trepidation. "Mark has heard what has been said. We can't allow him to crack the whip, as you say. I mean, where did he come from? How did he come to be your aide? Who is he?"

The President shuffled around in his chair nervously, trying to decide which leg to cross. "Well," he said, "he was recommended by a contact in the White House Personnel Department. You know how it is. I haven't got the time to …"

"Who?" interjected the CIA Director.

"Who what?"

"Recommended him to you?"

"Not who, but how," confessed the President. "He was recommended by email."

"Shit!" exclaimed the CIA Director.

"Indeed so," agreed Mandeville, and he proceeded to push the President for the vehicle navigation tracing code.

Chapter 12

Mandeville opened his eyes as he felt the Lord's presence appear on the screen of Seeker One. "My Lord," he said, "welcome."

"It may not be the welcome you envisage, Mandeville," replied the Lord.

"You're not blissful, my Lord," observed Mandeville.

"That is one way of expressing my disapproval," said the Lord.

Mandeville gazed at the Lord with irritation at his untimely intervention.

"You look worried, Mandeville. And so you should be. You appear to be losing the plot. I'm displeased with the way you have lost control of the virtual beings."

"Control, my Lord? And to which virtual beings do you refer?"

"Cunningham, for one. He presented Mark with your book of revelations. We agreed that the book would remain hidden. We agreed you would only present Mark with the agreed passages and allow him to write the book in his own words for the humans to read. Is there a problem with the humanoid, Cunningham, relating to the quantum terminal?"

"Indeed, there has been a technical problem with Cunningham. His mind is stronger than I thought, which allows him to override the signals from the terminal. However, he will weaken fatally as a result of his efforts. His natural course will continue through the vortex to the end. His virtual being on Earth will evaporate. Although, on second thoughts, I shall delay his trip through the vortex. Cunningham can serve me here on Seeker One."

"Too late, Mandeville," informed the Lord. "The damage has been inflicted."

"This is true," replied Mandeville, with confidence. "But, I have made adjustments that will accelerate the process of expanding military rule. And, of course, your need to be the only God."

The Lord struggled to accept Mandeville's confidence and understand his statement. "I wonder if I made the wrong choice in installing you to head my Second Coming. You attempt to brush me aside, favouring your own goal, which clouds your judgement."

"In what way, my Lord?" asked Mandeville.

"Mark appears to have more power than you thought," said the Lord, "and may succeed in acquiring the pause he wants …"

"He will," interrupted Mandeville. "You, my Lord, have created a window of freedom by your untimely appearance. My concentration is now diverted to you and not to the matter in hand."

The Lord was angry with Mandeville's accusation. A loud clap of thunder boomed through the screen and shook Seeker One for a few seconds. How dare Mandeville? thought the Lord. He stretches my patience, as he did on Earth. "This is why you have the humanoids at the terminals, the quantum and the virtual beings to aid you while you are preoccupied."

Mandeville remained calm and collected his thoughts: he panics at the slightest blip and appears to have no vision. "Mark is not a virtual being," informed Mandeville, "so he can't be controlled through the quantum. I have to control the situations he creates and those that I create for him. The virtual beings can assist but they can't become too closely involved with a human."

"Are you sure?" enquired the Lord. "We only assume that is the case. Our belief has not been thoroughly tested."

"No, I'm not sure," admitted Mandeville, "and neither are the virtual beings. Maybe we will soon find out if the virtual and the real can genuinely come together. Time will tell."

The Lord pondered on Mandeville's answer, clasping his hands tightly together. "I'm not convinced we will achieve our goals, given the current situation. I fear that Mark can outmanoeuvre you."

"How can he?" quizzed Mandeville. "He can only outmanoeuvre himself. As far as he's concerned, I'm a figment of his imagination. He battles with his own conscience. Is the book of revelations his or mine? Does he hide behind Mandeville to expose the truth behind military rule? These are questions to himself that I conjure up to confuse. Do not worry, my Lord, I'm convinced we will achieve our goals."

"Then convince me of your confidence, Mandeville," commanded the Lord.

Mandeville sighed. I could do with a cigarette right now, he thought. "I allow the enemy to advance," he said suddenly. "This provides a false sense of security and contempt towards any attack they thought would come. Eventually, the enemy lays its own trap and, at the precise moment, I strike, taking the advantage when their guard is most exposed. This is the method I will use to track Mark's movements with the help of David. I shall watch and wait for the opportunity to take control."

"You are going to allow his pause?"

"Exactly," answered Mandeville. "I have concluded that a more fruitful battlefield exists out of the book and back in his imagination of reality, which disappoints him due to the short visit into the book of revelations."

"So, will he write ...?"

"No, my Lord," interrupted Mandeville. "Tactics have been reformulated in response to changing events. He can help me in other ways ..."

"Me, me, me," thundered the Lord. "It is all about you and your goal. Have you forgotten your side of our bargain?"

"Priorities, my Lord," rebuffed Mandeville, with a stern look on his face. "If ... when he is returned to his reality, he will realise that he can go in and out of the book as he chooses ..."

"That's dangerous," interrupted the Lord. "An unforeseen development." The Lord hesitated in a moment of frustration and then voiced his realisation. "He could change things - make it difficult for you."

"Precisely," concurred Mandeville calmly. "I'm encouraged by your understanding. However, despite your hindrance, I have the situation under control. Trust me ..."

"The Lord thundered and then laughed. "Trust, Mandeville?" he queried. "All around me has lain betrayal, from the first day of my known existence, from those I trusted. You are not immune from my apprehension as regards your possible betrayal of me. While our worlds are divided by time, then you have the advantage. Eventually the two worlds will unite and I shall reign as the one God. There can only be one, Mandeville. You would do well to remember that."

"And it will be so, my Lord," replied Mandeville reassuringly. "Only ..."

"Only what?"

"Only you can unite the two-year time zone that has been created ..."

"I see. I thought ..."

"You thought I was about to give you an ultimatum," continued Mandeville. "Not the case, my Lord. I was about to ask for your patience and for you to refrain from bringing the time zone together until we have succeeded in our preparations. The UK must be in my control before we unite our future."

The Lord listened with a suspicious ear and thought: he grovels for my tolerance and expects me to waver what I desire. "I know," he said.

"You know everything, my Lord," stated Mandeville. "To what circumstance do you refer?"

"I know that David runs after Mark. David deserts the post in which I placed him in order to protect and guard over you on Earth." A roll of thunder cracked again. "You have renounced my command and taken away his God-given responsibility."

"David follows to help my cause ... our cause," explained Mandeville calmly, despite the roll of thunderous disapproval. "David will provide only the information I wish Mark to possess. Eventually he will destroy Rashid, which will recall Malik to his dungeon in hell."

"Why should Mark aspire to do what is alien to him?" asked the Lord. "It's a tall order to direct. Remember, he still has the human capacity to decide."

"Desperation, my Lord," said Mandeville, smiling. "It's a human capacity I exploit effectively. In fact, I'm proud of my talent to do so. Anyhow, the book is already published, which is something he won't expect on his return to his imagined reality. When the impact of the publication has been comprehended, he will imagine that the slaying of Rashid will change events, thus freeing him of suspicion ..."

"Suspicion?"

"The humans think that he is the author of the book of revelations, which will link him to the BLA due to the mention of the Middle East's intentions."

"Um," pondered the Lord, and he bowed his head in thought. This is indeed a suitable plan, which helps my desire to return Malik to isolation. Without an overlord like Rashid, Malik cannot contain his presence on the surface. Also, Rashid's demise would work towards Allah's withdrawal.

Mandeville urged the Lord to speak.

Eventually the Lord raised his bowed head. "How can you be sure?" he asked. "I would be dispirited if your worthy plan failed."

Mandeville smiled again. Fail? he thought. No, no. Never again. This time ...

The Lord coaxed Mandeville to speak by clicking his fingers in rapid succession.

"Sorry," apologised Mandeville. He then explained his guarantee of Mark's obedience. "He will imagine his daughter is in danger." Mandeville laughed. "Having a family secures co-operation."

"I understand, Mandeville," said the Lord. "If needs must, then ..."

"The needs outweigh any sentimentality, my Lord," interjected Mandeville, before the Lord had time to think again. Mandeville continued to engross the Lord. "I can deal with your threat on Earth, my Lord," he said, "but you must deal with your threat within the council of the realm who betray you."

"Ah!" breathed the Lord softly, with a sudden daze of realisation. "Zealot? He couldn't accept the punishment of being retired from his position in the first council. Idle and wounded, he betrayed his Lord and the white-eyed by conspiring with the red-eyed supporters of Allah. Do not brood, Mandeville. Zealot will join his new compatriot, Malik, in hell." The Lord appeared pleased and convinced of Mandeville's conviction, but felt compelled to add a protective clause. "I have one condition, Mandeville," announced the Lord. "Only then will I be satisfied and able to grant you my patience."

"Oh!" exclaimed Mandeville, not expecting an ultimatum. "And what is it, my Lord?"

"The author, Mark," revealed the Lord, "must be guided through the vortex and diverted to Seeker One."

Mandeville paused, well aware of the consequences of this request. I need a human contact on Earth, he thought. Dammit! "Your request is a high price to pay ..."

"A price you have to pay, Mandeville," insisted the Lord. "A guarantee against betrayal."

"You drive a hard bargain," responded Mandeville. But one I can compensate for, he thought. Mandeville paused before giving his agreement.

The Lord grew impatient at Mandeville's delay. "This is my demand, Mandeville. It is non-negotiable."

Mandeville wanted a few more seconds to consider the sacrifice he was about to hand over before acquiescing to the Lord's demand. He noticed the Lord's anxiety building up to a clap of thunder. "Okay, my Lord." Mandeville paused again and smiled. "You have your sacrificial lamb." But not the sheep, he thought. "However ..."

The Lord sighed. "However what?"

"You realise that you will delay the preparations?" enlightened Mandeville, placing his own price on the Lord.

"Your preparations, Mandeville," reminded the Lord.

"Yes."

The Lord conceded. "No matter," he said, "so long as my end of our arrangement is complete, then so be it ..." The Lord fell silent and stretched his back, which produced an audible sound of cracking bone. "I'm becoming tired of our conversation," he continued, "which has come to an end. A necessary but appetising matter requires my attention."

"My Lord," said Mandeville, and bowed his head. You go and feed the weakness within your council to the lions, he thought. Fill your time, which will deflect concern away from me. Mandeville chuckled as the Lord's image disappeared and he waited for the screen to return to its blank status. "Cunningham," he said in his mind. Soon after Mandeville's silent command, Cunningham appeared on the bridge of Seeker One. Standing to attention in front of Mandeville, Cunningham's white eyes stared into the eyes of Mandeville. Mandeville sniggered. "Still have the urge, Cunningham?" he asked.

"Urge?"

"I read your thoughts and your stare tells a story of a failed mission. Anyway, we are here now: a new mission in a new time. Prepare a place for the author, Mark ..."

"Come again?"

"You understand," continued Mandeville. "Let's not get into a long conversation like we entered into at the Oval Office ..."

"That was your trait, Mandeville," retorted Cunningham.

Mandeville exaggerated his facial expression. "Just get the terminal ready for his arrival. And prepare the virtual Mark for descent to Earth. Got it?"

"Got it, Mandeville," replied Cunningham, stepping back to exit the bridge.

"No mistakes," cautioned Mandeville, in a loud tone of voice. "You are on borrowed time."

Cunningham continued to exit in silence.

Silent whispers filled the depths of the Lord's White House. The council members felt an unease about the Lord's return from speaking with Mandeville. Zealot entered the lower lobby, where the council members met and held talks amongst themselves. "Where have you been, Zealot?" asked the new number one councillor, Malachi.

"What business is it of yours, Malachi," replied Zealot. "You have only been selected as the Lord's messenger to the council, and not an adviser as I was. Besides, I have retired from the council and its politics. Your concern for me is no longer a matter for the gathered members, who look uncomfortable. They respect my privacy. You, on the other hand, make me feel uneasy, being the Lord's spy."

Malachi thought: he makes my task all the easier with his resentful attitude. "My concern," he said, with chilling composure, "is a matter for the members." He signalled towards them with open arms and then returned his attention to Zealot. "You still frequent our meetings as an adviser and friend, yet you dare to accuse me. What we want to know is: who do you spy for, Zealot?"

Zealot laughed and paced in a circular motion. He stopped, placing his hands behind his back in a defensive pose. "Ah," he pondered, "the whisperings were not only about the Lord but also about my role within the lobby." Zealot stared at Malachi, prompting a swift response without thought.

"Well," replied Malachi, "as an elder of the council you are expected and welcomed." Malachi produced a friendly smile, which Zealot accepted with mistrust. "Your presence," continued Malachi, "has receded in recent times when you were required to attend a forum. Your absences become our concern. The members find it unacceptable ..."

"Speak for yourself, Malachi," interrupted Zealot angrily, suspecting Malachi's friendly smile a con.

"I speak for us all, as you did. But you dabble elsewhere and shirk your responsibility towards the council and the Lord." Malachi sighed with disappointment. "I benefited from your knowledge of the Lord, which helps when we are in session ..."

"Ha!" exclaimed Zealot. "You are all fools. Malachi traps me into thinking I'm of importance, as did the Lord. My experience and advice are void among the residents of this house of the Lord. I was verbally crucified for my thoughts, which were thrown back into my face." Zealot became overwrought with passion from his anger, feeling his every word. "As with the Lord's son, my pure policy of harmony, love and peace was no longer accepted and was deemed unimportant. The Lord has chosen Mandeville to fulfil his destiny. You all fall to your knees and grovel in his misdirected journey ..."

"Silence," interjected Malachi, perturbed by Zealot's words. "You are at ease with blasphemy and betrayal, which you plague us with ..."

"This is absurdity. You all convene to judge as one - puppets at the control of Malachi and your minds poisoned by the Lord. Well, judge this: consider an alternative to the management at the top ..."

The members howled with disgust and covered their ears. "Devil's talk," said one.

"No!" shouted Zealot. The members lowered their hands from their ears. "Any talk of change is looked on as infiltration by the devil. Come out from the dark and see the light I can create before it's too late."

"You are the devil's advocate," shrieked the same member.

Zealot laughed.

"This is no laughing matter, believer of the red-eyed," said Malachi accusingly.

"Not the devil," replied Zealot. God, their minds are closed, he thought. "I'm talking about a new God with strength and direction; the one our Lord is afraid of and battles to defeat instead of embracing for the good of all."

"Our Lord battles in defence of his realm on behalf of his believers," explained Malachi. "There can only be one ..."

"Where have I heard that before?"

"One you were devoted to ..."

"And I am, Malachi, I am. I'm devoted to saving our Lord from the alliance with Mandeville, his Second Coming." Zealot scoffed with laughter. "Mandeville advocates war and destruction. Am I the only one here who cares? Am I the only one who dares to speak the truth and see the light? You all appear deaf, dumb and blind to what is happening. Mandeville is using the Lord. The Lord is using Mandeville. Wake up!"

"We are wide awake, Zealot," informed Malachi, "and, to be honest, bored with your sermon. The Lord is wise ..."

Zealot laughed again at Malachi's tunnelled vision. "The Lord's wisdom deserts him and he allows Mandeville to sit on the throne of power and dictate. Can't you see that?"

"No, Zealot," replied Malachi. "You are poisoned and this decays your soul."

The other members whispered in agreement.

Zealot noticed the whisperings and the nodding of heads. "You dare to place me on trial?" he questioned, accusingly. "I'm the elder and most experienced of you all." Zealot waited for a response.

Malachi paused and stared at Zealot's desperate expression. Then he sighed with a look of sadness on his face. "If ... your statement is true, Zealot," he said, "we can't argue against it. So why wander into the depths of doom?"

"I don't need your sympathy, Malachi," replied Zealot. "Your sympathy disguises treachery towards me."

Malachi's saddened expression turned to glee at Zealot's rebellion. "Oh, but you do, Zealot ..."

"What?"

"Listen to your council. The Lord commands it."

"The Lord can no longer command me to do anything. My faith has gone."

"Is this a confession, Zealot?" asked Malachi, with hope.

"No," replied Zealot confidently. "Not a confession but a fact."

"It doesn't matter how you interpret it. The Lord is displeased."

"Really?" said Zealot flippantly. "He has no hold over me. Do you not know the law? Retirement is freedom from the official duties of the council."

The members whispered again.

"Stop this whispering," demanded Zealot. "If you have anything to say, then say it."

"Their words are not for you," enlightened Malachi. "Anyway, laws change according to the circumstances in which we find ourselves. You have betrayed your Lord - a Judas among his flock; a flock who have the honour of residing in his house, which you no longer have."

"What do you say, Zealot?" asked a council member. "Think carefully before we whisper again."

"I see," said Zealot, realising the meaning behind the whisperings. "He requires understanding before ..." Zealot paused and thought: I'm doomed either way. "So be it, Malachi. Whisper this." Zealot paused again and clasped his hands. He continued, "You have to betray those who refuse to listen and understand about a better way without suffering ..."

Malachi interrupted, much to Zealot's annoyance. "Suffering produces a godly way on the path of life ..."

Zealot vociferated with frustration against Malachi. "You interrupt my defence so that the Lord only hears your prosecution within the whispers. The devil is in you all. Mandeville is the devil's advocate who invades and controls the Lord's realm, controls the Lord, controls the humans and the virtual. You are all doomed when Rashid and Malik pave the way for their God. I tried to intercept in the Lord's name ..."

"Nonsense," roared the Lord, with a sudden interruption and dramatic entrance. "You anger me beyond my patience. You wanted to stop my Second Coming. You wanted to prevent the coming together of the two worlds, past and future, where there can be only one."

Zealot laughed and tears flowed from his eyes as the fear of God drained from his body. "Mandeville will be the one, my Lord," he said. "Are you so blinded by expectation?" Zealot attempted a hopeless escape.

"Restrain him," demanded the Lord.

The council members restrained Zealot and brought him before the Lord.

"My Lord," said Malachi, "show no mercy. He wished to take the devil's path and escape his ..."

"Who are you to advise me, your Lord?" erupted the Lord. "You only replaced Zealot as a messenger. My heart is heavy but I know what must be done." The Lord instructed the council members to release their grip on Zealot. "Stand free, Zealot," announced the Lord, and he stared into Zealot's eyes.

Zealot stared back, knowing that the Lord's hypnosis would fail. "Forgive me, my Lord."

The Lord stared in disbelief. "It cannot be," he said, "it cannot be. I had hope of your redemption from my gaze, which reflects your red eyes." The Lord bowed his head with sorrow, raised his right arm and then lifted his head to face Zealot. His sorrow turned to vengeance as he saw a sign of the red-eyed enemy smiling to accept his fate. "It has to be, my lost friend, my lost soul."

From out of nowhere, the spear of the Lord's son appeared in his right hand, pure white with a silver point and stained with the blood of Christ.

Zealot's fear returned. "The spear of sacrifice," he whispered.

The Lord exclaimed. "Zealot the Judas. Betray me no more." The Lord then cast the spear with all his might and anger, plunging it into Zealot's heart.

Rays of bright light appeared from Zealot's wound, followed by the blood of mortal man. Zealot tried his best to fight the wrath of the Lord and called on Malik, crying out in a voice that was not his own. "Rashid will survive."

The Lord clasped his hands and whispered to the devil, "Take your demon angel, who is banished from my house."

The Lord opened his hands to catch the rays of light, which disappeared into his body. He felt the pain of choice between life and death, portraying an image of a crucifix. He stared towards Zealot and a ray of light discharged from the white eyes of the Lord.

Zealot cried out in pain, surrounded by the light. After a few moments the light dissipated and Zealot, now banished, had disappeared into thin air.

The Lord returned to his normal stance and paused for a while in silence. Then he spoke to the members of his council. "Let this be a lesson to you all. I shall say to you what I reminded Mandeville. There can be only one God."

The council bowed their heads in silence, afeared by what they had just witnessed.

"Be gone with you now," ordered the Lord. "Return to your lodgings and pray for a stronger faith. Leave me to rest and meditate."

Silently, the council retired from the Lord's presence.

Malachi entered his room alone and sat on the hard wooden bed. He closed his eyes and called on Mandeville, appearing on the screen of Seeker One.

Mandeville withdrew from his suspended animation. "Ah, Malachi," he said, "a good day's work. We have eliminated a threat of goodness and weakened the humans' faith, which will make them vulnerable and more accepting towards military rule."

"I don't understand," said Malachi.

"He, Zealot, was the Lord's second in command of the realm. Prayers that the Lord could not deal with were passed on to Zealot. These will not be answered and anarchy will increase among the humans, which can be manipulated towards my cause. And Rashid will have to look elsewhere for an alliance. Um … I wonder where?"

"I see," replied Malachi. "The Lord was blinded by our prosecution and acted on it. He was not aware of Zealot's motives."

"It was the Lord's anger," enlightened Mandeville, "that weakened his wisdom. His frustration increases, which sanctions his reliance on his Second Coming and also on me as controller of Seeker One. Indeed, Zealot tried to infiltrate the devil's realm to strike a deal to prevent the Second Coming and halt the advance of Allah. Obviously, it didn't work."

"Zealot called on Malik," said Malachi, "but was forsaken. Also, that voice …"

"Rashid's voice," interrupted Mandeville. "Zealot was not calling for help. It was a realisation that Malik and Rashid would block any deal with the devil struck from the Lord's realm." Mandeville laughed.

"What is so funny?" asked Malachi.

"You have much to learn," replied Mandeville. "It should have been my name he called out. It was I, before you were promoted, that planted the seed of betrayal. Zealot was a threat and needed eliminating." Mandeville noticed the expression of confusion written on Malachi's face.

"I must confess my embarrassment as regards my ignorance, Mandeville," said Malachi. "Indeed, I have much to learn. But why dispose of …?"

Mandeville interrupted with a loud sigh. "Your embarrassment comes from only being a messenger and a spy. Useful, but you deliver without understanding."

Malachi looked displeased. "You treat me as though a child. You forget, I'm the first contact with the Lord from the council …"

"That's better," interrupted Mandeville. "A sign of forcefulness."

"So, explain the message of betrayal."

"The humans hide behind religion: their Gods, disciples and religious leaders, as I once did," replied Mandeville, "but I had my own reasons. Anyhow, I have come to understand that if they didn't have the cover of religion then reality would shine through. They have lost the guidance of the disciple, Zealot, and his quest for goodness. The Lord and I need each other. The Lord needs his Second Coming to eliminate his rivals, and I need to achieve military rule. Thus, one ruler from the heavens; one ruler on Earth."

"So," concluded Malachi, "you have no aspirations towards becoming God?"

"Ha, no!" replied Mandeville dismissively. "Where is the power in that? I'm here to control the humans and to become the one leader of the world. It's all about my ambition for America to rule the waves." Mandeville paused and stared into the eyes of Malachi. "Um," he continued thoughtfully, "I think that is enough for now. Some ignorance on your part is beneficial to me. However, now that I have given you a brief explanation and understanding, you are mine ..."

"I resent ..."

"Resent nothing, Malachi. You are my contact ..." Mandeville paused, with a smile of achievement. "You are my spy within the council and as regards what the Lord says."

"Don't presume that I'll agree."

Mandeville's smile turned into a quiet guffaw of laughter. "You also have much to learn about me. You witnessed Zealot's fate. Now, if I were to have a discreet word with the Lord ..."

"But it was your doing ..."

"And your message of deliverance. Whom would the Lord believe: a messenger or his chosen one that sits on the throne of Seeker One? Besides, if I feel you are becoming a threat to me ..."

"All right," conceded Malachi, intimidated by the blatant threats.

"Good," said Mandeville, with an air of satisfaction. "You have made the right choice. I'm sure you will benefit from my employ."

"What choice do I have? Let's hope the Lord keeps your favour, for both of our sakes."

"Don't worry," pledged Mandeville, "I won't be caught out again as I was on Earth. I will never allow others to plot my destiny. The Lord will be weak and will need to rest after his display. Time for me to continue the book of revelations."

"Never say never, Mandeville," advised Malachi. He smiled and faded from the screen.

Chapter 13

Mark, the President's aide within the book of revelations, arrived at the Pentagon car park and sat motionless in the X5, contemplating his next move. He stared out of the windscreen towards the building. What am I really looking for, he thought, and where in Mandeville's office do I find it? Anything, I suppose, to do with this dammed book. Maybe he's kept a diary or notes on a manuscript. Um ... anyway, it was a nice drive here in this posh car. I should keep driving in the hope of finding an exit from this madness. Mark paused from his thoughts, rolled a cigarette, lit it and inhaled deeply. "Still," he said to himself, "I've got to get in there first." Mark exited the X5, followed by a cloud of smoke, and headed towards the Pentagon doors.

Mark entered the foyer of the Pentagon and approached the security barriers. He reached into his pocket and yielded a credit card type object to the approaching the security guard.

"Hi," welcomed the security guard. "You are ... erm ..." The security guard was racking his brains to find an answer. "Ah!" remembered the guard. "Mark, isn't it?"

"Yes," replied Mark confidently. "You remember me?"

"Sort of ..."

"Sorry," interjected Mark, "I can't remember your name. Ignorant of me really. But we were ushered away quickly the last time we were here."

"My name is Mike," he said, pointing to his name badge and pausing for thought. "That's it," he continued, enlightened by Mark's mention of his previous visit. "You were with the President. God, how could I forget? You were his aide on the day in question."

Mark breathed a sigh of relief, happy to have struck a rapport with the guard. "Correct," he said. "You obviously have a good eye for detail."

"I do," agreed Mike, "and I certainly do in this instance ..."

"Really, what ...?

"Well," continued Mike, "it's not every night that an aide of the President appears uninvited, assuming he owns the building. Aide or no aide, you can't just walk in here as you please. An aide follows the one he is aiding. So what are you doing on these premises, Mark?"

Mark suddenly realised that a Pentagon guard cannot be taken in by simple rapport. He paused to formulate a convincing reply, knowing that Mike had the advantage.

"Well?" prompted Mike.

Mark smiled like a typical condescending aide to a politician. "Mike," he said, "not necessarily. You see, I'm not just any aide. I'm the President's aide and as such convey his authority. In fact, I aid anyone to whom he appoints me ..."

"Such as who?" retorted Mike.

"Mandeville, for instance. I've been given a job to do, orders from the top, which I must carry out. So here I am with this card, which gives me clearance to enter and do my job." Mark noticed the guard giving the situation some serious thought and hoped that the name-dropping would convince him to retreat.

"I'm not sure," said Mike, rubbing his chin with a nervous hand. "I haven't had any communication informing me of your right to clearance."

"Typical," complained Mark. "David told me he would ..."

"David?"

"Yes, David. You know - he's General Mandeville's aide. Well, more of an advise, I think."

"Okay already," declared Mike. "I realise who he is, but ..."

"But nothing, Mike," interrupted Mark, observing that he seemed to be gaining the advantage. "Are you aware of this weekend's important meeting?"

"Meeting?"

"Yes, meeting," stipulated Mark, "at the presidential retreat. All the top brass are there at this very moment ... including General Mandeville. Anyway, they need to see files that have been left in Mandeville's office. That, Mike, is my mission as a mere aide."

The guard began to ponder once again, but was interrupted by the phone ringing at his desk. "Stay here," he instructed. "Don't move."

Mark exhaled loudly. "You are wasting valuable time, Mike," he shouted towards the guard as he made towards his desk. "The President is an impatient man ... not to mention Mandeville."

"Enough already," ordered Mike. "Wait!" Mike answered the telephone call, which was brief and marked by silence from the guard's end. Mike replaced the receiver and walked back to where Mark was waiting. "Okay," he said disappointedly, "swipe through. Just doing my job, understand?"

"Of course I understand," sympathised Mark. "Good work, Mike. I shall mention your vigilance." Mark swiped the card, but it didn't work. He laughed nervously. "Damn!" he exclaimed. "Would you credit it?"

"Here, allow me," offered Mike calmly. He used his own card to allow passage for Mark.

"Thanks," said Mark, with slight embarrassment and relief. Phew, thought Mark as he made his way across the foyer towards his destination, thank God for the interruption. Maybe his pizza is on the way.

Mark arrived outside the reception to Mandeville's office. To his surprise, he noticed that the door was slightly ajar. Still, it makes my job easier, he thought. Mark continued through the small reception area until he reached Mandeville's office door. He twisted the doorknob. "Shit!" he whispered to himself. "It's locked." Mark glanced around the sides of the door. No keypad, he observed, only a key lock within the knob. There must be some keys around here somewhere.

Mark moved to the desk in the reception area and searched the drawers. Nothing. Where are they? Don't want to be too long or Mike will become suspicious. Mark began to panic and sat in the chair to compose himself. Scanning the surface of the desk, he noticed a bunch of keys sitting in the out tray. "Unbelievable," he said. "Who would have thought it?" Mark picked up the keys and tried each one until the lock finally opened. He entered Mandeville's office and headed straight for the filing cabinet. "Now I'm getting somewhere," he whispered as the drawers opened freely. However, he thought, it would be a more positive sign if one of the drawers were locked. Mark looked around the office, searching for clues of a possible secret hiding place for sensitive documents. Suddenly, a noise came from the door knob. Mark moved swiftly to the side of the door so that he would be concealed when it opened.

The door opened with considerable force and hit Mark hard. "Arrgh!" he sounded as David coolly made his way to Mandeville's desk and sat down. "Really, Mark," commented David, having heard Mark's cry and observing him rubbing his bashed nose. "Hardly spy material, are you?"

"How …?"

"How?" repeated David. "All too easy, Mark. An effortless piece of detective work and arrangement. And - voila! - here I am. Besides, my conclusion was proved correct when I heard you talking to yourself. Do you realise that humans can get locked up for that, as well as for breaking and entering?"

"I didn't break anything," replied Mark, "apart from my nose and my ego."

"Um," reflected David, laughing. "Fortunate you had a guiding hand ..."

"Such as?"

"At the risk of denting your ego even more, a phone call to the guard, Mike ..."

"You interfering bastard! I ..."

"Tut, tut, tut, Mark," interrupted David. "That is no way to thank me. Oh, and the keys - not too unbelievable, just convenient. Anyhow, your protection was better served by allowing you in. I mean, if the wrong people got to know of you from the guard ... well, who knows?"

"Why should I thank you?" responded Mark. "Are you really protecting me? Maybe you've come here to stop me from finding any embarrassing papers?"

"The book, Mark, is it not?"

"Whatever," responded Mark dismissively.

David laughed sarcastically. "You know it is. Let's stop pretending. You know who and what I am. You can't get out, Mark. You are in the book, as your designated character, until the end. You can't change history by acquiring research from this office and writing your own imagined account. Cunningham's so-called deal is nonexistent."

"Cunningham?" queried Mark, with suspicion, followed by realisation. You? Then again ..." Mark paused, observing David's smiling response. "You followed me into the book."

"I was already here, Mark. I serve and protect Mandeville wherever he is, in the future or in the past. Remember the quantum multiple of the virtual. We are here, there and everywhere."

Mark moved to the desk, sought out a cigarette and lit it with Mandeville's ornate table lighter.

"As for Cunningham," said David, watching Mark's desperation, "he's cunning ..." David paused and grinned. "Get it?"

Mark was unimpressed and simply continued to smoke and listen.

David's grin subsided. "Never mind. His selfish treachery was turned to our advantage to get you here for the knowledge and truth that the humans believe you wrote. His role in the book of revelations won't change. Mandeville won't allow it."

Mark stubbed the cigarette in the ashtray and sat in the chair opposite David. "Mandeville?" he asked quietly.

"What about him?" enquired David.

"Oh, I don't know," said Mark, with a defeated tone of voice. "Something isn't right ..."

"Indeed it is not," interjected David. "This is a pause in the book that shouldn't happen. The point is, I have to stop your attempt to get back; stop you putting the book down and taking matters into your own hands."

"Thank you, thank you, David," declared Mark brightly.

"For what?"

"Acknowledgement," revealed Mark. "Acknowledgement that I have the power to do so and that you're scared I may succeed. Besides, what's the point in stopping me? You don't need me."

"Yes we do, Mark," replied David, "and you need us. You can't allow yourself to pass up an opportunity like this. You are intrigued and involved. You are needed for the future. This book is your analysis and basis for writing our future." David looked at his watch. "Your fun is over. The time allowed for this pause is over, Mark." David laughed.

"What's so funny?"

"You have had the mug of tea you normally indulge in between chapters." David stared at Mark. "You will, eventually, find out what everybody's role was."

"That's it," said Mark. "Find out. Mandeville never had any intention of allowing me to write your history of understanding ..."

"Hurry!" exclaimed David, choosing to ignore Mark's presumption and looking at his watch again. "You have a gap in which to walk safely out of here unopposed. I suggest you go." David reached for the keyboard to Mandeville's computer and logged on. "I can head them off."

Mark was concerned. "Who?" he asked.

"The red-eyed," answered David. "They are coming for you ..."

"Ridiculous ..."

"Not so. They have intercepted the pause you have created and have realised you're not going to write their words by being in this book."

"No, no," said Mark, "this is your fault. What was said and agreed in the meeting makes it your fault."

"There's no more time for conversation, Mark," informed David.

"Yes there is," replied Mark, rising from the chair and standing close to David. "You can provide the time using the computer. Isn't that so, David?"

David paused, staring at Mark. He's calling my bluff, he thought. "I can try," he said, but I can't promise anything."

"That's good enough for me," replied Mark. "Now, I suggest you start tapping." Mark watched as David tapped the keys on the keyboard, out of Mark's vision. After a flurry of hand movements, David paused. "Well?" quizzed Mark. "Why have you stopped?"

"I'm waiting for approval to enter a code, if you don't mind? A few seconds, that's all."

Mark waited and concentrated on David's hands. He must be waiting to enter the Seeker One code, he thought. Suddenly, David started pounding the keyboard again. Mark counted the number of times that David tapped before a break.

David stopped again. "Right, I'm in," he announced.

Mark turned away and stood a short distance from David. He mentally recounted David's last action on the keys. Nine, he thought to himself. Definitely nine.

"Okay," said David, jolting Mark from his thoughts. "What is so important that you should risk remaining in the pause you think you created?"

Mark was slightly stunned by David's calmness, suggesting he was in total control of the virtual beings and situation. "What do you mean, think?" he asked, deflected from the subject of the meeting.

"You can't really create a pause," answered David. "Once you are in the Network's realm, you can't escape."

Of course I can, thought Mark. I'm not virtual, I'm human. I have my own mind. "I don't believe that," he responded. "I don't believe you. There must be a way, and there is - I can see it in your eyes."

David smiled inwardly. "There is," he revealed, "but it's complicated."

"Can't be too hard," contradicted Mark.

"Well, firstly," replied David, exposing his smile. "You need the code ..."

"Ah!" exclaimed Mark. "The mysterious code. Where have I heard that before?"

"You have?"

"Yes," admitted Mark, "just before I was given the book of revelations. Something about controlling an operative on board Seeker One."

"Forget it, Mark," advised David. "Another of Cunningham's cons. You'll never get the code anyway ..."

"So it does exist? I'm sure you just said it was a con."

David was becoming agitated at having to be so careful in responding to Mark's questioning. Can't give too much away, he thought. "I admire your stubbornness, Mark," he said, "but once you have the code you need to know which operative to control, which would not help your cause, being human."

"What do you mean?" probed Mark.

"Wake up, Mark," instructed David. "Think back to when this first started. The first contact."

Mark paused, thinking desperately. "Mandeville?" he questioned suddenly. "He must be the operative. I concluded that he was controlling the events in my life ..."

David laughed, interrupting Mark's desperate conclusion. "Close, but not close enough. He appoints both permanent and temporary operatives ..."

"Temporary?" interjected Mark, with concern.

"I've said too much," decided David.

"Don't stop now," demanded Mark, frustrated at David's vagueness.

"Um ..." David paused, looking at his watch to determine the moment. "Time is ticking by, Mark. An operative on board Seeker One will break this pause, one way or another."

Mark rubbed his chin and then looked to the heavens for inspiration. Is he bluffing or not? wondered Mark. Come on, Mandeville ... Mark's thought stopped and he returned his attention to David. "So," he said, staring into David's eyes, "you need me; Mandeville needs me. I suggest you conclude this debate and give me the answer."

David smiled and swivelled the chair around to break Mark's stare. After one revolution, he came to a stop, facing Mark again. "Okay," he said, "have it your way. All of a sudden you have the courage to demand ..."

"You are the ones who make demands on those who want answers."

"Payment, Mark," corrected David. "It's payback time for those who are told the answers. Will your courage extend to our settlement, our payment on demand?"

"I'll risk it, David," answered Mark confidently.

"A name and birth date are entered after the code and this connects you to the operative controlling the virtual ..."

"Now I'm getting somewhere," concluded Mark. "I'm getting more information than I'd hoped for, thanks to your presence. You have been most helpful. Better than rummaging through this office."

David shook his head. "You'll get nowhere, Mark," cautioned David. "You can't change or stop what has happened or is about to happen."

"Change?"

"I know you'll try something," replied David. "But what will it be? Something from the meeting, perhaps. It must be, due to your sudden retreat. Something shocked you."

Mark knew what David was getting at. "Yes, it did," confessed Mark. "You are about to open the gates to hell through an act of destruction …"

"Actually," interrupted David, "we are trying to close them. The towers are sacred to the West and not a way in for invaders from the East. If we don't act now, then the one they call Malik will rise."

He's already risen, thought Mark, and the red-eyed are on their way here to stop me. "What makes you so sure I'm going to do something? Maybe I don't want to play this game anymore …"

"Game?" interjected David loudly. "It's not a game …" David's attention was diverted towards the computer screen.

"What is it?" asked Mark.

"Whoops! Time out," announced David, with a grimace. "The computer informs me that they are close." David noticed Mark looking towards the door. "You can't escape without my help, Mark."

Mark glared back at David and uttered forcefully, "How many humans and virtual beings are you actually protecting? How can your judgement be trusted?"

"Time out, Mark," repeated David, with a tuneful pitch.

"Sod your time out," retorted Mark. "You are controlling the fucking advance of the red-eyed. You just want me to stay in the book …" Mark paused. I have to get out, get eliminated, he thought. If it doesn't work, then I'll be out of the game anyway.

"What are you thinking, Mark?" enquired David. "We play off each other in order to get the desired result. It's the oldest trick in the book. Whom are you going to play off, Mark? Me?"

"I'll take my chances with my own judgement." Mark started towards the door.

"Wait!" shouted David. "You'll need this."

Mark turned and noticed a gun in David's hand. "What? You're joking," he said, "I'm no shootist."

"They don't know that," replied David, and he threw Mark the gun.

"No, but you do," commented Mark.

David laughed. "You're learning, Mark," he uttered, through his laughter. "But can you be sure? Besides, I'll be right behind you." David tapped furiously on the keyboard. "There, we have a 60-second gap to get through the door and make our escape back to the retreat. Ready when you are, Mark."

Mark paused for a second. "No way," he said. He rushed towards David and knocked him and the chair to the floor. In a rush of adrenalin, Mark hit David over the head with the gun, knocking him unconscious. "I want to go home," whispered Mark, "hopefully." Mark turned his attention to the computer screen and noticed some written instructions. Think, he thought. In a fit of inspiration, Mark closed the window. An instruction appeared to save the changes: yes or no. Mark clicked not to save the changes.

"Arrgh," moaned David as he came round and tried to move. "What are you doing?"

Mark ignored David and ran for the door, wrenching it open. He rushed into the corridor, waving the gun.

"There!" shouted a voice. "Careful, he's got a gun. Shoot!

Mark felt a piercing, hot pain. "Shit!" he yelled as he fell to the floor.

David heard the commotion out in the corridor, picked himself up and installed himself behind the computer. Once again, he furiously tapped on the keys.

A red-eyed walked over to where Mark lay. "Who the hell is he?" he asked his colleague.

"God knows," replied the colleague. "Let's look in the office. The one we want may still be in there."

The red-eyed entered the office and scanned the area. "Dammit!" they growled in unison.

David knocked on the door to General Mandeville's quarters at the presidential retreat.

"Come," said Mandeville.

David entered the room smiling and poured himself a drink.

"Has Mark returned with you?" asked Mandeville.

David swallowed his drink in one gulp and sat down to rest. "No," he answered, with delight. "He's eliminated from this chapter, as desired. It was a close call, though - nearly got caught ..." David paused and grinned. "Even had to pretend to be knocked out."

"Good," praised Mandeville. "Cunningham's plan has failed miserably and has been dealt with effectively."

David stretched his legs and breathed a sigh of relief. "Now we can virtually continue with the meeting and our plans without fear of intervention. The towers are doomed."

"Well," said Mandeville, "I'll drink to that, David."

Chapter 14

"Arrgh!" shrieked Mark, as he was cast back into his imagined reality. "It was supposed to be about the oil, not the towers." Mark observed his surroundings. He looked out of the living room's bay window and scanned the front garden and the street beyond. I'm back, he thought. It worked. He examined his upper torso with his hands and, with relief, whispered, "Nothing is wrong with me. That's it. All I have to do is get eliminated and I can go in and out of the book as I please." Mark closed the book and placed it on the nest of tables next to him. He fixed his stare on the book and a sudden realisation hit him: but not back to the same chapter, he thought. Still, I'm back to sabotage Mandeville's attempt to con the humans in my world. They can't believe what Mandeville has professed in the book of revelations. In fact, they don't need to know. I have the only physical copy. I can write my own account to contradict his so-called revelations. Surely it was never an issue of the East taking over the West ... or was it ...? Mark's thoughts were interrupted by a thunderous knock on the front door. "Shit!" he whispered, annoyed at the interruption. Another knock reverberated. "Okay, okay," shouted Mark. "Give me a chance to get there."

Outside the front door stood two people, who smiled at each other on hearing the irritated tone of Mark's response.

Mark eventually opened the door, having peeped out of the window to see whom he was about to confront and decided that there was no imminent threat. He came face to face with a man and woman.

"Mark, I presume?" asked Detective Inspector Una Francombe. She smiled, enhancing her friendly facial features.

"Yes," replied Mark. "But who wants to know?"

Sergeant William Fisher held up his identification badge. "We do," he said. "I'm Sergeant Fisher and this is Detective Inspector Francombe."

"Hello, Mark," said Detective Inspector Francombe, producing her identification badge. "We are from Scotland Yard and would like a chat with you if you don't mind."

Sergeant Fisher displayed signs of slight frustration at Francombe's nice approach, thinking they should instead just barge in and get straight to the point. "Of course he doesn't," he said, rubbing his hands together.

"It's cold standing here, Mark," commented Francombe. "This won't take long."

Mark gazed at the Detective Inspector for a second or two, thinking she reminded him of someone, although not anyone related to his present predicament. The absence of eye shades and thus confirmation of eye colour gave Mark confidence to let them in. "Yes, it is cold," he agreed. "Please, come in." Mark escorted them into the living room and invited them to sit down.

"Nice place," commented Sergeant Fisher. "You writers always seem to have a nice place." He smiled at Mark.

Mark kept his composure, although he was wondering how they knew he was a writer. "Like a cup of tea?" he asked as a polite formality, hoping they wouldn't accept.

"Yes, that would be lovely," answered Francombe.

Fisher looked and felt irritated. "Well," he muttered, "we don't really have the ..."

"It's all right, Mark," interrupted Francombe, with a soothing voice. "You carry on. A hot drink will warm us up."

Mark smiled at Detective Inspector Francombe and nodded his head. I like her, he thought ... although she could just be the nice one in a typical police good guy/bad guy double act. Mark moved swiftly to the kitchen, relieved to distance himself for the time being. He switched on the kettle and gathered the mugs and tea bags. Mugs! thought Mark. Oh, they won't mind: they look like mug-type of people. Mark chuckled to himself while waiting for the kettle to boil. Then suddenly he realised something and rushed back into the living room, interrupting his visitors' conversation. "My wife? My kids?" he quizzed in a panic.

Detective Inspector Francombe reassured him. "Nothing like that, Mark. As far as I know, they're fine."

"Phew!" Mark said faintly, with relief. "I thought ..."

"I think that's the kettle boiling, Mark."

"Oh, yes. I'll ..."

"You do that," interjected Fisher, looking at his watch. After Mark had vanished from the living room, the Sergeant looked at Francombe, nodding towards the small nest of tables next to Mark's chair. Fisher made a fleeting remark. "Looks as if he's been reading his own book. How vain is that?"

"I don't think it's vanity, Fisher," contested Francombe. "Authors have to read through for mistakes."

Fisher smirked. "Really," he commented. "A bit late for that. Anyway, how would you know?"

"My son is an author. Well, a struggling author. I shared the process with him."

Fisher raised his eyebrows. "Um ... I didn't know that."

"No, you wouldn't," said Francombe defensively. "Private life, and all that."

Fisher smiled sarcastically. "I understand," he remarked. "Best to keep one's private life under wraps, especially in this job. You just never know what might come to light."

"What do you mean?" queried Francombe. "You think ..."

"No, of course not," reassured Fisher. "Anyway, the whole book is one hell of a mistake if you ask me ..."

"I'm not," interjected Francombe. "Besides, we have to focus on getting him down to the Yard."

"Yes, I agree. Home turf for us, which will make things difficult for him. We can really get to work on him then."

Francombe looked at Fisher with disdain at his fervour for interrogation and said, "We'll get to that in a due course, albeit softly, softly. In the meantime, I want Guy to meet him. I've arranged for Guy to sit in on the interview ..."

"Guy? That crazy crackpot of a psycho ...?"

"Now, now, William," responded Francombe. She was about to explain her tactics when Mark appeared with a tray of tea, sugar and milk. "Here, let me help you." Francombe moved the book from the small nest of tables and placed it on a nearby cupboard to make room for the tray.

"Proper nice," commented Fisher, reclining into his seat and crossing his legs. "Milk and two sugars, please."

Mark directed a disapproving look at Fisher. Arrogant prat, he thought. "Actually," he said, "I forgot to ask if you took milk and sugar, so I put it all on the tray. Nothing posh about it."

"Practical, Mark," said Francombe, with a smile.

"Exactly," agreed Mark. "Now, just help yourselves." Mark was keen to serve Francombe with her tea, seeing as she was so affable, but he decided against the idea in fear of being branded a guilty butler by Fisher.

Fisher stirred his tea loudly while remaining vocally silent.

Francombe smiled at Mark after taking a sip of her tea, silently preferring it to be weaker.

Mark observed that the two of them looked like children waiting to be told off. So, after an awkward lull, he decided to speak first. "So, if my family are safe, what do you want?"

Fisher moved to the edge of his seat and placed his empty mug on the tray. "Nice cuppa," he commented. "We need you to answer a few, if not a lot, of questions on certain matters that have come to our attention."

"Well, fire away," instructed Mark.

Francombe cupped her hands around her mug of tea and gazed at Mark with her blue sparkly eyes.

Here we go, thought Mark. The nice act is about to begin. I must say, though, she's very convincing.

"The thing is, Mark," said Francombe softly, pausing for a few seconds. "We need to conduct this interview at Scotland Yard."

"Really?" declared Mark. "Why?"

"It's a sensitive matter, Mark," said Fisher, in a louder tone of voice than Francombe. "It's best done at the station, official like. And also for your protection. Don't want any accusations of police brutality do we?"

Mark couldn't think straight and started to worry. "Now?" he asked.

"Of course, now," retorted Fisher. "We haven't just come around here for a cup of tea and biscuits ... oh, we didn't get any of the latter. Still, no time now. We have to go, Mark."

Mark looked to Francombe for some support, which was not forthcoming. Then why would she? he thought. After all, she's not my ... Mark paused from his thoughts and looked at his watch, knowing that he had no choice but to go with them. Besides, he was intrigued about the 'sensitive matter'. "How long will it take?" he asked. "I ..."

Not long, Mark," interrupted Fisher. "Although the longer we stay here ... Well, you understand."

"No, I don't actually," admitted Mark. "Are you charging me with something? If not, I can refuse to come with you."

Fisher laughed. "Oh, I think you'll come."

Mark noticed the confident look on Fisher's face.

"Listen to me," said Francombe, with a comforting tone. "We are not charging you with anything. As we said, we just want you to help with our enquiries."

She's trying the friendly approach again, thought Mark. Still, it's not working. "I'm sorry," stated Mark firmly, "but I need to know exactly what your enquiries are about. Otherwise I'm going nowhere." Mark stared at Fisher. "Do you understand?"

Fisher glanced at Francombe, silently asking for help.

Francombe nodded her head in approval. "Fisher will give you a brief outline," she said. "But no details until we arrive at the Yard."

"Well?" prompted Mark, looking expectantly at Fisher. "I'm waiting."

Fisher ground his teeth in annoyance at Mark's unexpected rebellious streak. How about I give him a slap? he thought. We're getting too soft these days. "Does the A12 ring any bells in your head, Mark?" he asked aggressively.

Mark remained silent. What do they know? he thought. Are they real or virtual? Mind you, they don't have the traits of a virtual. Cunningham! Is this what he was warning me about? Damn! I can't remember.

"Well?" requested Fisher sarcastically, scoring a point. "I'm waiting for the bell to chime."

"Not again," replied Mark with a sigh, searching for his own answers.

Fisher's face adopted a smug look. "What do you mean, not again?"

Mark was panicking inside, desperately searching for an appropriate response.

"What do you mean?" repeated Fisher.

"One of your lot," answered Mark, glancing at the book on the cupboard. I have to protect it, he thought. "Yes, a detective has already been to see me. We cleared it."

"Cleared what exactly?" asked Fisher.

"He explained that my car was on the CCTV footage and wanted to know if I had seen anything."

"Really?" responded Fisher. He, too, glanced at the book. "The thing is, no one could have retrieved the footage so quickly. So tell me, is Cunningham …"

"Cunningham?"

"Your detective, Mark," responded Francombe. "Is he a contact of some kind or a figment of your imagination?"

"No, can't be his imagination, Una," stated Fisher confidently. "Just like his book of revelations is not his imagination. Isn't that right, Mark?"

"It's not my book," resounded Mark. "And how …?"

"Never mind, I'm shifting away from the point in question. Cunningham?"

"Like I said, he's a copper," reiterated Mark.

"No he isn't, Mark," informed Francombe.

Damn! thought Mark. "He isn't?" queried Mark, acting surprised.

"No, I'm afraid not, Mark," responded Francombe, preparing to land a bombshell. "We saw the news interview." Francombe paused to see if there was any reaction from Mark's body language. Nothing, she thought, and continued, "We believe he was at the scene all along and was masquerading as a Chief Inspector. The cheek of it! Anyway, this facade was adopted in order to obtain the advantage, remove the reporters and clear the area ..."

"Advantage to what?" interrupted Mark.

"That is something we're not quite sure about. But let me finish. By the time we arrived, as I pointed out, the accident scene had been cleared. In fact, there was no longer any evidence of an incident."

Shit! thought Mark, I've just landed myself in it.

Francombe sensed a reaction from Mark. "We believe the BLA ..."

"BLA?" retorted Mark. "Where has that come from?"

Francombe glanced towards the book. "In time, Mark, in time. As I was going to say, the BLA appear to be a highly organised group, and not strictly British. We have a lot of concerns, Mark. Ones that need clarification."

"I'm being stitched up," declared Mark suddenly, with anger. "And, you know more than you're letting on."

"Stitched up?" enquired Fisher. "Come on, we're the ones feeling hard done by. I'm becoming annoyed, as I suspect you know more than we do. Now, you can either come with us of your own free will, or we can arrest you on suspicion ..."

"Of what?" retaliated Mark. "My imagination?"

Fisher stretched his neck, feeling his shirt collar tighten. "You sarcastic bast ..."

"Okay," surrendered Mark, holding his hands up. "I'll come with you. I, too, want to get to the bottom of this confusion."

"We all do, Mark," said Francombe. "It's our, and your, destiny to do so."

Mark looked into Francombe's eyes. She talks like a virtual, he thought, but she's not.

"So, shall we go?" suggested Francombe.

"Yes," replied Mark apprehensively.

Detective Inspector Francombe, Sergeant Fisher and Mark assembled around the unmarked police car parked outside Mark's house.

"How will I get home?" asked Mark, waiting for the car door to be unlocked.

"That's a bit premature," replied Fisher, fumbling around in his pockets for the car keys.

"Well," reminded Mark, "you said it wouldn't take long."

Francombe tapped on the car roof to attract Mark's attention. "Circumstances change, Mark," she said sympathetically.

The car doors made a loud clunking sound, indicating that they had at last unlocked.

Francombe gestured towards the rear car door with her hand. "Now, if you would get into the car, please," she said, "we can move on. And don't worry, Mark. If there is a car available, you will be brought back …"

"If not," interrupted Fisher, "it'll be Shanks's pony, or the cell."

Cell! thought Mark. I don't like the sound of that. How much do they know, and how can they?

"Get in the car," demanded Fisher, observing Mark's hesitation.

"Wait!" exclaimed Mark, realising his rights.

"Oh, I'm getting in," retorted Francombe, looking at her watch.

Fisher sighed with great annoyance. "Do I have to drag you into the car? Besides, wait for what?"

"I'm allowed a phone call, aren't I?"

"Um …" pondered Fisher, "when we get to the Yard. The journey will allow you time to think whom to call. And consider your predicament. Again, get in the car … please."

Mark perused the open street with a desperate thought of escape.

"Don't even think about it, Mark," cautioned Fisher, demonstrating his experience. "You wouldn't get far."

Mark's shoulders slumped in surrender. He knew at this point that his options were exhausted. He therefore succumbed to Fisher's impatience and repeated requests to enter the police vehicle.

Eventually the unmarked police car sped away from Mark's home and towards Scotland Yard.

Mark reclined in his seat and watched the passing scenery. This journey to Scotland Yard, he thought, is going to take about an hour. Um … never been there before. Should be interesting, if nothing else. Mark was starting to feel more positive, but realised he'd have to have his wits about him. I could just fall asleep. Better not: it will dull the brain. I know, I'll have a chat with my captors - especially Detective Inspector Francombe. I feel I can relate to her. Not Fisher, though. I just feel like winding him up the wrong way.

"Okay in the back?" asked Fisher, as he drove swiftly through the streets.

"As okay as I can be," replied Mark, adjusting his position to sit up straight. "No siren then? The traffic will get busier soon, so it'll give you a chance to show off your manhood."

"Very funny, Mark," retorted Fisher, briefly squinting through the driver's rear-view mirror before focusing his concentration on the road ahead.

"Never mind, William," said Francombe, with a slight grin on her face. "Just ignore him. Concentrate on your driving."

"I'm trying to."

Mark stared at Francombe from behind the driver's seat.

Francombe noticed Mark's fixation from the corner of her eye. "Is there something you want to ask, Mark?"

"Nothing in particular," responded Mark, still gazing at Francombe.

"In that case," she said, "would you mind not staring at me. It's rather offputting."

"Sorry," apologised Mark. "It's just that ..." Mark paused, taking in the likeness. "It doesn't matter." She does, though, he thought. Especially when she was younger with a smooth, clean complexion, cheeky smile, piercing blue eyes and greying hair. Then there was her flawless demeanour and kind attitude ... Yes, she was a perfect lady.

Francombe turned slightly to look at Mark. "You're still staring, Mark," she reminded him gently. "If you have anything to say that you think might help you, then say it."

"No," answered Mark, "it has nothing to do with your injustice ..."

"That's a good one," interrupted Fisher, laughing.

"Shush, William," instructed Francombe. "Just drive."

Her defence of him made Mark smile.

"So, if it's not our injustice, then what?"

"You remind me of my mother," confessed Mark, looking sad.

"Is that what you were just thinking about, Mark? Your mother ...?"

"Normally the case," interrupted Fisher. "Criminals often get an attack of sentiment."

Francombe and Mark ignored Fisher's comment. Francombe wanted to gain Mark's confidence. "How is she?" she asked.

"Dead," answered Mark firmly.

Francombe appeared embarrassed for a few seconds. "I'm sorry to hear that, Mark," she said, with sympathy.

"No need," replied Mark sternly. "You weren't to know."

"Well, I should have," confessed Francombe, "if someone had done their research properly." Francombe glanced towards Fisher.

Mark noticed Francombe's fleeting glance. "I can imagine," he replied, wanting to score a hit. "Anyway, talking of research, you don't appear the type to be a Detective Inspector."

"Here we go," retorted Fisher. "He's putting on the act of an author."

"Drive!" exclaimed Francombe. "Keep your comments to yourself. For now, at least."

"Don't be taken in by it, Mark," warned Fisher, unable to respect a command.

"By what?" asked Mark, interested in Fisher's ability to prompt a reaction.

"It's all an act," replied Fisher, still focusing on the road ahead. "She's as hard as nails really."

Mark was determined not to agree with Fisher, even if he wanted to. "I doubt it," he said quietly. "More like firm but fair."

Fisher laughed. "What, like your mother was?"

"Piss off, arsehole!"

"Wow! Listen to him," said Fisher. "Touched a raw nerve, eh?"

"Of course ..."

"A friendly warning, Mark," retorted Fisher. "Your mother she is not."

Mark thought Fisher's warning a strange one.

"Type?" enquired Francombe.

"Sorry?" requested Mark.

"You mentioned I wasn't the type to be a DI. That was before we were so rudely interrupted."

Mark became calm again. "Well ..." Mark cast his mind back. "Oh, yes. I was going to say you're too nice. Quiet even. Besides, I'm not really bothered now. I don't care how you two develop this act of yours. It's becoming tiresome and boring." Mark yawned ... and then yawned again.

"Actions speak louder than words," stated Francombe, wanting to continue the conversation.

"True, I suppose," responded Mark reluctantly. "Except in his case." Mark nodded towards Fisher.

Francombe giggled.

"Mock all you want," remarked Fisher. "At least there are no false impressions with me, mate. I say it as I see it ..."

"That's original ..."

"This is the real world, Mark, not one of your books or perfect essays. If I get it wrong, I get it wrong, and move on."

Francombe was finding the fact that Mark was getting under Fisher's skin quite amusing. "More often than not, William," she commented.

Fisher smiled and looked at Francombe with affection for a second. "I haven't got the woman's touch."

"Eyes forward," suggested Francombe, returning a smile.

"Oh God!" groaned Mark. "Sick! Talk about sucking up."

Fisher glared at Mark via the driver's mirror.

Mark stared back, taking in Fisher's features. He has a stern look about him, he thought, with his chiselled chin, long face, short parted hair and staring brown eyes. He must be about six feet tall with a straight, rigid back, which matches his straight talking. "Anyway," continued Mark, thinking back to his original enquiry. "What's your story, Detective Inspector Francombe?" Mark paused and lowered the window. "Mind if I smoke?"

"Jesus! Guy's going to love this one," remarked Fisher.

"Guy?"

"In due course, Mark," intervened Francombe. "Someone you are going to meet."

"Sounds interesting," said Mark. He held up a cigarette. "So?"

"If you must," conceded Francombe.

Mark lit the cigarette, inhaled deeply, and then attempted to blow the smoke out of the window but it was sucked straight back into the car, annoying the other passengers. "I'm ready for your story now," he said.

Francombe looked at her dainty watch. "There's not enough time now, Mark. Another time, perhaps." Francombe seemed more distant and quiet.

She's probably had enough, thought Mark, or it's part of the act.

"Yes, Mark, I agree," said Fisher. "We're nearly there. I suggest you remain quiet for the remainder of the journey and enjoy what's left of your freedom."

"What?"

"Ignore him, Mark," advised Francombe, breaking her silence. "I'm sure we'll get to the bottom of this."

"Whatever," commented Fisher, relishing the fact that he was able to drive the last few miles in peace.

Chapter 15

Mark observed the surroundings from the car window as they approached Scotland Yard.

"So," he said, breaking the silence.

Sergeant Fisher sighed and stated, "You're supposed to keep quiet."

Mark ignored the Sergeant. "I didn't realise it was so close to the Houses of Parliament."

"What?" replied Fisher, with the minimum of interest.

"Scotland Yard. I've only seen it on the telly. You know, with a reporter standing in front of it. Ah! And there it is: the famous rotating sign of Broadway."

"Very funny," commented Fisher sarcastically.

"I also didn't realise how tall the building was." Mark paused and counted. "Twenty floors," he concluded.

"Is there a point to all of your meaningless chatter?" asked Fisher.

"Yes, there is actually."

"And what would that be, Mark?" intervened Francombe.

"Why have we come here rather than to a normal police station?"

"Because you are not normal," jested Fisher. "And perhaps you are visualising your escape?"

Francombe concealed a laugh and then said, "My office is here, Mark, along with my team."

"Team?"

"Never mind that now," interrupted Fisher, after parking the car. "Out you get."

Mark promptly followed Fisher's abrupt order and walked around the car to open the door for Francombe. He smiled and indicated the way with his extended arm.

"Thank you, Mark," said Francombe, exiting the car.

"Please!" exclaimed Fisher. "You won't score any brownie points with her."

"He's obviously a gentleman, William," retorted Francombe. "However, that is not in question."

"Exactly," concurred Fisher. "Just because he shows off doesn't mean he's innocent."

Francombe shook her head at Fisher and then turned her attention towards Mark. "This way," she said softly, indicating the way forward.

"Wait!" hollered Fisher, while securing the car.

Francombe and Mark stopped walking and turned around to face Fisher.

"We should cuff him, Una," suggested Fisher. "He might want to escape …"

"Escape?"

"Yes. He thought about it at Mandeville Road."

Um, of course, thought Francombe, Mandeville Road. "No," she answered, returning from her thoughts. "Don't be silly. He hasn't been charged. And stop obsessing over the issue of escape."

"Yes, ma'am. You know best," retorted Fisher, and he breezed on ahead of Francombe and Mark.

Francombe squinted her eyes. Really, she thought, sometimes, he's too sarcastic, demonstrating a low form of wit. Francombe looked at her dainty watch.

"That's nice," noted Mark. "It's similar to …"

"Come on," instructed Francombe, interrupting what she thought Mark was about to say.

Mark was escorted by Sergeant Fisher into a small room, accessed from Detective Inspector Francombe's office. The room was used for interviewing suspects whom Francombe and Fisher believed could assist with their enquiries. Mark scanned the room with slight trepidation. It was more or less a 12-foot completely uninviting cube. A table and four chairs furnished a corner spot opposite the doorway, with a single chair placed on its own against an adjacent wall. The walls were bare and painted white due to the lack of natural light coming in from the high narrow window. The floor was covered with cheap-looking laminate wood flooring, which was stained with cigarette burns. Clusters of spotlights were fixed to the ceiling, which was also painted white and was fitted with a wood and steel rotating fan.

"Go and sit down, Mark," requested Fisher, lighting a cigarette.

Mark sat down on the hard upright chair, its padding worn down. Mark looked over at the other chairs, but they were in the same state of disrepair. I'll stay where I am, he thought. Mark sat straight and rigid with his forearms resting on the table top.

Fisher stood still and silent in the middle of the room, smoking his cigarette and allowing the ash to fall to the floor, which he dispersed with a flick of his foot. He retrieved an unopened packet of cigarettes and threw it onto the table. "Help yourself," he said dismissively. "There's an ashtray on top of the voice recorder."

Mark looked at the large black box sitting on the table and spotted the cheap accessory that Fisher mentioned. "I'm not allowed to use the floor then?" he asked.

Fisher grinned before he answered. "There's not usually one in here - especially when she's around. That's why I'm sneaking one in and using the floor."

"She'll never notice," taunted Mark.

"Not if you have one. I'm supposed to be giving up."

"I see," comprehended Mark. "There must be a deal here somewhere ..."

"What? Trying to con a copper, eh? Nice try, but this department don't do deals. So just have a fag and calm down."

"I will," stated Mark, "seeing as I'm waiting. But waiting for what?"

"Francombe, of course," answered Fisher, thinking Mark should know. "She's just confirming an appointment."

"Personal?"

"It'd be none of your business if it was," scolded Fisher. "However, you will get to know soon enough."

Mark raised his eyebrows. He's evasive and then he teases, he thought. I won't ask: he'll be expecting it. Mark opened the packet of cigarettes, extracted one and lit it with his own lighter.

Fisher stared at Mark as if to ask why he hadn't responded to his tease.

Mark inhaled on his cigarette, allowing the smoke to escape through his nostrils. "There," he said to Fisher, "Francombe will never know. Just don't breathe on her."

"You think I'm scared of her?"

"I doubt it," replied Mark.

Fisher smiled. "Good," he said, "'cause I'm not."

"You're scared of being found out, that's all."

"Ha!" retorted Fisher, "Bollocks! What would you know? You don't know me."

"Not yet, Sergeant Fisher," tormented Mark, "not yet." Mark observed Fisher's silence, surprised at the absence of a counter-attack. "Maybe," pushed Mark, "it's not about the fags. Maybe you had a fag because you were nervous and needed to calm down. Maybe you're worried I'll find out who you two really are."

Maybe nothing, Mark," fired Fisher. "You're searching through thin air. Besides, you're the one sitting at the wrong side of the table. We're here to ask you 'maybe' questions."

"We? Who are we?"

"You know who we are. But we don't know who you are."

"Yes," agreed Mark. He paused for a few seconds. "The thing is," he continued, "it's whom or what you are associated with that I don't know. And that's a troublesome thought, Sergeant Fisher."

Fisher smiled again. "Then we have the upper hand, Mark, don't we?"

Mark returned a smile. "It depends on who's dealing the cards …"

The sound of approaching footsteps interrupted Mark's flow.

"Gentlemen," announced Francombe, walking swiftly to the table. "Sorry to have kept you waiting. I hope my Sergeant has entertained you, Mark?"

"He has," replied Mark quietly.

"Good," said Francombe positively.

"Be careful, Una," warned Fisher. "He asks too many questions. You'll be lucky to get a word in edgeways."

"I'm sure I will, Sergeant," replied Francombe confidently. "You just have to know when. Isn't that right, Mark? I mean, your General knows how close to let the enemy get before he strikes."

Mark stared, taken aback by Francombe's comment.

"Anyway, more of that later," continued Francombe. "Now, what questions have you been asking, Mark?"

Fisher walked to the table and sat next to Francombe. She's up for this, he thought. She's got the bit between her teeth and is going to let him have it.

Mark reached for the ashtray and placed it on the table in front of him. "You don't mind, do you?" he asked the Detective Inspector.

Francombe reached for a switch located on the wall near to where she was sitting and pressed it forcefully. "No," she replied with understanding, as the fan whirled into action. "I don't suppose you're trying to give it up?"

"No chance," answered Mark, "unlike your Sergeant."

Fisher remained silent, intent on just observing for the time being.

"So, Mark, what questions do you want answering?" enquired Francombe, smiling.

Mark returned a knowing smile. "Who are you and what do you really want with me? I mean, Detective Inspector is not a Scotland Yard rank. At least, I don't think so."

"What do you think it is then, Mark?" asked Francombe.

"CID, of course," replied Mark, stating the obvious.

"Well," pondered Francombe, "we are all interlinked around the force."

"That doesn't answer my question," rebuffed Mark.

Fisher leant forward across the table, closer to Mark, with a suspicious look. "You seem to know your stuff."

"Of course I do," said Mark, with a confident tone. "I'm a writer."

"Oh, of course," granted Fisher sarcastically, "but I wonder about the subject of your material ..."

"Really?"

Fisher moved back to his original position and suggested, "Is it a story, or is it a warning?"

"Warning?"

Francombe observed patiently, though inwardly irritated by Fisher's intervention and lack of tact.

"Like that film," he teased.

Francombe frowned. "Like what film, Sergeant?"

"*Basic Instinct*," replied Fisher confidently.

Francombe shook her head slowly. "I said we'd get to the purpose later on ..."

"Hang on," interrupted Mark, amused. "I'm interested to know why he chose that title. Besides, I don't have the legs, Sergeant."

"Very funny," retorted Fisher. "But I'm glad you know who she is. She writes about a crime, which she commits in real life."

"I'm aware of that," responded Mark, "but what has that to do with anything? Please tell me you've more to talk about than an ageing film about a tart."

"The relevance, Mark," said Fisher, "is that it's about a crime within a crime, which ..."

"Later," intervened Francombe, her patience spent.

"Later, later," repeated Fisher. "What's all this 'later' about?"

Francombe tapped Fisher's foot with her own under the table. Then she wrote something on a notepad and showed it to Fisher away from Mark's view, which read: "Waiting for Guy".

Fisher nodded with realisation.

"Anyway, where were we?" enquired Francombe. "Oh, yes. Who are we?"

"Would you like me to answer that?" jested Mark.

"Well, do you want to know or not?"

"Depends if you think it's relevant or just wasting time."

Francombe grinned at Mark's presumptuousness. "It will help you to understand as we move forward," she explained. "You see, Fisher and I are connected to the territorial support group, CO20. We investigate the aftermath of terrorist actions and their political implications. We detect and bring to justice …"

"Hence the ranks, Mark," interjected Fisher.

"We also assist MI5 and MI6," continued Francombe. "So, now you have an idea about who and what you are confronted with."

"Intimidated, you mean," suggested Mark sternly.

"We are not here to intimidate you, Mark," assured Francombe. "We just want you to help us with our enquires. Then you can be on your way."

"Way where?" asked Mark pensively.

"That depends on the outcome …"

At that moment, a series of light taps could be heard on the door.

Francombe's face beamed. "That must be Guy," she speculated, and she requested the guest to enter.

The door opened to reveal a large figure of a man: tall, stout and dressed in a scruffy suit. His appearance and manner matched his dress code. "Hello, Una," said Guy, as he walked into the office. He sat down on the lone chair, sighed and then paused. He immediately lit a cigarette and muttered, "This had better be good."

"What was that?" probed Fisher, feeling overshadowed.

Guy exhaled his smoke towards Fisher. "You've dragged me away from an interesting session with a young Muslim. He was about to open up and squeal his guts out before I … Anyway, don't let me hold you up. Please continue."

"We haven't even started yet," complained Fisher. "Francombe was too busy waiting for you."

"Well, you'd better get on with it," prompted Guy, "and I'll intervene when I feel it's necessary, or when you run out of ideas."

"Bloody cheek," commented Fisher under his breath.

Francombe smiled at Guy. "Good to see you again, Guy," she said. "This one will quench your interest."

Guy remained silent and smiled back at Francombe.

"Excuse me!" exclaimed Mark.

"Ah, yes," responded Francombe. "This is Guy. He's a psychiatrist."

"Really," replied Mark. Mark tried to make eye contact through the tinted glasses Guy was wearing. Too dark, he thought, and so he kept any suspicions to himself. "Anyway, I agree with the fat man over there. Let's just get on with it."

"Mark, really," said Francombe, dismayed at his derogatory comment. "It's not like you to be insulting."

"How would you know?"

"Just a guess," concluded Francombe, wanting to move forward with the interview. "So, the day in question?"

"Day?"

"You were travelling along the A12, remember?" said Fisher, in a loud tone of voice.

Mark leered at Fisher. "That is correct, Sergeant. In fact, I use that road frequently. But, you already know that."

"Indeed we do," confessed Fisher, glancing through a pile of papers.

Mark took particular notice of Fisher's fingers as he turned the pages. Looks like some kind of statement, he thought. Am I being stitched up here? I can't remember … I haven't given one. Mark paused again, searching the depths of his mind. Mandeville! Has he tampered with the police computers to set up this interview? Mark looked at Guy out of the corner of his eye, searching for some kind of clue.

"You are a writer," continued Fisher, interrupting Mark's concerns.

"I prefer author," corrected Mark. "But, yes. I write books. Fiction, of course."

Fisher started flicking through further pages of the report in front of him, allowing Francombe to continue the conversation.

"I have read your first published book, which I enjoyed," informed Francombe.

"First?" queried Mark, with slight confusion.

Francombe picked up on Mark's reaction. "Well, your book is your first publication?"

"Yes."

"I found it very interesting from the perspective of getting to know you and how your mind works …"

"That's more evident in the second one, Una," interrupted Guy. "I preferred it to his first."

"Not now, Guy," commented Francombe. "You'll get your chance."

Mark frowned. What is he on about? Second one? He scrutinised Guy discreetly once again. Ah! Is that the clue I'm looking for? Does he know about the book of revelations? Play it cool. Let them reveal whatever they think they know.

"Something to say, Mark?" asked Guy.

Mark ignored him and turned his attention to Francombe. "Aren't we moving away from the point of questioning about my movements?"

"In time, Mark," said Francombe. "I just want to get a mental profile of who and what I'm dealing with."

"Well, Una, nothing out of the ordinary," replied Mark. "You don't mind me calling you Una?"

"Actually I do. My title or surname will suffice."

Guy smiled. I'm enjoying this, he thought, as he lit another cigarette.

"I wouldn't call you ordinary, Mark," declared Francombe. "In fact, I admire what you have achieved. It can't have been easy working on your part-time occupation as well as being a full-time bus driver ..."

"Cover up, more like," interrupted Fisher. "Who would suspect a bus driver?"

God! Where is this leading to? thought Mark. "I can see you've done your homework. That can't have taken long, eh Sergeant?"

"I have done the homework, Mark," clarified Francombe.

Mark was more impressed.

Francombe continued. "I have to delve into the background of the people, or suspects, I have to question. Research, you might say. Something you are familiar with. You must read a lot of books in order to compile your research and feed your imagination. Also relying on computers."

"Of course I do. That's obvious."

"Yes, excuse me for stating the obvious," reflected Francombe. "It's what we coppers do before we get behind the obvious."

"Point taken," said Mark. "Carry on."

"Like you, I have to use computers. Not that I'm totally compatible with them. Must be my age. Anyway, let's get back to the A12."

"As you like," agreed Mark. Shit! he thought, she's landing a whole lot of hints. "You should confront your fear of computers, Detective Inspector. Once you've overcome that hurdle you'll find they're very useful, informative and essential to everyday life - not to mention manipulative. Your age shouldn't be a barrier."

"Manipulative? Strange you should use that term. Are you referring to hacking?"

"Ah!" realised Mark. "Someone has hacked into your computers. A mole maybe? Or an informant?"

"It doesn't matter how we received the information," said Fisher, glancing over the paperwork towards Mark. He placed the pages neatly on the desk, satisfied that he had digested the intelligence they contained. "It's interesting reading, Mark. Backs up our own investigation."

"Which is?"

"We traced the footage from the cameras that serve the area in which you were driving. Apparently your journey, prior to the explosion, started from the docklands. Do you want to elaborate on this revelation, Mark?"

Mark smiled nervously. "Well ... I ..."

"Got lost?" interrupted Fisher.

Mark shrugged his shoulders.

"I mean," continued Fisher, "that is not the location of your daughter's university, is it?"

"No," answered Mark quietly.

"I put it to you that this location in the docklands is where the base for the BLA is situated."

Mark laughed. "Really? I don't think so."

Fisher rested his hand on the pile of paperwork. "I would think very carefully before you come up with a fictitious answer."

"Fictitious?" queried Mark, noticing Fisher's reference to the sheets of paper.

"I can see your mind working overtime, looking for a cover-up."

"It's nothing so intriguing, Sergeant. Research, that's all."

"Not according to our information, Mark."

Mark pondered for a few moments and then asked, "Who sent you your information?"

Guy made a short grunting noise. "Someone who wants you to do something?" he quizzed, and then looked to the heavens.

Francombe giggled. "You lay the blame at his door, Guy?"

Guy shrugged his shoulders. "Who else is there?"

"Never mind, you two," said Fisher. "I'm waiting for an answer, Mark."

Mark stared at Guy for a few anxious moments. Do I have my own answer, he thought, and can I trust these people, one of whom is possibly a virtual? Anyway, I can con them with the imagined truth they want to hear. It's the only way I'm going to get out of this place.

"Well? I'm still waiting," announced Fisher impatiently

"I was taken," said Mark suddenly, breaking from his thoughts.

Ah! thought Fisher, my bluff about the cameras has worked.

"Taken? Were you forced?"

"Kind of."

"Either you were or you weren't. Which is it?"

"Well, I wasn't in a position to refuse them. Besides, I was curious."

"Yeah, don't tell me. Anyway, who were they?"

"Two men, looked like agents. Turned out they were interested in my outlook for the future."

"BLA representatives," suggested Francombe. "Did they want to recruit you?"

"Yes and no," teased Mark.

"Explain," requested Francombe.

"The BLA is a guise of the Network ..."

The noise of turning pages interrupted Mark.

"Ah, yes," said Fisher, "there is a reference to the Network ... Yes, here it is."

"There is your hacker," suggested Mark, "your informant. In which case, you know everything there is to know."

"But we need your confirmation, Mark," said Francombe.

"I don't think I need to," replied Mark confidently. "I guess what is written there is pretty unbelievable. You couldn't make a charge stick ..."

"I think otherwise," retorted Fisher. He opened a drawer and retrieved two books, which he slammed onto the table. "Now, you give us the confirmation we want."

Mark looked at the top book with amazement and shock and then threw an accusation at Fisher. "You took that from my home."

"No," replied Fisher. "It's published and on the shelves. We bought the damn thing."

"That's impossible. I have the only copy."

"Not so, Mark. People are reading it; believing it," rebuffed Fisher, distorting the facts.

Nice one! thought Francombe, expressionless.

"Well, if that's the case ... it proves I didn't write it," declared Mark confidently.

Fisher held up *The Book of Revelations* so that Mark could see the cover. "In your name - see? Both this and *Military Rule* are blueprints for the activities of the BLA."

"How would you know? Have you read them?"

"I have," revealed Francombe, "but not all of *Revelations*, just enough material to link the Middle East conspiracy with the BLA. However, I read the whole of *Military Rule* afterwards, which convinced me even more."

"Rubbish!" exclaimed Mark, and then he paused with frustration. "*Military Rule* has nothing to do with this so-called BLA organisation, which I suspect is a fabrication."

Fisher held the papers in his hand and waved them at Mark. "This is not fabrication, Mark. It's all here in black and white. Let's cut to the chase. This game of cat and mouse has gone on too long. It's becoming tedious and is getting us nowhere." Fisher laid the papers back down on the desk and turned over a few pages until he found the section he was looking for. "Rashid, Malik and David. Are these colleagues of yours?"

"No, but Rashid wanted my services to help promote the rise of Allah as the one God. That was my conclusion and I agreed just to get out of there. Everything since then has been informed to me."

"Informed?"

"Yes," confirmed Mark. "The news, email, Cunningham ..."

"Mandeville?" interrupted Guy, fixing a knowing look on Mark.

"Ah, Mandeville," tormented Francombe. "I think that's a code name for someone else ..."

"God!" shouted Mark. "You haven't got a fucking clue. It's written in front of you but you just don't get it. Look beyond your contact lenses."

"How do you know I wear ...?"

"Never mind that," continued Mark. "I'll spell it out. *Military Rule*, one God, Seeker One and the Second Coming: Mandeville is real and you had better be afraid. The BLA is a front for Allah's quest to be the one God ahead of our Lord ..."

"There's no need to be like that, Mark," retorted Francombe, with a stern look that one would give a naughty child. "I have been kind and understanding towards you."

Mark stared into Francombe's eyes, which seemed to sparkle. Shit! he thought. I wouldn't have spoken to my mother in that way. "Sorry," he said, with sincerity. "I only want ..."

Guy clapped his hands. "You think that is the truth, Mark?"

Mark's stare moved towards Guy. "I have a feeling I should speak to 'Fitz'," he said.

"Really? Why do you feel the urge to do that, Mark?" asked Guy.

"You understand more than these two. Besides, Francombe wants you to get your teeth into me. Virtually speaking, I mean."

Guy laughed. "I'm not a vampire. I don't want to draw blood."

Maybe, maybe not. But another form of human who believes that imagination leads to reality."

"Indeed," agreed Guy. "I'm a psychiatrist who deals with people like you …"

"Enough of this crap," snapped Fisher. "Reality check, Mark. He's the real thing: not an actor reading from a script. You're wrapped up in your fiction and assuming the truth, which is a lie to convince us that you are only a writer."

Mark banged his fist on the desk in frustration. "You wouldn't know the truth if it hit you on your big nose!"

"Looked in the mirror lately, Mark?"

Francombe intervened, pleased with Mark's request. "We need to calm down and have a break. This is getting us nowhere fast. Fisher, you stay and keep an eye on Mark. When we return, Guy can resume the interview. Understand?"

"Okay, thanks," agreed Fisher. He then spoke into the voice recorder before switching it off. "Detective Inspector Francombe and Guy have left the room."

Francombe escorted Guy into her office. "Take a seat," she offered, gesturing towards a chair. "I felt we needed to confer."

"Fascinating," said Guy, as Francombe sat at her desk. "He actually believes in his fiction …" Guy paused. "Can we be heard? The interview room's very close."

"No," replied Francombe, "there's a corridor between us."

Guy noticed a vacant expression on Francombe's face. "You are not convinced?" he asked.

"Um …" pondered Francombe. "Any writer believes in his work."

"Not when he's found out that the reason behind his belief is a lie. He wants to confront Mandeville's deceit. We are just helping him on his way. He's ready. He trusts you and suspects me."

"Suspects you?"

"As a virtual being from the Network, which helps the cause." Guy laughed.

"I see," said Francombe. "So, you think he's ready to lead us to the BLA and its leader, Rashid?"

Guy removed his tinted glasses and rubbed his eyes. "Damn things," he moaned. "I should get a new pair."

"You should try laser treatment, then you won't need glasses. Shame to hide those big brown eyes of yours."

"Actually, I'm undergoing treatment that will eventually mean I can do away with shades. It's just a matter of time. Anyway, I imagine it's what you want?"

"My eyes are fine with contacts," said Francombe.

"No," retorted Guy, replacing his glasses. "Mark?"

"Oh! Sorry, yes. After your little chat, I will release him."

"You really believe he's involved in the BLA?"

"Without a doubt," replied Francombe. "We just lack the evidence. He's right though, we can't convict him on the basis of books and a hacker's email."

"Excellent," commented Guy, with glee. "He just needs a final push, which I'll provide. He'll lead you straight to them."

"You mentioned Mandeville. Do you believe in him?"

"It is Mark's reference I'm using, that's all. So long as he believes in him …"

"I see …"

"What is wrong? Not going soft?"

"Nothing," lied Francombe, feeling uneasy at Guy's sudden outburst. "Let's not delay any longer."

"Don't worry, Una," consoled Guy, "we will all get his co-operation. Come! Let's go back in there."

Mark glanced towards the door, distracted from his thoughts about what he must do. He noticed the large figure of Guy enter the interview room, followed by Francombe, who returned to her seat.

Fisher leant over to switch on the voice recorder again.

Francombe blocked Fisher's intention. "Leave it off," she whispered.

Guy stopped short of the table and stared at Mark. "Um …" he mumbled, dragging on a cigarette.

Fisher turned to face Guy. "Hello again, Guy. This one has your interest then?"

"Might do," replied Guy, pondering his mental script. "It certainly has the makings of an interesting case." Guy dropped his smouldering cigarette butt and stamped on it with a heavy foot.

Francombe emitted a sigh of disapproval, anticipating yet another burn on the floor.

Mark smiled, almost breaking into a snigger.

"Do you find all of this amusing, Mark?" asked Guy.

"Hilarious," answered Mark, aiming a deep stare at Guy. "I guess your analysis is coming my way."

Guy returned to his position on the lone chair. "Indeed it is. I have to continue with this farce." Guy crossed his arms across his ample chest before surmising, "I believe you are creating your own world because you are pissed off with this one. You are one of these 'I want to change the world' buffoons."

"Who isn't?"

"I understand, Mark. But you have to make the best of what you have."

"The best of it?" scoffed Mark. "Ha! The best has gone, long gone."

"Meaning?"

"Look around you," suggested Mark. "In fact you must be very busy, coining it in. This place is full of mad people. Virtuals maybe?"

"Which place?" taunted Guy. "This one?"

"Up there or down here," replied Mark, proffering a choice. "Does it matter?"

Guy grunted, followed by a cough, and then asked, "Up there? What do you mean 'up there'?"

"The Lord's domain," retorted Mark, surprisingly.

Guy remained calm. "I see," he said. "You blame God for our mad world."

"Nonsense, Guy," rebuffed Mark. "You know nothing."

"Really?"

"Yes, really. If you knew me, or had been told about me, you'd know that I don't blame God." Mark laughed. "How can you blame something you don't believe in?"

"So what is to blame? Or, indeed, who?" enquired Guy.

"Humans' belief in religion and their chosen images."

Guy shifted around on his chair to stem the numbness in his buttocks. "Humans …?" he quizzed. "Um … interesting." Guy stared at Mark.

Mark smiled. "Go on."

"You don't consider yourself human?"

Mark's smile turned to laughter. "Of course I do," he answered, and then he paused.

"But?"

"Maybe I'm preparing not to be? I disassociate myself from the selfish mentality that breeds destruction."

Guy stared upwards into space.

"Too much for you to digest? Looking for enlightenment?"

Guy unfolded his arms, retrieved a cigarette and lit it, taking time to inhale and exhale before responding. "No," he replied eventually. "Just evaluating."

"And?"

"I think you want to be up there within the lion's den."

"Where? What is up there, Guy? This is the second time you've mentioned 'up there'." Mark also stared upwards, and then commented, "Are you homesick and eager to conclude your mission?"

"This is heavy stuff, Mark," stated Guy. "What are you getting at?"

Francombe and Fisher observed intently.

Mark shot from the hip. "Do you want me dead?"

Guy felt both shocked and embarrassed. "Certainly not, Mark," he responded emphatically. "Come on! I'm only suggesting that you want to be 'up there' in mind only. A form of escapism from Earth's frustrations."

"Is that what you're here for then, to decide on my mind's conclusion?"

Guy's brow became moist with sweat. "Phew!" he exclaimed. "You should have become a shrink. You would do well: coin it in!"

"Ah, but you think I'm on the other side as a psychopath," deduced Mark. "You want to discredit me before the humans lose faith and belief, believing that the book of revelations is more relevant than the Lord's distortions. You know the book is not mine. You know the book is written by another hand. This, Guy, all around us … this is my book. You are only a character within it, playing out my imagining and dialogue."

Guy was about to stamp out his cigarette on the floor.

"Use this, please," instructed Francombe, passing him the ashtray.

Guy obliged, smiled and handed the ashtray back to Francombe.

Mark stared as Francombe retrieved the ashtray.

"Have one if you must, Mark," pre-empted Francombe.

"Thanks, I will," said Mark.

Guy spoke while Mark lit his cigarette. "So, you think I'm a virtual being?"

"Stop!" exclaimed Mark, after lighting his cigarette.

"Stop?"

"Too many clues, Guy," explained Mark. "You are as subtle as a pig." Mark glanced at Francombe. "Don't you think so?" he asked her.

"Dear me," responded Francombe. "Leave me out of this one. Guy has the floor. It's way above my head."

"I don't think so, Detective Inspector," said Mark. "Why else would you bring 'Fitz' into the frame …?"

"Clues, Mark," interrupted Guy.

Mark smiled with satisfaction, but remained silent.

"Take your time, Mark," quipped Guy, looking at his watch.

"You are trying to shape my destiny, Guy," contemplated Mark. He then looked at Francombe and said. "And yours, Una."

"Mine?"

"You want to know if my imagination is real. Hence, your investigation. However, you can't prove or charge anything. So the second option is to prevent military rule; or, in fact, embrace it and set me up for entrapment. Which is it, Inspector?"

"Well …"

"No," interrupted Mark, "don't answer. You might incriminate yourself." Mark glanced at the voice recorder.

"Sorry, mate," lied Fisher, "it's off."

Mark frowned. Typical, he thought. They have to be conspiring.

"How, Mark?" continued Francombe. "How, apart from the fact that no one else knows about it, will I incriminate myself?"

"By allowing me to go ahead and find my destiny, which will create a new case for you to solve. Basically, you will become involved in conspiracy."

Francombe's eyes lit up with excitement, followed by a cheeky grin. She gazed towards Guy. "Oh dear," she said, "he's better than you. He should be on my team."

"Understandably," replied Guy. "He's a writer with an overstretched imagination. What a bitch … but I'll live with it." Guy looked again at his watch. Things to do, he thought. "Time out," he announced. "I'm off to the nearest pub to order myself the largest of whiskies in order to drown my sorrows."

Mark laughed inwardly. "More like celebration, Guy," disputed Mark. "You pretend to be beaten when you know you've won."

Guy smiled awkwardly as he rose from the chair. He hesitated to brush some ash from his crumpled jacket and then headed for the door, remaining silent.

"See you in the Lord's domain," muttered Mark faintly.

Guy turned to face Mark. "Sorry, I didn't hear that."

"Nothing," replied Mark. "See you around."

"Um …" mumbled Guy, and then he disappeared.

"Can I also go, Detective Inspector Francombe?" asked Mark. "Unless you intend to charge me with writing a book I didn't write."

Francombe remained silent, looking beyond the open door.

"Somehow I don't think so," observed Mark. "Besides, the imagined truth is no longer shocking: too much water under the bridge in terms of ghastly government."

Francombe had been listening to Mark while appearing distracted. "There is still the question of a link with the BLA," she said, as she turned her head from the doorway.

"Too many clues and no evidence, Inspector … yet, anyway."

"Meaning?"

"You know what I mean," suggested Mark. "You'll get your evidence by using me as bait …"

"There is this," interrupted Fisher, jabbing his finger on the papers.

Mark surveyed them with contempt. "Anyone could have sent those," he said. "But we know who did, don't we? And it's pretty unbelievable."

"Actually, I don't," revealed Fisher.

"Oh, haven't you been paying attention, William?" interjected Francombe. Fisher's expression was a picture of confusion as he asked, "Who was it?" Francombe ignored him. "Okay," she said to Mark, "I'll let you go."

"Of course you will. You will follow my destiny and pick up the pieces for your evidence."

"Are you sure, Una?" asked Fisher, with reservations.

"Women's intuition, Fisher," replied Francombe. "And a gut feeling …"

"Really?" mocked Fisher.

"Or guidance," posited Mark. "Manipulation even."

"Guidance?" voiced Francombe, and then guessed, "Oh, from up there?"

"Maybe it's Guy?" queried Mark, throwing in another possibility for Francombe to think about. "Even your own intuition. As I said, Guy is as subtle as a pig - but you? You are more like an angel, a messenger with the traits of my …" Mark smiled during a slight pause of possible realisation. "Mandeville chose well," continued Mark. "You don't have to spell it out."

"Don't be silly," remarked Francombe.

"He's fucking mad," grunted Fisher. "Ignore him. He's playing with your mind, gathering a plot."

"Mad enough to do your job, Sergeant."

Fisher rubbed his chin with his hand. Francombe is using him, he thought. I could be jeopardising her plan.

"Lost for words, Sergeant?" enquired Mark.

Fisher picked up the papers, folded them and placed them inside his pocket. "Unlike you," he said, "I'm guided by reality and my immediate superior."

"Good for you, Sergeant ..."

"You can go now," announced Francombe. "But I'll see you again. You can count on it."

"Thank you," said Mark. "One last thing ..."

"Go on."

"When you read the book of revelations ... I can't remember if I've asked you already ..."

"If you have it doesn't matter," interrupted Francombe. "Ask again."

"Did you feel strange, or anything other than you would when normally reading a book?"

"Nothing that I can recollect," answered Francombe. "Like what?"

"Being a part of it?"

"No."

"Oh well, never mind," responded Mark. "Goodbye. Guess I'm using public transport then?"

"Do you mind, Mark?" said Francombe. "It's just that we ..."

"It's just as well I still have my staff pass, isn't it?"

"Thank you, Mark."

Mark left the interview room.

"So," said Fisher, "he'll lead us to Rashid's headquarters and then we move in to collar the lot."

"Yes," replied Francombe softly. "Among other things ..." Francombe paused, looking thoughtful.

"You don't sound so sure," observed Fisher. "And your vacant look tends to back up my suspicions."

"You don't appear convinced," retorted Francombe.

"The interview didn't go as I'd expected. But you seemed quite comfortable with it ... almost as if you and Guy had rehearsed it."

"We had to get to him, get his co-operation ..."

"Exactly," grunted Fisher. "I wasn't part of 'we'."

"You played your part, unwittingly."

"Thanks, but I have trouble understanding what is reality and what is fiction. You two lost me along the way."

"I know," said Francombe. "Now that Mark has gone, I wonder myself. Reality into fiction or fiction into reality. He's using the books to ... No, sorry. He's using his imagined reality to write the books."

"But he said he didn't write the book of revelations."

"So he did," agreed Francombe. "Do we believe him?"

"Not until we find this Mandeville figure. Which, I suspect, we won't."

"No, not in this time," speculated Francombe.

Fisher scratched his head. "Oh, I don't know," he said, followed by a sigh. "Maybe we could try to trace Mandeville. We could see if he's on any of our records."

"I doubt he will be, William," replied Francombe. "Firstly, it could be a false name. Secondly, he's just Mark's character. And thirdly ..."

"Yes?"

"We haven't got the time. We have to move now and get to where we think the headquarters is situated. I'm sure we'll see him there. The thing is, I feel I need more."

"More of what?"

"More from him ... Mark."

"Is it a strange feeling?" asked Fisher sarcastically. "Anyway, you may still catch him. He can't have got far."

"Yes, I could try," agreed Francombe, hesitating for a few moments before darting out of the room.

"I'll wait here then," shouted Fisher. "Make sure you don't scare him off."

Francombe rushed across the narrow corridor into her office and headed for the door. Then she suddenly stopped in her tracks. "Mark!" she spouted.

"I knew you would come after me."

Francombe caught her breath from the shock. "You earwigged," she said.

"Who knows?" teased Mark.

"Knows what, Mark? I'm not sure I know anything after what went on in there. So talk to me."

Mark sneered. "That's what we've been doing for the last ... I don't know ... few hours?"

"Not really," responded Francombe.

"It felt like hours."

"No, no," said Francombe. "I'm referring to the conversation, the interview. I think there were too many voices. What I mean is: talk to me, alone and now."

"Now!" exclaimed Mark, meaning something different. "Now it's all about the revelations and what I think is happening."

"What's that?"

"People, or humans, can't read past the first revelation until it's either solved or discredited. That, I think, is Mandeville's intention."

"Why? How …?"

"Whoever reads the book will become so shocked that they'll put it down in disgust, and then become afraid. Even with my imagination, I had to come out of the book."

"Come out?"

"Ah! I see the confusion in your handsome face, Una. However, think back."

Francombe tried to think but hit a dead end. Feeling mentally exhausted, she sat down at her desk and sighed as she reclined in the chair. "About what?" she asked.

"Remember …" Mark paused, experiencing a sense of protection towards Francombe. "Remember," he continued, "I asked if you felt strange when you read the book."

"Yes, I do," replied Francombe. "And, if I remember correctly, I said I didn't."

Mark frowned, as he'd hoped that Francombe might have changed her mind. Looking straight into her eyes, he said, "Let your imagination run wild …"

"Sorry?"

"Oh, just some advice I received a long time ago. Anyway, I know you can go beyond the first revelation."

"There's more?"

"Oh yes …"

"I knew it!"

"There's enough material in there for you to investigate, detect and solve. In fact, you could make a career out of it. Once you … we have solved this first revelation then you'll have the imagination to move on."

"Which it isn't," reminded Francombe.

"Isn't what?"

"It's not solved," retorted Francombe.

Mark continued to stare into Francombe's eyes. "It will be," guaranteed Mark.

Francombe remained silent, returning Mark's stare with anticipation. Give me confirmation, she thought.

Mark smiled, as though he knew what Francombe was urging. "I'll go after Rashid," announced Mark, "and Malik will return to hell. Allah will lose his supporting disciples."

Although Francombe was pleased to hear Mark's decree, she felt concerned. "It's not safe for you to do so," she cautioned. "It could be dangerous."

Mark threw her a line of reassurance. "They are only virtual," he stated, "imagined even. Besides, who is the BLA? What does the 'British' in its name mean exactly …?"

"We were hoping you would know," said Francombe, missing the point.

"British?" repeated Mark. "Is it Muslim, Jewish, African, Caribbean, Eastern European, Scottish, Welsh … and not forgetting the Irish? The list is endless. Any of these groups could form a British Liberation Army."

"Ah!" realised Francombe. "But we know … well, we have a pretty good idea that it's …"

"Only what Mandeville wants us to believe, here and now. Anyway, I was just being fastidious."

"And Rashid," remembered Francombe, "according to you …"

"Me?"

"His aim is to target the Prime Minister?"

"Conducted by Mandeville," said Mark. "You're right, of course. We do know which group it is. Mandeville uses the Middle East for conspiracy, deceit and manipulation. And he isn't finished yet."

"At the risk of just humouring you, how do you know?" asked Francombe.

"Because I'm convinced that imagination is the foundation of reality," answered Mark. "I believe … imagine that Mandeville influenced the writing of *Military Rule*. His return proves this. And so Mandeville, the Lord, Seeker One and the virtual beings do exist, but two years ahead of us. However, Mandeville is creating a world of virtual beings in our here and now to control our time. He knows, or I believe, that the Lord will eventually accomplish his quest of being the one God and thus unite the two worlds. When this happens, Mandeville will have control of the situation. But exactly how, I'm not yet sure."

"Are you sure you're not sure, Mark?" quizzed Francombe.

Mark hesitated, not really wanting to confess his theory. "Well," he said, "I have an idea that Mandeville will recreate himself …"

"Become a virtual being? Surely not in our time?"

"No," answered Mark faintly. "Worse than that."

"What could be worse?"

"In his time, two years ahead," disclosed Mark, "ready for the uniting of time."

Francombe remained silent, contemplating Mark's theory. Is this just a guess or his imagination conjuring up his knowledge of the facts?

Mark observed Francombe's silence, which seemed to signify that she was looking for a way to disbelieve. "Think about it," prompted Mark. "He is still alive … here and now. He hasn't, as yet, travelled through the vortex. That happened in 2008."

Francombe lit up with excitement. "Then we can go after him now." She looked intently at Mark. "Can't we?"

Mark shook his head. "No," he responded. He paused and noticed Francombe's disappointment. "If he gets a whiff of suspicion, he'll have the advantage. Believe me, I know."

"We could set up a covert operation …"

"Who would believe two years on? Besides, we can't change the past: every hour, day, week and month that passes becomes history. We have to fight him in the future."

"Fight him?"

"Yes."

"How do I know that you really want to fight him? How do I know that you don't want to become one with your creation?"

"Because of what I'm about to do," answered Mark convincingly.

"Proves nothing," retorted Francombe anxiously.

Mark sighed and held Francombe's hand. "Trust," he stated deeply. "You have to trust as a mother would."

Francombe gazed into Mark's eyes. "No," she said, releasing Mark's grip. "We have to do something now. But what?" Mark's eyes seemed to give Francombe her answer. "You can't contemplate …"

"I have to," intervened Mark, guessing Francombe's conclusion. "Although it's not guaranteed that I will succeed in slaying Rashid. I am, indeed, being influenced by Mandeville. But I also sense another influence."

Francombe's intrigue came to the fore and her eyebrows rose. "Who? What?" she asked.

"It's who," replied Mark.

"Tell me," insisted Francombe.

"Guy," revealed Mark. "Guy is a virtual …"

Francombe laughed. "You're clutching at straws, Mark," she declared.

"No," continued Mark, "I'm certain he is. However, I don't understand what his mission is. Maybe just to watch?"

"So," said Francombe, "where does his influence come into it?"

"He pushed me," answered Mark. "You were there to see it. He talked about my destiny, to achieve what I must do. But why? In the end, he admitted defeat but knew he'd won."

"I'll talk to him," suggested Francombe. "But what about? I'm not sure he'll take kindly to an accusation of being a virtual."

Mark sighed. "Your intentions are good," he said. "At least I think they are …"

"Mark!" exclaimed Francombe, interrupting his doubts.

"Oh, never mind," continued Mark. "Besides, he's gone …" Mark paused for a while and then continued, "Not for good, however. Um … I wonder …?"

"Wonder what? Did you think he might've gone back up there?"

"Initially. However, I believe he'll be in the shadows, watching. Maybe you won't need to approach him: he'll talk to you after the …"

"Then you mustn't go ahead with your plot," interrupted Francombe, envisioning the worst scenario.

"I have to," retorted Mark. "The plot should continue; my imagination of the truth must continue. How else can I write and come to the conclusion?"

Francombe was worried but at the same time excited. "If it goes wrong," she said, "what will happen?"

"What I imagine will happen."

Francombe looked on expectantly. "Well?"

"I'll travel through the vortex into Seeker One and become a virtual being in our time."

"I can't allow it," declared Francombe firmly.

Mark laughed. "You have to," he revealed. "I've imagined your role …"

"Role?"

"A human contact in a virtual world … as I was … am. You will have a contact between the two worlds."

Francombe looked confused. "Who?" she blurted out.

"Me!" proclaimed Mark. "Don't you get it? Or do you? Anyway, let me spell it out for you to confirm your wish …"

"My wish?"

"Yes," continued Mark, clasping his hands together. "Me in Seeker One and my virtual here in your … our time." Mark looked for a sign of comprehension in Francombe's facial expression, but it wasn't forthcoming. "So," he continued, "together - collectively - we could stop Mandeville's dictatorship."

Francombe's expression indicated that the penny had finally dropped.

"Bingo!" hollered Mark, but he then noticed that Francombe's air of realisation had transformed into a grimace. "What is it? Am I wrong?"

Francombe's furrowed brow smoothed and the grimace was replaced by a look of concern. "No, Mark," she answered, "I doubt you could be wrong about all of this. However ..."

"However what?"

"I'm concerned about your family ..."

"Why? What do you know?" Mark's thoughts started racing. "Are they in danger ...? Yes, I suppose they could be ..."

"Calm down, Mark," said Francombe, with authority. "It's nothing like that. I meant if things go wrong ..."

"They won't. It's all in here," responded Mark, pointing a finger to his temple. "I'll still be here for them."

"Only as a virtual," commented Francombe.

Mark smiled. "But me, nonetheless." Mark paused and stared at Francombe for a while.

"What is it?" she asked.

"Your emotional concern surprises me," replied Mark. "After all, you are a ..."

"A slight blip," retorted Francombe. "Anyway, it's all part of the job: getting to know one's subject and all that."

"Of course," said Mark. "Is that what I am, someone to be studied and controlled?"

"If we're getting down to basics, then yes, you are. And don't forget: I'm conducting an investigation here ..."

Mark laughed. "Conspiracy more like," he countered.

Francombe ignored Mark's accusation. "So," she continued, "how does one spot a virtual ... Guy, for instance?"

"White-eyed or red-eyed," answered Mark, with a cooler attitude. Any sense of warmth towards Francombe was starting to fade. "That's why they wear shades to cover their eyes."

"Ah!" exclaimed Francombe. "Then he can't be. I've seen Guy's eyes and they're brown."

"Cast your mind back to what I've said," instructed Mark.

"About what?"

"About allowing your imagination to run wild," reminded Mark. "You see, the typical human can't detect or visualise anything deeper than what they see on the surface. The majority don't understand what is going on. You will understand more when you and Guy talk - but not until after my mission. The outcome could dictate his content; dictate his actions."

"You talk as though he were the key to my investigation."

"What investigation? It's all a set-up, something to which I'm privy."

"The BLA, Mark. Or have you forgotten? There's still the doubt about you and your association with it."

Mark smiled confidently. "We are all associated with it and Mandeville controls it. The BLA is the link to securing his success in the UK and the rest of Europe."

"Even so," mused Francombe, "set-up or no set-up, it's there."

"Yes," confirmed Mark, "there for you to continue investigating along with the revelations. He wants you to unmask the evil, or so-called evil, that will plunge humans into the depths of civil unrest. Then he will strike and command military rule."

"I don't have to, Mark," suggested Francombe.

"But you do. You have no choice. This is his history from two years hence. You can't change history - his or ours."

"No," retorted Francombe stubbornly. "We can walk away and let it be."

"You don't really believe that," challenged Mark. "Besides, I don't believe you'll walk away. It's not in you to give up. You're just trying to protect me - get me out of harm's way."

Francombe smiled knowingly. He's right, she thought. This is too big for me to walk away from ...

"He's good," said Mark, interrupting Francombe's thoughts.

"Good?"

"Yes, he chose well," replied Mark. "He knew I couldn't refuse you, which makes it easy for you to plot, investigate and solve in order to carry out our destiny. We must go along with his ensconce and get close to him ..."

"Fight him in the future," remembered Francombe.

"Exactly," verified Mark. "Beat him at his own game of letting the enemy get close. Then strike."

Francombe looked coy and stared at Mark with her twinkling eyes.

"You don't agree? Do you wish to walk away?"

"No, not really," confirmed Francombe. "Especially after what you said about not refusing me. Why is that?"

"You already know."

"You are confused, Mark," warned Francombe gracefully. "And I think

181

you have an added objective."

"Such as?"

"The death of your mother has clouded your judgement. You hope to find her."

Mark felt a tear trickle onto his cheek and took in a deep, manly breath. "You're way off the mark: I'm totally focused. Anyway, my mother would not stoop to say such a thing. She had too much decorum for that. Maybe it's not my mother that you remind me of but someone from the book? Maybe we read it at the same time?"

"It's all in your head, Mark," stated Francombe. "You never forget your mother, no matter where you are or what you're doing. You're looking for something that's not there."

Mark frowned. "You're right, of course. But I have to try to do what I have to do."

"Yes," agreed Francombe, "defeat Mandeville."

"I feel that is a long way off," said Mark. "We have to get through this first: smash the first revelation and take it from there."

"We?" questioned Francombe, putting on an act of naivety.

Mark raised his eyebrows and tutted at Francombe. "Come now," he said, "you know what you said in your private conversation with Guy. And, I'm guessing, with Fisher after I'd left the interview room."

"Obviously. But ..."

Mark placed his finger to his lips for a second and then said, "But nothing. Don't incriminate yourself. I can only guess what you said, but I have a good idea ..."

"No doubt ..."

"Hence this little heart to heart, eh?" Mark paused and gazed into Francombe's staring eyes. "So," he concluded, "I'll say goodbye, Detective Inspector Francombe."

"For now, Mark," replied Francombe. "We still need some answers from you to keep the Chief Constable at bay."

What a load of bollocks. Just let me go, thought Mark. She's stretching out a long goodbye; looking for guarantees. "No doubt," he responded, with a smile. "However, make sure you keep your distance."

"Is that a sign of concern I'm hearing from you, Mark?" asked Francombe.

Mark smiled again. "I'll see you from hell, Una," replied Mark, as he made for the door. There was nothing more to say. He left Francombe's office and headed for home.

"Fisher," hollered Francombe.

Fisher rushed back into the interview room from the connecting corridor. "Yes, Detective Inspector," he replied, with a raised voice.

Francombe relocated to the doorway that led into the corridor from her office. "Lock the interview room and come into my office," she instructed him, noticing the scent of Fisher's aftershave wafting in the air. So, she thought, he's been listening.

"Okay," said Fisher, "give me a minute ..."

"Now, Fisher, now."

Fisher eventually entered Francombe's office, slightly ruffled. She was sitting behind her desk and so took a seat facing her. "Here, the keys," he said, placing them just in front of her. Francombe held out her hand.

"They're there," informed Fisher, pointing to the keys he'd just deposited.

Francombe frowned at Fisher. "The tape?" she prompted.

Fisher retrieved the tape from his jacket pocket, placed it in Francombe's hand and remained silent.

"Thank you, William," acknowledged Francombe. "I'll destroy this later. It serves no purpose ..."

"Francombe!"

"I smelt your poor aftershave in the corridor," cautioned Francombe. "Was it your intention to keep quiet about the tape?"

"I just ..."

"I understand," interrupted Francombe. "However, I was trying to keep you distanced from this one and uncorrupted. If it goes belly up, then ..."

"No need, Francombe," assured Fisher. "I'm with you all the way, as always."

"I hope so, William," said Francombe. His close relationship with the chief has now become a concern, she thought. Still, it's a risk I'll have to take.

Fisher observed Francombe's contemplation. "Don't worry, Una," he said, "you can trust me. You know you can."

"Of course, William," replied Francombe. "Lots to think about and plan."

"Of course there is, Francombe," declared Fisher sarcastically. "So I suggest we get to work and stop wasting time."

"Um," acknowledged Francombe, looking at her watch. She then responded with a lie: "We need to set up surveillance at the docklands. Two teams working with us should suffice."

"You're sure he'll go there?" queried Fisher.

"Oh, yes, it's his destiny."

Chapter 16

Mark arrived home from his interview with Francombe, having endured hours of suffering using the public transport system.

"Where have you been?" questioned Sandar, acknowledging Mark's arrival from the dining room.

Mark delayed his answer. He was frozen to the spot as he stood in the living room, gazing at the copy of the book of revelations. What? How? he thought. Christ! They must have their own copy! If they have, then who else …?

"Well?" reiterated Sandar.

Mark dispelled his thoughts and walked into the dining room. "Hello, doll," he said, and sat next to her in his usual place at the dining table. He lit a cigarette while observing Sandar's suspicious demeanour. "You're home early," he said, exhaling smoke.

"You knew I would be," replied Sandar. "You have to go and collect Cara, remember?"

"Yes, I know," retorted Mark, trying to avoid the inevitable questioning. "I think I'll make some tea." He moved to the kitchen and switched on the kettle. "Want one?" he shouted.

Sandar followed Mark into the kitchen. "Don't evade the question, Mark," she said. "You're acting strange. I called a few times and got no answer. I was worried."

Mark grabbed the mugs of freshly made tea and returned to his seat in the dining room.

"Mark!" exclaimed Sandar.

"Come and sit down, doll," requested Mark. He waited until Sander had settled next to him. "You wouldn't believe me," he continued. "Anyway, it doesn't matter: I'm home now and back to reality."

"Mark?"

Mark gazed into Sandar's eyes, realising he couldn't evade her examination, much like Francombe's before. "Oh, hang on then," he said, and he went to retrieve the book from the living room. "It's all about this," he continued, "and the contents within it."

"What do you mean?" asked Sandar, confused.

"The police ..."

"Police?"

"Oh, don't worry," reassured Mark, "it's nothing; all sorted out. They thought I'd written it and questioned me about it. Like I said, all cleared up now."

"Are you sure?" enquired Sandar.

"No problem."

"I think there is, Mark," speculated Sandar.

"No, really. After my chat with Detective Inspector Francombe ..."

"Francombe?" queried Sandar, and then she sighed. "Oh, Mark. That's what I mean. You're still grieving and you're taking your work too seriously. I managed to ignore it before, but I can't now."

"Ignore what?"

"Us, Mark," clarified Sandar. "You're starting to live in your fiction and you're forgetting what's around you."

"Don't be silly," defended Mark. "Of course I'm not. I just want to get it finished."

"At what or whose expense?" reflected Sandar. "You need to take a rest, concentrate on your family and Christmas."

Mark remained silent, almost sulking. He stared through the window into the garden, drinking a sip of tea.

"Come on, darling," said Sandar, rubbing Mark's thigh. "I'm not asking you to stop completely."

Mark sighed. "Yes, you're right, doll," contemplated Mark, looking to the future. "I do need a break ..."

"Good," interrupted Sandar, with a consoling smile. "Sort it and come back to us. I miss your attention ..."

"I will, doll, I will. Sorry." Mark leant over and kissed Sandar. "Now," he continued, "I'll just check my email before collecting Cara."

"Oh, Mark," groaned Sandar, "what have I just said?"

"Well, you might have something," replied Mark cheerfully. "Just checking. I won't be long."

"Whatever," retorted Sandar. "I have things to get on with."

Mark retired to the bedroom, sat at his desk, switched on the laptop computer and waited until his desktop icons appeared on the screen. Mark guided the arrow towards the Internet icon, double-clicked and waited. The modem connected. "You have email," said a posh voice. Mark opened his email account and a subject heading caught his eye straight away: 'Danger! Read, Mark'. What is this? he thought. Slightly perturbed, he quickly opened the email, which read: "Your daughter is in danger, Mark."

Mark was startled but remained calm. Another ploy? he wondered. That fucking Guy maybe? Or could it be Cunningham? Whoever it is, they know I have to act on it. Shit! It's stopping me trying out the code for Seeker One: no time. Oh what the hell! It doesn't matter now: I have to hurry. I know, I'll call Francombe. Damn, no. She won't believe me, or she could even be in on it. Either way, I'll call her from the car. I have to go along with it. Mark deleted the email, shut down the laptop, quickly descended downstairs and approached Sandar. "I'm off now," he said, kissing her on the cheek.

"Oh, all right then," replied Sandar. "Isn't it too early?"

"Well, traffic and all that," responded Mark. "I don't want to turn up too late."

"I suppose so, darling," said Sandar. "Oh, anything for me?"

"Sorry?"

"Email? Any email for me?"

"No, doll, I checked and there's nothing there," lied Mark.

"Make sure Cara has packed everything she needs," requested Sandar.

"Yes, yes, doll, I will," assured Mark.

"Only saying," said Sandar. "Off you go then. Take care. Love you."

"Bye, doll. Love you too," said Mark, then he swiftly left the house.

Mark arrived at his daughter's university and parked the car within the allocated parking space. I hope I'm not too late, he thought. He got out of the car, stretched and took a look around. "No sign of Francombe," he commented to himself. "Never mind, no time to hang around waiting." He continued to make his way to the block complex where his daughter resided. On arrival, he pressed the intercom button for Cara's block - number 42 - and waited for a response. "Come on," he said quietly, "answer." Mark scanned his wristwatch quickly and tried the intercom again. He was beginning to wonder if he'd recalled the number correctly when the door made a buzzing sound to indicate that the lock had been released for entry. Phew! he thought. She must be okay. He raced up the three flights of stairs, expecting to see Cara standing by the block's doorway, but there was no sign of her. Mark rushed to the block door and banged on it repeatedly with his fist. "Cara! Cara!" he shouted. Eventually the door opened and he found himself face to face with a student of Middle Eastern appearance. "Can I help you?" he said, yawning.

I don't recognise this chap, Mark thought. "Yes, hopefully," replied Mark, feeling slightly confused. "I'm looking for Cara. Do you know her?"

"Who's asking?"

"I'm her father," answered Mark. "Well?"

"Do you know her room number?"

"Of course I bloody ..."

"Then go and knock."

"Thank you," grunted Mark sarcastically. "So, if you don't mind moving out of the way ...?"

"Help yourself," shrugged the student, making way for Mark to pass.

Mark approached Cara's door and knocked softly.

The student laughed. "More force, father of Cara," he said. "She won't hear that if she's wearing headphones."

Mark tried again. "Cara!" he shouted.

"It appears she's not in," commented the student, stating the obvious.

"Maybe she's on her way back from a lecture?" suggested Mark, hopefully. "Mind you, she's not supposed to have one at this time. And she knew I was coming." Mark noticed the student suddenly smiling. "You know something?"

"She's gone," revealed the student, shrugging his shoulders.

"You piece of shit!" exclaimed Mark. "You made me go through all this farce knowing ..."

"She could have come back since I noticed ... Anyway, why should I help you, English dog? Ha! Calling me a piece of shit."

"Sorry," apologised Mark hastily. "I'm in a bit of a panic, that's all. I'm sure you understand."

"That's no excuse. But yes, I understand about daughters ..."

"Since?"

"What?"

"You said 'since I noticed'. Noticed what?"

"I noticed her getting into a car."

"Car?"

"I thought it must have been you, her father, coming to pick her up."

"Do you know my car?" shouted Mark.

"Um, afraid not," confessed the student. "I just assumed ..."

"You're lying," accused Mark, before lunging at the student's neck with his frightened hands. "What do you know? What do you know?"

The student gasped for air. "Get off," he struggled to say.

Mark tightened his hold on the student and banged his head against the wall. "What car was it?"

"Black," whispered the student, through a restricted airway.

"Black did you say?" enquired Mark, releasing his grip.

The student pushed Mark away from him. "You madman!" he exclaimed, rubbing his neck with soothing strokes of his hand. "I'm saying nothing more. Now fuck off!"

Mark steadied himself. "You people soon grasp the English language ..."

"What do you mean 'you people'?"

"Oh, I don't know. You tell me."

"I come here for asylum from my invaded country. So, I am a consequence of Western policy. It's your fault we are here ... ignorant pig!"

"We?" mused Mark. "The black car? That signifies the children of Allah, the BLA and the virtual beings. You and my daughter are being used to point me in the direction I have to go, I think."

"You and your kind talk in riddles; you're wrong in the head and become ignorant. Allah spits in your faces for this. Go where you must, so long as it's away from me ... far away!"

"Damn!" exclaimed Mark. "I know where! I always have." He made for the exit door.

The student reached for the door, opened it and waved his hand for Mark to pass. "Piss off," he said, "and find your daughter."

Mark swiftly passed the student and made his way down the stairway to return to his car.

The student watched from the doorway until Mark had disappeared from sight. Satisfied that he had gone, the student then shut the door and turned to face the figure of a man who had appeared from the kitchen/lounge area. "Did I do good, big man?" he asked.

"Yes, indeed. Excellent. The virgins will be proud to receive you."

Detective Inspector Francombe and Sergeant Fisher drove into the university campus and parked beside Mark's car.

"Is that his car, Sergeant?" asked Francombe.

Fisher removed his seat belt and exited the car. He scanned the area with keen eyes, then walked around Mark's car and inspected the number plate. Fisher returned to the squad car and leant in through the open door. "Yes, ma'am. It fits the description he gave to you over the phone, as well as the parking and building area."

"No need to keep calling me, ma'am, William," instructed Francombe, getting out of the car. "Besides, I haven't reached that rank yet."

"I like calling you ma'am, ma'am," replied Fisher.

Francombe smiled. "Oh, well I'm not arguing the point," she said.

"He's not around here," observed Fisher. "Maybe he's found her and is inside her room? Do you know which room it is?"

"No," replied Francombe. "His call was very brief and hurried. I guess he was driving at the time."

"Naughty boy," joked Fisher. "Guess I'll have to go and find out which room it is from the security gate. I'm sure they have the savvy to trace her room."

"Good idea, Sergeant," agreed Francombe. "I'll wait here. Pointless wandering around aimlessly."

"Okay, see you in a jiff," replied Fisher, as he headed off towards the security gate on foot. Oh! You'd better call the team at the docklands and let then know what's happening."

"Will do," responded Francombe, although she had no intention of actually doing that. She settled back in the front car seat, sighed. We're just going through the motions, she thought, feeling quite bored. She was jolted suddenly from her musings by repeated knocking on the window. "What the ...?"

"She's gone, she's gone!" yelled Mark.

Francombe turned the ignition key and lowered the car window. "Mark!" she exclaimed. "Gone where?"

"Don't know exactly ... but ..."

"Hang on," said Francombe, clambering out of the car. "How do you know your daughter has gone?"

"Eh?"

"Well, saying she's gone means she's not on the campus. Someone must have told you she's left the campus."

Mark paced around, scratched his head and looked to the heavens.

"Pull yourself together, Mark," advised Francombe. "You need to stay calm and explain the facts clearly."

Mark stood still and took a few deep breaths. "That's easier said ..."

"Never mind," retorted Francombe. "Who told you?"

"The guy ..." Mark paused for thought: Guy ...? No, being silly. How could he ...?

"Mark?"

"Sorry, just had a thought," continued Mark. "Anyway, there was a student

189

from the room opposite Cara's ... Seemed to know more than he was prepared to let on."

"Really," commented Francombe patronisingly. "Did he manage to tell you anything?"

"Only that she was seen getting into a car ... a black car. That's all I could get out of him."

"What do you mean 'get out of him'?"

"Well," replied Mark defensively, "he did annoy me. And the fact that he was of Middle Eastern appearance didn't help. Plus, I hadn't seen him before. I felt he was an intruder and found him quite intimidating."

"Um ..." pondered Francombe. "You should think before you act ..."

"Oh, really. Just like the state does."

Francombe ignored the change of subject. "That's not the point. Now, do you know if Cara accepted a lift of her own free will?"

"I don't know ... How could I? He just said ... God! This is getting us nowhere."

"I agree," conceded Francombe. "You're not concentrating on the questions. You're too upset."

"Is it any wonder?"

"You need to look at the bigger picture," suggested Francombe. "Remember our little chat and what was said? That's what you need to concentrate on."

"Easier said than done, Detective Inspector," responded Mark. "Maybe you have an angle on this one?" Mark stared at Francombe in the hope of seeing a confirmatory facial expression.

Francombe momentarily looked away towards the block of rooms. "I'm as much in the dark as you, Mark," she said abruptly. "Come, show me to his room."

"What good will that do?"

"At the moment I'm more objective than you," replied Francombe. "You should've tried to extract more information from him."

"I doubt that any would've been forthcoming," maintained Mark. "It was as if he was reading from some script."

Francombe pondered for a while.

"Well, are we going?" asked Mark, with frustration.

"Yes, come on," instructed Francombe, and she headed towards the accommodation block.

"What were you thinking about?" asked Mark, catching up with her.

"If you think that your mystery student was quoting his lines," posited Francombe, "then maybe your daughter is safe … in no danger?"

"I hope you're right," said Mark, far from convinced.

When Francombe and Mark arrived at the main door, someone was just exiting. "Quick! Grab the door," urged Mark. "It'll save us buzzing for entry."

Francombe hastily did as instructed, barely noticing the figure that had just passed them.

They made their way up to the top floor landing and Francombe pressed the button next to the door to gain access.

"I hope he's still there," said Mark, catching his breath from the short climb.

"Somehow I doubt it," predicted Francombe.

"Then why …?"

" Process of elimination," answered Francombe. "If he's not there, then we can search the room for clues."

"How," quizzed Mark, "if we can't get in …?"

"Fisher should be on his way with the key," revealed Francombe, looking at her watch. "Actually, he's taking his time. He should be here already." At that precise moment, Francombe's mobile phone rang. "Yes? What is it?"

"Hello to you too," answered Fisher. "Anyway, I'm still waiting for this shabby lot to help me with my enquiry …"

"Hold on," interrupted Francombe, "I can hear movement. Never mind that now. Get back to the car. I'll meet you there." Francombe terminated the call and banged on the door. "Police! Open up! Now!"

The door opened, revealing a young British Asian woman. "Okay I'm here," she announced. "What's the rush? Who are you and what do you want?"

Francombe looked at Mark. "Obviously not the student you had words with."

"No," confirmed Mark.

"Oh, it's you again," stated the young woman.

"What?" exclaimed Mark. "I didn't see you before."

"I was in the kitchen. I heard everything."

Francombe held up her identification badge for the young woman to see. "I'm Detective Inspector Francombe," she announced. "Francombe will do. "What is your name?"

"Tracy," answered the young woman.

"Really!" blurted Mark.

"Yes, really. I was born in the UK."

Mark frowned. "I didn't mean that ..."

"Anyway," interrupted Francombe, "how do you know it was this gentleman? You said you were in the kitchen."

"Well, when he became aggressive ..."

"Frustrated. I was frustrated," corrected Mark.

"That's of no consequence," said Francombe. "Carry on, Tracy."

Tracy continued, "I heard the noise, so took a peek. When I saw the fight, I withdrew out of sight."

Francombe faced Mark. "You didn't see her?"

"What does it matter?" countered Mark. "The one we want isn't here."

"Tracy," said Francombe, "do you know the student this gentleman had his hands on?"

Mark tutted loudly.

Tracy appeared unsure. "No," she replied. "Possibly a visitor."

"Was there anyone else in the kitchen with you?" enquired Francombe.

"Erm ... no," lied Tracy. " Why would there be?"

"It's a communal kitchen," observed Francombe.

"Yes it is," admitted Tracy, "but most people have gone home for Christmas."

"But not you, Tracy?"

"I'm on my way," she answered. "Only I can't get into my room."

"Room? Which room?" asked Francombe suspiciously.

"This one," responded Tracy, with irritation. "I can't find my key. I was just about to get the spare one from the office ..."

Mark sighed loudly. "This is not helping. We're getting nowhere."

"Patience, Mark," advised Francombe calmly.

"Has this got something to do with Cara?" asked Tracy suddenly. "Only I'd hoped you might be here to help me gain access to room."

Um, thought Francombe. She keeps going on about the room, but I strongly suspect that it's not hers. "Yes," said Francombe, eventually answering Tracy's question. "Do you know her? Can you tell us anything about her disappearance?"

"Yes, I do know her," Tracy responded with a lie.

Francombe glanced at Mark.

"I don't know many of her friends, if any," admitted Mark, answering Francombe's glance. "There are loads of students here."

"Well I do," said Tracy convincingly, "and I didn't realise she'd disappeared. I thought she was going home."

"Here we go," retorted Mark. "The script again ..."

"Shush, Mark," interrupted Francombe. "Let me handle this."

"Handle what?" asked Tracy, staring at Francombe.

"Are you going to tell us what you supposedly know, Tracy?" asked Francombe softly.

"There's no supposing about it," rebuffed Tracy, acting irritated. "I know what I saw."

"Well?" pushed Francombe.

"I saw her getting into a car when I was walking past towards the block. Is she in trouble for doing so?"

"I don't know yet," replied Francombe, "but possibly. It depends on the leads we ascertain. Now, the car: what can you tell me about it?"

"Like what?" enquired Tracy hesitantly.

Oh, she's good, thought Francombe. "It's not a difficult question, Tracy," she said. "Colour, make, any distinguishing marks, that kind of thing. You know, simple observations that I'm sure you could pick up on."

Tracy smiled at Francombe's scathing remark, resisting the temptation to bite back. "Let me think for a moment," she said. "Ah yes, I remember ... It was a sedan ... sorry, a saloon. Actually, it looked like a van ..."

"A people carrier maybe?" interrupted Mark. "Could it have been a Voyager?"

"Yes, that's it," confirmed Tracy. "Black with tinted windows."

"Did it have any markings?" asked Francombe.

"Markings?"

"Writing, advertising? Anything?"

"No," answered Tracy, "it was plain, sinister looking ..."

"She's taking the piss," interjected Mark, "and she knows it. God! We're getting nowhere ..."

"So you keep saying, Mark," retorted Francombe. "We're already at nowhere, but that's where one begins to get somewhere."

Mark frowned. Where did she read that? he thought.

"It had lots of aerials on it," said Tracy abruptly. "Yes, I thought he must be into gadgets or something ..."

"He?" queried Francombe.

"Yes, he," stated Tracy. "A man was sitting in the driver's seat."

"Anyone else?"

"Erm ..."

"Please think," urged Francombe, with irritation. "It could be very important. Don't forget: a young lady could be in grave danger."

"Two more, I think," estimated Tracy, "but I can't be sure. Besides, I wasn't taking that much notice. After all, I didn't suspect any foul play. I just kept on walking. And that's it. I can't tell you any more."

"Well, that will have to do then, Tracy," said Francombe, concluding her questioning. "Thank you."

Tracy conveyed a sympathetic look towards Mark. "Sorry, I couldn't be of any more help," she uttered, placing her hand on his arm. "I'm sure she will be okay. A misunderstanding maybe? Things will turn out the way we … you want."

"Great," replied Mark sarcastically. "No need to worry then, if you're so sure." He tugged his arm away from Tracy's hand and walked away.

"Don't mind him, Tracy," said Francombe, before departing. "He's got a lot on his mind." Francombe smiled and winked at her. "Goodbye."

"Sure he has," replied Tracy, as Francombe turned away. "As we all do. Goodbye to you too, Detective Inspector." Tracy smiled to herself and glanced at her watch. Give them a few minutes, she thought. Time to get out of here before she returns.

Francombe finally caught up with Mark, finding him smoking a cigarette and pacing around on a grassed area outside the building block. "There you are," she said, observing his politically incorrect habit. "I could nick you for that, Mark."

"For what?" enquired Mark, rebelliously exhaling smoke in Francombe's direction.

"Never mind," replied Francombe, "but finish it off quickly while we walk back to the car. Fisher should be there waiting for us."

"Oh yes," said Mark. "But what can we tell him? A black car, a sedan … no, a saloon … or is it a Voyager? Who can tell? As I keep saying, Detective Inspector, we are still at nowhere."

"Not exactly," answered Francombe confidently. "Come on, back to the car."

Mark respectfully obeyed and walked by her side, matching her brisk pace. He started thinking back to the moment they entered the building. "That man coming quickly out of the door …" he said to Francombe.

Francombe slowed her pace. "What about him?" she asked, almost dismissing the question.

"Exactly," retorted Mark. "You ignored him. You didn't even glance at him. Strange. It's a natural reaction to look, don't you think? I would've thought it would be a simple observation for you. Mind you, in your defence, he was in a hurry."

"What are you getting at, Mark? Did you recognise him or something?"

"Vaguely," answered Mark. "Mind you, it could've just been my imagination. But a figure … an appearance that might've sparked some sort of recognition."

"Um …" contemplated Francombe, slowing her pace even more. "Can't say. However, your suspicion could tie in with her attitude."

"What?" exclaimed Mark. "You're now supposing that they're connected, even though you didn't see him? You think she was coached, like I did?"

Francombe reached out and caught hold of Mark's arm, bringing them to a halt.

"What is it?" asked Mark.

"She wasn't expecting us," speculated Francombe, "but was prepared. She was in the middle of doing something and, I suspect, we disturbed her …"

"Doing what?"

"Can't say, but," realised Francombe, "she's not a student."

"Really!" exclaimed Mark. "Have I tickled your suspicion all of a sudden. So, what makes you think that?"

"Her language was distant," surmised Francombe, gazing with thought. "Um … she said 'people' instead of fellow students, mates or friends."

"Hang on," said Mark, Francombe's method of deduction losing him somewhat. "People?"

"Yes," replied Francombe, "she said, 'most people have gone home for Christmas'. Also, she said 'the block' rather than 'my block'."

"Um … you have a point," agreed Mark. "Your imagination is nearly as good as mine."

Francombe smiled.

"And another thing," continued Mark. "The man, or men, in the car. How would she know if the windows were so heavily tinted?"

"She didn't say heavily tinted, Mark," recalled Francombe.

"Oh," said Mark, with doubt. "Sorry, my mistake."

"Easily done," comforted Francombe. Could he have recognised the vehicle she tried to describe? she wondered. Francombe looked at her watch. "Come on," she said, "Fisher will be getting impatient."

"At last!" chimed Fisher, observing the two arrivals. "What's been going on? I was about to come searching for you."

"I was doing my job, William," explained Francombe sarcastically.

"Oh, I see," replied Fisher. "I'm again the victim of your scathing attacks. Lowest form of wit, you know. Besides, you …"

"Yes, William," interrupted Francombe, "I know." Francombe opened the back door of the car and instructed Mark to get in.

Mark obediently followed the order and sat in silence as Francombe and Fisher settled themselves in the front seats.

"So, what have you found out?" asked Fisher, turning towards Francombe.

"I'm not quite sure," answered Francombe, looking thoughtful.

Yes you are, thought Mark, observing from behind. "Tell him about the car …"

Francombe raised her hand to silence Mark and said, "Just let us do our job please."

"Car? What car?" enquired Fisher excitedly.

Francombe looked thoughtful again. Eventually she had an idea. "Get onto our database people," she said. "See if any car has been supplied in the last few hours from the car pool."

"Supplied to whom exactly?" asked Fisher, slightly confused.

"I'm not sure yet," responded Francombe. "That's what I want to ascertain."

"Okay, I'm onto it," responded Fisher. He exited the car, retrieved his mobile phone from his pocket and began his enquiries.

Mark leant over to look out of the window towards Fisher. Come on, get on with it, he thought.

Francombe noticed Mark's obvious impatience. "Don't worry," she said, in a professional manner. "We'll get to the bottom of this."

Mark remained silent. I think I have done already, he thought. I know where the car has gone. She's stalling. But why? Whom is she trying to finger?

After a short lull, Fisher climbed back into the car.

"Well?" asked Francombe impatiently.

"Standard issues have been pooled from various agencies," revealed Fisher, "but it would've helped if I knew exactly what car you're after."

"Is that all you've come up with?" probed Francombe. "Standard issue?" I know there's more, she thought.

"Not quite," confessed Fisher, winking at Francombe. "Three operational cars were used by MI6 during the last few hours or so."

"Really? What makes of car, William?"

"Two Fords and a Voyager," answered Fisher. "Only …"

"Only what?"

"Well, apparently the Voyager's tracking system isn't working. Or it's been turned off."

"Bingo!" hollered Francombe. "I had a hunch they might have something to do with it. Damn!"

"Now what?" queried Fisher.

"Where's it going?" continued Francombe. "Or where has it gone?"

"What? That's ridiculous," commented Mark, listening from the rear. "What would they want with my daughter?"

"Oh, Mark," replied Francombe, with an undermining tone of voice. "Your daughter is safe - I'm sure of it. I don't even think she's been taken anywhere."

Mark grimaced and said, "I can't risk thinking that."

"Exactly. That's my point," replied Francombe, definite in her surmise. "That's what they want."

"Um," uttered Mark. They? They are not MI6. Unless MI6 are after Rashid after scrutinising the book. But how? How would they have the revelations? Mark stared at Francombe from behind as she spoke to Fisher, his thoughts continuing to analyse the situation. Maybe it was MI6 that took me? Maybe they've placed undercover agents within the BLA? Or what if they're assisting Rashid …?

"Are you all right, Mark?" asked Francombe, noticing the lack of vocal contributions from the back.

"Yes," answered Mark, not wanting to divulge his exact thoughts. "Just hoping you're right about Cara, that's all. I don't want to be given any false hopes."

"Nothing is guaranteed in this job, Mark …"

"No, it isn't," interrupted Fisher. "Especially, if we keep wandering away from the matter at hand. We need to find out the exact location of the Voyager."

"Well," noted Francombe, returning from her digression, "we can't go through the usual channels, as that would cause too much suspicion."

"Tracy!" spouted Mark.

"Who?" enquired Fisher. "Is there …?"

"Of course," realised Francombe.

"What is going on?" retorted Fisher, glancing at Mark. "I don't like the fact that he knows more than I do."

"Stop being childish, William," scolded Francombe. "Mark just happened to be there ... The room ... We've to go back, Sergeant, and carry out further investigations to find the answer."

"She's probably gone by now," remarked Mark, "done a bunk! Especially in light of your deductions."

"You could be right," agreed Francombe. "Still, we have to go back. It's in the script, isn't it, Mark?"

"If you say so ..."

"God!" interjected Fisher. "You two talk in riddles ..."

"Which have to be solved, Sergeant," stated Francombe.

"Um," persisted Fisher, "I prefer straight talking; talk you can understand."

There was a lull while Francombe contemplated her next move. Eventually, and with concern, she spoke. "You stay here, Mark. I feel you need time on your own."

"Fine by me," replied Mark, and then he smiled. "Off you go then."

"Oh dear," said Fisher, with a sharp tongue. "I hope I haven't offended you, Mark."

"Hardly! I imagine it's over your head."

"You imagine too much for your own good ..."

"Like - you are on a wild goose chase one thinks, Sergeant."

"Enough you two," interrupted Francombe. "There's no time for this. Come on, Sergeant."

I agree, thought Mark, and he watched as Francombe and Fisher walked away from the car.

Francombe glanced back towards Mark, who was now leaning against the car smoking a cigarette. He's going to get caught out, she thought.

"Is he still there?" asked Fisher.

Francombe hastened her walking pace. "For now," she said worriedly.

Fisher stepped up his own pace to keep up with Francombe. "No need to fret, Una," he advised. "I placed a tracking device under his car while I was checking it."

"Well done, Sergeant," replied Francombe, slightly relieved. "I don't want to ... we don't want to lose him. Now, let me fill you in on what happened earlier ..."

Mark sighed with impatience as Francombe and Fisher finally disappeared out of sight. At last, he thought, it's time. Mark closed his eyes and imagined his next move. "Time for time to stand still again," he whispered.

Fisher banged on the door of the so-called student's room, which Francombe had pointed out. "No answer," he said. "No signs of life."

"That doesn't surprise me," commented Francombe. "Someone left in a hurry, leaving the two main doors open. Or, they were purposely left open after my first visit with Mark."

"What now?" urged Fisher.

"Wait here," instructed Francombe, "while I go and check the kitchen and lounge area."

"What the hell for?" muttered Fisher. "There's no one here."

"I heard that, Fisher," said Francombe, as she stepped into the kitchen and lounge area. "I might find some keys left on the worktop or something." Francombe scoured the room, which seemed unusually clean for students' quarters. "She's been thorough, Sergeant," shouted Francombe. "Left no clues at all."

"Who?" hollered Fisher.

"Tracy, of course," replied Francombe, as she returned to Fisher.

"Oh, I see," remembered Fisher. "She's probably long gone by now. So, that's it then?"

"No," retorted Francombe, "that's not it! You'll have to break down the door."

Fisher chuckled. "How do you suggest I do that, ma'am? I'm somewhat lacking in the Mr Universe department."

"Find something!"

Just then a security guard appears. "I have the key," he gasped, out of breath from his climb up the stairway.

"Good man," said Fisher, relieved to receive it at last.

"Oh, by the way," remembered the guard. "That car you asked me to look out for ..."

"Yes, what about it?" interrupted Fisher expectantly.

"It drove out of the gate," explained the guard, "as I was making my way here."

Francombe stared at Fisher. "Never mind that now," she said dismissively. "Open the door."

Fisher opened the door and entered the room, which was enveloped in darkness due to the curtains having been pulled across the window.

Francombe followed. "Open the curtains," she instructed hastily.

Fisher moaned at the obvious order received and opened the curtains, a cascade of light pouring into the room.

Francombe froze as her dazzled eyes caught sight of a body lying on the bed.

"I'll wake him up," offered Fisher.

"I don't think that will be necessary, Sergeant," suggested Francombe instinctively. "I suspect he's dead. Check for me please, William."

Fisher moved close to the body, knowing that Francombe, even with all her experience, hated the sight of corpses. Fisher checked for a pulse and then frowned. "Your suspicions are correct, Una," he confirmed. "He's dead."

Francombe looked away and shut her eyes tightly for a few seconds, feeling a surge of guilt.

"Are you okay?" asked Fisher compassionately.

"Yes, yes," replied Francombe, opening her eyes and returning her focus to the body. "It's what lies behind this that concerns me."

"So," surmised Fisher, "this was the student that Mark spoke to?"

"Again," deduced Francombe, "he wasn't a student."

Fisher looked confused and retrieved his mobile phone.

"What do you think you're doing?" demanded Francombe accusingly.

"Calling for the crime squad, of course," answered Fisher bluntly.

"No you don't," retorted Francombe. "Call our own. They can sort out this mess for the time being."

"Our own?" contemplated Fisher scornfully. "That means a cover-up, eliminating evidence ..."

"Excuse me!" spouted the security guard from the corridor. "Can I go now?"

"No!" replied Fisher loudly, moving to the doorway. "You need to stay here for a while. Go and make tea or something." Fisher closed the door with considerable force.

"No need for that, Sergeant," rebuked Francombe, expecting a moral lecture.

"Yes there is, Una," disputed Fisher, feeling left out in the cold. "This is some kind of diversion or delaying tactic, isn't it?"

Francombe remained silent, looking guilty.

"You do know," determined Fisher, creating a lull while he observed the scene and gathered his thoughts. "That's why you were so pleased that I'd fitted a tracker ..."

"I had my suspicions, Sergeant," said Francombe, trying to assert her authority. "She kept on about the room."

"Bollocks! What's going on, Francombe?"

"Really!"

"Don't be obscure. It's gone beyond the language of the upper class and well educated. Talk to me, Una. It's as if you're just playing along with your own cooked-up scenario ... just like Mark."

"It's not my own, William," replied Francombe. "It's just a case we're involved in."

"One that has been planted on your desk, which means I have a hunch we're been used ... you've been used."

"Maybe," confessed Francombe, observing the body. "I guess he is Guy's young man."

"Eh? He's gay? Christ!"

"No, you silly man," retorted Francombe, familiar with Fisher's sudden outbursts of first thoughts. "Remember ...? I stopped Guy's session ..."

"Oh yes," realised Fisher, "I see. So now that I'm involved ..."

"Indeed you are, Sergeant," confirmed Francombe.

"Um ..." reflected Fisher. "You've made sure of it. I told you I'd support you."

Francombe tittered. "Even though you attempted to hang on to evidence that could help you answer awkward questions in the future from our superiors."

"Evidence? I don't ..."

"The tape?"

"Ah! The one you confiscated."

"I had to, William," explained Francombe. "There's too much at stake here; too much to gain, and too much to lose. I couldn't risk your using a moment of moral conscience against me." Francombe stared at Fisher with a twinkle in her eyes and confessed, "I need you with me on this one."

"And Guy?"

"And Guy."

"Mark?"

"We all need him. That's why ..."

"Why?"

"He must be helped with his imagined journey."

"Where to exactly?" probed Fisher, desperate for clarification.

Francombe smiled evasively. "Only time and his fate will tell," she said, looking at the ceiling and beyond. "We shall soon find out which path he finally chose ..."

"Or had chosen for him," challenged Fisher.

"How do you mean?"

"You are obviously and selfishly hoping for the one you want. So which direction is he going to take?"

"It's not a case of what I want, William," reprimanded Francombe. "But what is best for us all in our time."

"Now you need to explain what you mean."

"To stop military rule. Here and now," replied Francombe.

"Can you be sure of that?" queried Fisher. "Can you be sure it's what he wants? After all, there's the pending case about his involvement with the BLA and this Mandeville character."

"Um, I understand what you're saying," admitted Francombe, "which begs the question: are they his friend or foe?"

"In which case," warned Fisher, "you're taking a gamble in your alliance with Mark."

Francombe shivered, becoming uneasy with remaining in the room. "Let's step outside ..."

"Not yet," pounced Fisher, blocking the door and behaving like a prison guard. "I haven't got all the answers."

"No one has, William," explained Francombe calmly. "This is a risk worth taking ... if he survives and returns. Just think about it for a while, William. Risk is what we deal in to obtain the answers to solve the mysteries, isn't it?"

Fisher lingered in silence as if accepting Francombe's explanation.

Francombe allowed Fisher's hesitation to take its course, hoping that his thoughts would reach a favourable conclusion.

"What now, ma'am?" asked Fisher suddenly, fumbling with his mobile phone.

"We track him, William," answered Francombe, smiling.

Fisher pressed the call button on his mobile phone with a nervous twitch, noted by Francombe. "So, who are you are calling, William?" she asked apprehensively.

Fisher shrugged his shoulders. "What the hell," he responded, with evident obedience. "As usual, I have to look after you. I'm calling our boys, of course."

"Thank you, William," said Francombe gratefully.

As soon as Fisher had finished his call, he opened the door and exited the room. "You there!" he hollered towards the security guard.

The security guard appeared hastily from the kitchen/lounge area. "Yes, what is it?" he asked.

"We're leaving now," briefed Fisher. "I want you to stand guard outside the main entrance and wait for our colleagues to arrive. When they get here, show them to the room."

"Yes, sir," responded the security guard obligingly.

"Oh!" remembered Fisher. "And not a word to anyone. Understand?"

"You can rely on me," assured the guard, tapping the side of his nose with his finger. "Soul of discretion, Sergeant."

"Eh? How do you know ...?"

"I have eyes and ears," answered the guard, winking at Francombe as she followed Fisher.

"On your soul be it," concluded Fisher, as he and Francombe descended the stairway.

"Come on, come on, William," urged Francombe anxiously. "Get a move on."

Chapter 17

"You found it then," said David, approaching Mark from behind.

Mark turned, shocked to hear David's voice. "David!" he exclaimed, and then looked around at the building from the courtyard. "What happened here? It's derelict."

"Moved out! It was compromised," replied David matter-of-factly.

"As soon as I saw the gate, I knew," responded Mark. "Besides, the gate mysteriously opened when I drove the car close to it. Someone must have known?"

"Unfortunately, this will be your last visit," said David, evading Mark's suggestion. "The secret of secrets is no more."

"Moved where?" demanded Mark.

David smiled knowingly. "No, no," he teased. "That would be too easy."

"Evasive, as usual," noted Mark, undeterred. "Only a few organisations could dismantle a headquarters such as this so quickly. What do they call it? Ah, yes. Cut and run."

"They had to," said David. "As I said, it was compromised."

"Ha! Planned more like," commented Mark.

David paused. His initial thoughts were challenged by Mark's unexpected response, having anticipated that he would blame the book. He revised his reply. "So, who do you think?"

"The boss, of course: my creation; the one who controls you. You had me think that this is, or was, an MI5 base ... or MI6."

David grinned and teased again. "The boss! Maybe. In reality, possible."

"But this is not reality," lured Mark.

"What makes you say that, Mark?" enquired David, playing along.

"Because I have come for my daughter," replied Mark. "In reality, she would not have been abducted."

David laughed. "Sure of that, Mark? You must be. It's taken you a while to ask. Besides, this is the wrong place, wrong time. Can you risk thinking that this is not reality?"

"So where?" asked Mark urgently.

"I'll come back to that ..."

"You mean you don't know. Or you want to distance yourself from me, the book, Mandeville and Rashid ... let yourself off the hook."

"No, I'm still in the ..."

"Is there any shelter in this goddam place?" interrupted Mark, blowing warm air into his cupped hands. "Can we go inside? There's a definite chill in the air."

Let him think what he wants, thought David, but I'll still continue to feed him. "She's not in there," he said, suspecting Mark's true motives. "The building is locked tight. Still, you won't be here for much longer: you'll have to move on."

"As you do," accused Mark. "Like following me out of the book?"

"No," retorted David loudly. "You didn't listen. I'm still in it."

"Oh really? How?"

David smiled and nodded conceitedly. "I'm a virtual being," he said proudly. "Remember? We can multitask and be in more than one place at a time ... in any time ..."

"But not beyond your own future?"

Right!" exclaimed David, with annoyance. "But you know this."

"Of course,"

David sighed. "A feeble attempt, Mark."

"Oh?"

"You're trying to trip me up; confuse me; anger me. You humans are so inadequate."

"Hardly!" retaliated Mark. "Besides, you used to be one ..."

"To my horror after my enlightenment," confessed David.

"Anyhow," continued Mark, "I managed to come out of the book and created a pause to open the door ..."

"Only with my help ..."

"Ah, the code," declared Mark. "Which is?"

"Never mind that now," dismissed David. "It's of no consequence - yet. To continue, I'm about to help you again."

"Again! How?"

"Point you in the right direction," informed David, recollecting. "We didn't have time to talk in the book. So, here we are."

Mark paused and then voiced his realisation. "This is your selfish interlude," he remarked, "a time to gloat ..."

"Nonsense ..."

"What about?" continued Mark. "I don't have time for idle chat. My daughter's safety is ..."

"You've more time than you think," interrupted David, learnedly. "You have been given the scope to suspend time. Therefore, you can imagine your plot."

"God!" exclaimed Mark. "Now who's evading the issue?" Mark paused and stared into David's eyes. "My daughter?" he asked forcefully.

"Don't worry," reinforced David, "I wouldn't keep you here if she was at risk. Trust in the Lord, Mark."

Was Francombe right? thought Mark. Is she safe? Mark then realised what David had said. "Trust in the Lord?" he repeated. "As you did?"

"Of course, as we do now."

Mark laughed. "He stabbed you in the back and allowed the attack on Washington DC."

"He's entitled," deemed David. "Indeed, as you imagined, he didn't allow it, as such. It was an oversight: allowing his future Second Coming too much control and influence."

"More like incompetence," challenged Mark. "Mandeville was a blunderer, full of his own shit. It was he that allowed the destruction of Washington by misjudging his men and the situation."

"Granted," accepted David. "But as the great man that he is, and was, he took advantage of the situation you refer to. And now the excuse is there to be used."

"Here and now?"

"Partly," reasoned David. "There is also the Lord's excuse."

"Which is?"

"He believes that the UK wishes to protect the East and collaborate in the quasar plot."

"Rubbish!"

"Not so, Mark," argued David. "Rashid, the BLA, this building and the secret of secrets are the reasons behind the supposition. Collectively, they prove that the UK is a stronghold for the case for one God - the quasar plot. In turn, Mandeville will use this as grounds for imposing military rule here and in the rest of Europe - as you know. You think you've come to stop it, which you can't - not in reality, not here and not as a human."

Mark's facial expression seemed to reflect his comprehension. "So you're saying that it can only be stopped virtually?"

David raised his eyebrows. "Yes, I'm saying that you have started a war that you can't stop as a human. Hence the arranged alliance with Francombe

..."

"The human contact?"

"Yes," confirmed David, and he stared at Mark. "She agrees with what you have to do. But you are delaying the inevitable." David released his stare and continued, "So you need a push and guidance in the right direction. Consequently, here we are."

"I'm not delaying," responded Mark, "I'm considering the alternative. Do I? Don't I?"

"Ah!" realised David. "The meeting of the two Rashids, eye to eye, using the code to arrange the encounter."

"Something like that," replied Mark. "If a virtual being meets his double and they look each other in the eye, they die. Or cease to exist by deprogramming."

David laughed. "Virtually impossible," he quipped. "You know that."

"Not for certain," said Mark, with aspiration. "One can only try in the hope ..."

"I know the future, Mark," revealed David. "As a virtual being, I'm here, there and everywhere. You know, different timescales. There's no point using the code to duplicate Rashid at the same time ..."

"I'll rewrite," announced Mark desperately." God! Why did I say that? he thought.

David grinned at Mark's despair. "You can't," he said, knowing the outcome. "You're not in this time to do so as a human. You can't rewrite what's written, you can only continue the plot until its conclusion. That is why you need ... want to do what you have to do. This is it! Follow your destiny ..." David looked at his watch. "Francombe will be here soon."

"Of course, David. You would know that Francombe is on her way."

"Yes."

"What if I don't believe you?" challenged Mark.

"You have a tracker on your car, which you won't find," disclosed David.

"Another push?"

"You don't want her catching up with you, Mark," advised David, "and confusing your thoughts."

"Doubtful!" exclaimed Mark. "She wants me to ..."

"Indeed she does," interrupted David, second guessing Mark's conclusion regarding Francombe's expectations. "However, she's human and has attacks of moral conscience."

"I see," understood Mark. "She may try to stop me then?"

"Yes," answered David cautiously. "And try to fight off Rashid in the process, resulting in her death."

"Virtual can't kill human," tutored Mark.

"No," acknowledged David, "not directly. "But it can be arranged."

Mark wasn't sure how forthright David was being. I can't risk that happening, he thought. I need her in the future. Besides, I wouldn't want to be responsible if she were to ... "Okay," he said suddenly. "Where is my daughter?"

"She is safe," replied David confidently. "You will see her again if you seek your destiny."

"Another push, David?"

"If you wish to think so," baited David.

Mark paused and weighed up his options. "Why don't you just do the deed?" he enquired. "Job done!"

David sighed at Mark's simple outlook. "Because you, and you alone, have to be sure. You have to confront Rashid in order to decide. Destroy him now or look to the future. It's your choice."

"No pressure then. Besides, you said I couldn't destroy him."

"You would find a way if you really wanted to."

"As I said, no pressure."

"Not for the creative and curious mind ..."

"Hang on! You said you saw the future, which means you know the outcome. I have no choice."

"Yes you do, Mark," enlightened David. "Unlike the past, the future can be changed by the changing of minds, which equals choice of fate."

God, he's good, thought Mark. He knows I can choose to end it now and go back to a normal life in which I'll never write again, never be involved, never able to tell the world of future scheming and thus save it from the virtual beings. And save it from a godly fight. But do I want to end it? Francombe - she's the key to my destiny; the temptress introduced by Mandeville, who is developing quicker than I had imagined. What have I created? A new General God to rule the world? What was clear in my mind is now clouded by David's attempt to push me closer to my so-called destiny. Ha! I should adopt Mandeville's rule of sleeping with the enemy until such time as I can strike most effectively. The tools to do so are all up there ...

"Time out, Mark," announced David abruptly, interrupting Mark's decision-making thoughts.

Mark snapped out of his preoccupation. "Where do I go now?" he asked, passively seeking guidance.

"Shorditch Church," revealed David. "I believe you know where it is. Rashid is protected there by the masses who inhabit the area."

Mark appeared stunned by David's revelation. "Yes, I do," he answered dubiously. It's on the 149 route. But why a church? Why not the nearby mosque? That would make more sense."

David sniggered. "Look at yourself, Mark," he answered, stating the obvious. "You would not be allowed to enter a mosque, despite what is said about integration. Especially now, with the quasar plot. Also, he's a virtual being; seen the future. That is why it is almost impossible to kill us. More so on sacred ground."

That's a tempting factor in terms of my decision, thought Mark, before continuing, "But not Allah's sacred ground."

"He believes there is already only one God. So he is on holy ground and safe from confronting himself, free from the potentially deadly result of your actions. Still, that is not relevant now."

"Why hide in the Lord's house? Surely, according to Christ, all ground is holy or sacred?"

According to him. And there lay the problem."

"What?"

"One God claiming all ground. However, this claim is shunned; left to the belief of the individual human. The institutions advocate a house of worship to keep themselves safe and mysterious, preaching their own sermons of control. Why else would humans flock like sheep? The question is, which God will end up in which house?"

"Rashid is not a human anymore; he's a virtual, like you. Why should he care?"

"Exactly! His belief is true."

"Ah ...!"

David lifted his hand, looking at his watch again. "I calculate that Francombe is close. It's time for you to choose, Mark."

"Not really," agonised Mark. "I've been press-ganged towards my imagined destiny. What alternative do I have?"

"To change your mind ..."

"How?"

David retrieved a small object from his pocket. "Take this," he instructed, handing it to Mark.

Mark took the thin, pocket-sized, hinged case from David and opened it.

"A mirror!" exclaimed Mark. "What's this for?"

"I said, almost."

"Almost?"

"To kill a virtual," elucidated David reluctantly. "There is a weakness, as with all things."

"Which is?" asked Mark urgently.

"Make him angry; lose control. You're good at that."

"I don't know anything about him that I could use against him," said Mark cautiously. "It has to be personal to be effective. Besides, what would happen? I'm sure he's stronger than me."

"If you decide to, then ask about his brother and how Rashid came about."

"Okay," understood Mark. "So, I've made him angry, very angry. What then?"

"He'll emit a beam ..."

Mark laughed and imagined the scenario. "The spear of Christ?"

"Kind of," warned David seriously. "But not a spear or any other type of weapon."

"Well?"

"The eyes ... through the eyes," betrayed David. "Hold up the mirror to deflect the beam."

"And I'm going to have enough time to do so?"

"You'll know when the time comes. Use your imagination."

"I get it," said Mark glibly. "He'll end up looking at himself. Then - poof! - up in smoke."

"Exactly, Mark. You have the choice to decide." David extended his arm, pointing to the gateway. "Get in your car and go."

Mark hesitated before adhering to David's unconditional request. "Where are you going?"

"Wherever I'm commanded and energised. Now go. You're making me angry, which I can't afford."

Mark still hesitated, looking into David's eyes and risking his wrath.

"What is it?" asked David furiously.

Mark frowned. "You've seen the future. What will happen to Francombe when she arrives here?"

Nothing, Mark. Nothing! She just thinks that she's on a wild goose chase, chasing the tracker until she eventually catches up with the outcome. But the timing is of the utmost importance. You must go. If you delay any longer, the future will be changed. Everything has been explained." David suddenly walked away and disappeared into the building, putting an end to their encounter. "It's up to you," he shouted, then silence.

Bastard! thought Mark. It was open all along, and now there's no time to go in and look. He knows that. This is a choice. If I follow him ... Damn! There is no choice.

Mark arrived at Shorditch Church, parking his car illegally due to his haste to reach his objective, and ran inside.

Hello again, Mark," greeted Rashid serenely. "I've been waiting. It's so good to see you again. However, I'm disappointed ... You disappoint me, Mark."

"Really?" responded Mark. "Not that I'm sorry to hear you say so. Anyway, what about?"

"Um ..." pondered Rashid. "You forsake your book ..."

"It's not mine."

"You're bound to think that," continued Rashid, "because it has circulated from the future. Therefore, you have not written it yet. I wanted you to write a contradictory account for my cause and educate the humans with the truth."

"A con, you mean ..."

"Whatever, Mark. We could have worked together."

"How? By getting me into trouble, associating me with the BLA?"

"Not I," uncovered Rashid, "but Mandeville, your creation. Or even your own imagination. Anyway, I believe that time is of the essence. We are not here to reminisce but to decide on your destiny."

"Where's my daughter? That's what I'm here for."

Rashid laughed. "I don't think so. Besides, I believe you have been told that she is safe."

"You seem to believe quit a lot. It sounds as if you are all in this together."

"In a manner of speaking, we are," reasoned Rashid. "The same plot but different outcomes. But how do we conclude this little chapter, Mark? Are you here to kill me and deny me Allah's world?"

"Who knows?"

"You do, Mark," said Rashid confidently. "You know you can't kill me. However, I can kill you."

"Ah, but you can't."

"Not directly, as you know. I could always summon Malik to do the deed. Now, if he were to ... Well, you would end up going to hell. You don't want that, do you? All your efforts would have been for nothing, and I could continue the quasar plot in peace."

I hadn't thought of that one, mused Mark. None of them did. If this is his intention, then I'll have to use the mirror. I mustn't allow him to summon Malik: it would spoil the choice. Damn! This is why he gave me the mirror. Did he know ...?

"Run out of conversation, Mark?"

"Maybe we could renegotiate? Turn the clock back and start again?"

"Too late," responded Rashid. "It's a matter of trust."

"Exactly, Rashid," acknowledged Mark. "If you had been more open in the beginning ..."

"Open?"

"With information about yourself," continued Mark antagonistically. "If I don't know my subject properly, then I can't write or imagine."

"There is nothing for you to know," rebuffed Rashid, reluctant to share.

"So you just popped out of nowhere, just appeared. Ah, I know. You're just a figment of the imagination to be used by others. In other words, you're nothing." Mark stared into Rashid's eyes. They are beginning to stir, thought Mark. I need to keep him focused on me.

Rashid remained silent, containing his anger.

"Nothing to tell, Rashid?" prompted Mark. I hope there is time for this, he thought. If Francombe barges in, he'll have her without hesitation. I need to conclude this, and quickly.

"Like what?" asked Rashid, through gritted teeth.

Mark felt nervous, not knowing what to expect after posing David's suggested question. Mark placed his hand in his pocket in readiness.

"Well?" prompted Rashid, still angered. "Ask or forever hold your peace."

"Nothing out of the ordinary," replied Mark, damping down the tension. "I was wondering how you came to be - your background and family. For instance, do you have a sister, or a ... brother maybe?"

Rashid's defences disintegrated at the mere mention of his brother. He perched on a pew, his thoughts flooding back to the American-led invasion of his country. He became visibly uncomfortable as the scene in his head came to the fore.

Mark stood rigid, ready for the unexpected as he heard Rashid speak.

"It was a usual hot day in Baghdad," began Rashid, with sadness. "It was afternoon and we were hassling our father for permission to go out. Eventually he conceded to my brother's desire, and passion, to play football. You see, my younger brother had a gift, a gift from Allah ..."

"Had?" interrupted Mark.

"Allow me to finish," commanded Rashid, and he continued, "My brother had the skill of all the great football players put together. So, with elation, we went to our usual place in the street to act out the part of his heroes. We had a shabby ball and goalposts painted on a wall. We were having fun but practising hard because my little brother had dreams of playing for Manchester United. He called them the greatest team on Earth ... but only within the walls of our home. Outside those four walls, Iraq was the greatest team on Earth. My brother was showing off his skills while I had to try to take the ball away from him. Alas, my tackling skills were limited. We lost track of time and soon dusk was upon us. A few minutes more, we thought. My brother had his sights on a winning goal for his favourite team ..." Rashid paused to quell the rush of sad emotion, wiping away the tears.

Mark remained silent, hypnotised by Rashid's story.

Rashid took a deep breath and then resumed exposing his hidden secret. "My brother tricked the ball around me, passed me and scored a great goal between the painted goalposts. God, he was jubilant, waving his arms. I was clapping with encouragement, telling him he had just scored the winning goal and had become a hero for all to embrace ... Then they came. My brother called them fireworks. During our celebrations, we were thrown to the floor with mighty bangs sounding all around us. My brother lay flat on his back and I lay on my stomach looking towards him. I stretched my arms out in front of me, calling his name. I heard him say, "Look! Fireworks in honour of my goal." "No!" I shouted, as I looked closer at his body, now missing both legs and one arm. At that moment, an American trooper knelt beside my brother. My brother pointed out the fireworks. "Are you from Manchester United?" he asked the trooper. I listened to the trooper's words. "No, son," he said. The insult ripped through my body and I shouted at the top of my voice for him to leave my brother alone. The trooper told us he would get help as many soldiers rushed by us. I crawled over and lay on top of my brother. I was lucky: I only had minor injuries. I cried, and cried, and cried to Allah, praying for his help. My brother asked me what was wrong. "Your legs," I cried, "your legs." He had no idea until we both looked down together. I cannot describe that shriek of realisation. His dreams were shattered, his life in ruins. Suddenly, I heard a voice telling me to move away. I looked up to see a trooper pointing a gun at my brother's head. "No, no," I told him, "you can't." The trooper replied as though talking about an animal. "Look at him," he said, with no respect. "He's better off dead." I was defiant, but he threatened to kill me as well. I had an instant thought, as if Allah were speaking to me. I wouldn't be able to avenge my brother if were dead; I needed to stay alive. So reluctantly I moved and looked away. I heard a single shot after my brother's intensive pleadings. The trooper was so cool and robotic. He told me to go home and find my parents. He even suggested that they might be dead. I waited until he'd gone and then moved close to my brother. "Rashid," I said, "I will take your name and avenge your death by the invader from the West. Rashid will join with Allah and fight a holy war." I managed to stagger to my feet and watched the rain of bombs. After what seemed like an endless time, I shouted at the top of my voice, "Death to the West!"

"My God!" exclaimed Mark, finding it difficult to listen any longer.

Rashid jumped up from the pew. "My God?" he shouted. "Damn your God to hell!"

It appears to be working, thought Mark, and he continued to focus on the task at hand. "What of your parents?" he asked tentatively.

"No matter," responded Rashid more calmly. "But if you want the gory details of my headless father and raped mother ..."

"Surely not?"

Rashid stayed silent, collecting his thoughts of the present time. Then suddenly he laughed and stared Mark in the eye.

Mark placed his hand in his pocket and gripped the mirror.

Rashid stopped laughing. "You have tried and failed, Mark," he said. "You have not angered me enough to fall into your trap. Now you know what drives me. I'm a product of the aftermath of your invasion. I'm a terrorist with brains; too clever by half."

Mark sighed, unable to respond. How can I blame him? he thought. How could I ...?

Rashid drew a gun and pointed it at Mark.

"Shit!" exclaimed Mark, not expecting this twist. "You can't do it directly."

"I lied, like a good little terrorist."

"So you're not a virtual then?"

"Of course I am ..."

"Oh yes. How?"

"My own choice. Sound familiar? I wanted to fight Allah's war against your Lord within the realm of the Gods, so I committed suicide ..."

"Okay," interrupted Mark, "I get it. Don't want all the gory details."

"No, you don't get it! I wasn't a bomber. I shot myself, knowing my own guilt and sin. I seized a window of opportunity."

"Sin? If not a bomber, then what?"

"So you do want to feed your curiosity with the details?"

"I guess so," admitted Mark.

"My mother was not dead after the soldiers had finished with her. I wept and called her a Western whore ..."

"Um, that's bad ..."

"Ha! That's not all."

"Oh!"

"I killed her and faced her towards the West. You see what your empire-seeking generals have done, Mark? I was just one case. Think of the many thousands that feel as I do."

"No doubt ..."

"Now, kneel before me."

Before Mark could obey Rashid's deadly instruction, a shot rang out and a bullet penetrated his body. Mark cried out in burning pain, falling to the holy ground flat on his back. He looked around, confused.

"No!" shouted Rashid in frustration. "It was meant to be I who accompanied him into the vortex, as my servant, deliverer of my wrath."

Mark's pain began to ease. Who the hell is he shouting at, he wondered. Shit! Malik? Mark noticed a pair of brown leather shoes appear next to him. He looked up and saw another gun pointing at him, and then looked beyond the hand. "Guy?" he struggled to say. "Fucking Guy! Why? Not that it matters: I've been shot before and ..."

"Never mind that now," said Guy. "I know all about it."

Mark groaned.

"Don't worry, it'll pass," informed Guy.

"Glad to hear it," mocked Mark, "even though you're a liar just like him."

"Liar?"

"You're a damn virtual. I've known all along. So how can you shoot me?"

"It's not about lying, Mark," explained Guy. "It's all to do with the programming at the time in question ... like now. Besides, it's not to kill you, is it?"

"So why you?"

"Rashid has to remain pure, so his vengeance must be delivered by others. Also, I can't allow you to serve him. You are with me ... with us."

The questions and reasoning milling around Mark's mind faded into the background as he struggled to keep his eyes open.

Rashid pointed his gun at Guy. "I ought to kill you."

Guy smiled and lit a cigarette. He inhaled, then exhaled. "You won't, Rashid. Oh, you would like to all right, but you won't. Both you and I know that you have to remain without blood on your hands ... because it is God's way. That is why you have Malik. Where is he, by the way?"

"He's up the road ... in Allah's house."

"Of course! He's too evil to be in here." Guy inhaled more smoke, exhaling it again through his nostrils. He looked down at Mark and kicked him lightly in the ribcage. "He's on his way, Rashid. The transformation will soon be here. The Lord will work his magic, which I'm sure you don't want to be caught up in."

Rashid angled the gun once more at Guy. "I'm so close to pulling the trigger, even though it may not have any effect."

Guy tutted repeatedly.

"You appear so confident that I won't have you terminated. Why is that?"

"I support the late Zealot ..."

"Ah!" exclaimed Rashid, and then he smiled with realisation. "Um ... You also want vengeance against your Lord. Be careful: you may face the spear of Christ ..."

"And you, or Allah," contradicted Guy.

"Don't worry, Guy. We are safe: we're only servants. Allah and the Lord will have their time in space: a one-to-one battle to decide the fate of East and West."

"I fear that that is a long way off," said Guy, glancing down at Mark. "Mandeville's time has yet to run its course."

"You are right," contemplated Rashid. "The Lord's Second Coming to find the easy way out, to avoid the clash and to reign through the back door. His designs to use military rule to crush the Middle East will not work. Opposition will see to that now that I have been spared. In the end, there will only be one left standing."

A bright light appeared, blinding Guy for a few seconds. Once he had regained his focus, Rashid was gone. He took a last look at Mark. "Safe journey, partner, and I'll see you soon. I'll stay and greet the rest of the pack to welcome them into the plot." Guy took in a deep breath and closed his eyes. After a brief time of analysis, Guy breathed out and opened his eyes. Time to hide, he thought. The mist is on its way.

"Look," said Francombe, relieved. "There's Mark's car."

"And traffic cops," added Fisher.

"Good," responded Francombe. "They can stand guard. Quick, park behind his car."

Fisher looked behind after bringing the car to a halt. "I can't seem to detect the surveillance team, Francombe," he said sarcastically. Maybe they've got lost?"

"Leave it, William," ordered Francombe. "Just go and ask those two for now."

Francombe and Fisher hastily exited the car.

"You two! Over here," shouted Fisher, waving his arm.

"Who are you then?" asked one of the traffic cops arrogantly, as he approached Fisher.

Fisher held up his identification badge. "I'm sure you can recognise this," he said, and waited for an answer. "Well?"

"Yes, sir," observed the traffic cop.

"Good," responded Fisher. "I want you and your mate to stand guard outside the church doors. Understand?"

"Clear as a bell, Sergeant," acknowledged the traffic cop.

"Very funny …"

"Come on, Fisher!"

Francombe and Fisher ran into the church, prepared for any eventuality.

"What's all this?" quizzed Fisher, stopping abruptly and waving his hands.

"Some kind of smoke," answered Francombe.

"Doesn't smell like smoke," observed Fisher.

"That's because it isn't," informed Guy, stepping out from behind a pillar.

"Guy!" exclaimed Francombe. "What …? How …?"

"I can see you're shocked to see me, Francombe," said Guy. "Not as shocked as you appear, though …"

"She's not the only one," interrupted Fisher. "What do you know about this smoke?"

"Mist, Fisher. It's only mist."

"Okay, Guy," conceded Fisher, "if you're sure then I won't call for the fire brigade."

"No," responded Guy, looking at Fisher as if he were the loose screw among them, "there is no need to call anyone."

"Well, something's happened here," noted Fisher. "You look as if you've seen a ghost."

"Not a ghost, William," deduced Francombe, "but something similar, I guess." Francombe looked Guy straight in the eye, thinking about what Mark had told her and weighing up the whole scenario.

"Take your time, Una," advised Guy. "Think about what you see here and how you got here."

"Tracker!" exclaimed Fisher. "Simple really ..."

"I'll ask you not to join in, William," insisted Guy. "For the time being, at least."

Fisher held up his hands and withdrew a few paces. "I'll just listen for now then," he said. "Don't mind me."

Guy focused on Francombe and removed his tinted glasses, briefly rolling his eyes.

"White-eyed," said Francombe softly. "Mark was right. You are a virtual being. But I've known you for so long ..."

"Humans don't catch on unless they know what they're looking for," explained Guy tactfully.

"I have been used, haven't I? And I fell for it."

"Went for it," contradicted Guy. "You couldn't resist, which made things easy."

"Never mind, we're here now," accepted Francombe, and she looked around. "He was here?"

"You know he was, Una," said Fisher. "His car is outside." Fisher noticed Guy's stare. "Sorry, force of habit to butt in."

"It doesn't mean he came in ..."

"You're right, Una," interrupted Guy, "but he did. There's your confirmation."

"So, he went ahead with it?" asked Francombe, knowing the answer.

"Yes."

"You didn't feel the urge to protect him or stop him?"

"Getting cold feet, Francombe?" enquired Guy. "We have what we want: a contact, a spy. Of course I didn't stop him. Don't play the innocent with me, dear lady. Your ambition for the future - your goal - is achieved. We are the same: we want to halt Mandeville and we'll stop at nothing to do so."

"And Rashid? Where is Rashid? Have you dealt with him?"

"He's gone," replied Guy.

"You let him go?"

"Listen!" exclaimed Guy. "I was just here to observe and to see what choice Mark made. You think ..."

"I don't want to accuse you directly," proffered Francombe, becoming suspicious.

"Don't go down that road, Una," responded Guy, reeling her in. If anything, we can all be accused. We're in this together. And now we'll have to work together ..."

Fisher laughed. "What are we? The three musketeers?" he joked.

"Very funny, William," said Guy. "More like waking the dead."

Francombe sighed in disgust. "You two are being too flippant."

"Sorry," apologised Guy. "Poor joke. However, relevant."

"I don't find it funny that we're all privy to murder," remarked Francombe.

"Murder?" exclaimed Guy, emitting a guffaw. "That's a bit strong and melodramatic."

"Well, he had to die to get into the vortex," clarified Francombe. "Also, how do we know he'll not bypass the vortex and actually die?"

"He'll get there," assured Guy. "He's not pure. Besides, his imagination will steer him. Oh! That reminds me." Guy turned his attention towards Fisher and instructed him, "Get rid of those two cops outside. It's important to the plot."

"How did you know ...?"

"Never mind, just do it."

"Okay," retorted Fisher, receiving a nod from Francombe.

"What if he doesn't?" continued Francombe, repeating her question and clearly bothered by the possibility.

"I'll spell it out, Una," replied Guy, "once and for all, seeing as you're more concerned about yourself ..."

"I'm listening."

"It's the perfect crime," continued Guy. "How can you be accused when you're looking at the murdered in the eye and can hear him breathing?"

"Is that what I'm doing now: looking into the eyes of the dead?"

"There you are," confirmed Guy. "You have just convinced yourself that nothing happened here."

"If he comes back!"

"Ah! There lies the risk," teased Guy, impatient with Francombe's guilt. "However, you will be reassured when you leave this place, which should be now."

"Is that your foresight, Guy?"

"Indeed it is," corroborated Guy. "You see, It's an advantage to have allies like Mark, and me. Mandeville will think he's arrested Mark and is free to continue his quest. On the other hand, you have your link to the future ..."

"I've dismissed the traffic cops," announced Fisher, returning inside the church.

"Good," responded Guy. "Time for me to go."

"Where to?"

"It's not for you to know. And - to help you recover from your temporary guilt - out of sight, out of mind. But don't worry, Una. You will see me again." With that, Guy started to walk out of the church.

Francombe shouted after him, "Is your young Muslim friend coming back?"

Guy stopped and turned around to answer Francombe. "He's busy with his virgins," he mocked, "but yes, he'll be back. So, again, your conscience is cleared." Guy resumed his exit and disappeared.

Fisher looked around. "He's right," he said, "it's as if nothing happened here."

"Only in our minds, William," replied Francombe. "We have to deal with our conscience."

"Not in this job, Una," reminded Fisher. "Anyway, let's get out of here. I'm starting to get the shivers."

Francombe and Fisher left the church and headed towards their squad car. "I'll be a ..."

"What is it, William?" asked Francombe, with a sigh.

Mark's car ... it's gone!"

Francombe's spirits lightened and she smiled. "He's back ..."

"Or he never went," disputed Fisher. It doesn't prove ..."

"I think so, Sergeant," interrupted Francombe, believing she'd been freed from her guilt. "I'm sure of it."

"So, back to the tracking system?" queried Fisher, sounding indifferent.

No, William," answered Francombe. "We'll rest. Drop me off at home, and then you go home. We'll check up on him later when our heads are slightly clearer. We know where he lives."

"Okay, Detective Inspector," conceded Fisher. "Only ... one thing is bugging me."

"What's that?"

"I feel that Guy has a different agenda."

Mark noticed Cara walking his way as he parked the car in the university campus's car park. He got out of the car to greet her. Thank God! he thought. She's safe.

"There you are!" exclaimed Cara. "You're a bit late. Was there a lot of traffic or something?"

"Something like that," replied Mark. "Some kind of movement anyway."

"Eh?"

"Oh, don't mind me," commented Mark. "My mind is wandering. Besides, I'm just glad you're safe."

"Why shouldn't I be?" asked Cara, slightly bewildered.

"Just generalising, darling ... no worries."

"You'll have to stop thinking about your book, Dad," guessed Cara. "That's why your mind is all over the place. You ought to be careful: you'll start thinking it's your reality." Cara laughed. "I know, take a break for Christmas. Enjoy me being at home."

"Yes, darling, I always do," smiled Mark. "Um, I will. And get ready for work again."

"Oh, you just can't help it, can you?" accused Cara, in fun.

Mark sighed. "No, I suppose I can't. Anyway, where's your stuff?"

"Of course, I nearly forgot ..."

"How can you forget ...?" Mark grimaced, and then carried on talking. "How can you forget your bags, Car?"

"Are you sure you're okay, Dad?"

"Um, just a twinge in my chest," replied Mark, trying to rub away the pain. "Indigestion, I guess."

"You're run down, Dad," diagnosed Cara.

"Whatever! So, your bags?"

"I can't get them yet," informed Cara. Then a sudden realisation hit her. "Is that why you asked me if I was safe? ... But how could you have known?"

"Known what?"

"There's some kind of incident going on in my block. The security guard wouldn't let me in. He told me to come back later or leave it altogether. Doesn't matter: it's just bits and pieces that I can manage without. It's only for a couple of weeks after all."

"If you're sure," responded Mark, "then we can get going. Besides, we can always come back."

"We'll see," said Cara. "So, did you know?"

"Know what?"

"About the incident."

"I can't remember," contemplated Mark. "Must've been told on the way in, I imagine."

"Blimey, Dad!"

"Sorry, darling," said Mark, directing Cara to the car. "I'll be okay once I'm back home and feeling more settled."

Mark and Cara climbed into the car. Mark secured his seat belt and then paused before starting the engine. He sighed as the feeling of pain in his chest began to subside. Thank God for that, he thought.

"Let's go then," urged Cara loudly, "before there are any more hold-ups. Mum will be waiting."

Mark smiled, started the engine and embarked on the route home.

Chapter 18

Virtual being, Cunningham, approached Mandeville's throne on the bridge of Seeker One and announced, "Mark is inside the vaults and hooked up to his terminal, which is now programmed to control his virtual being."

Mandeville remained silent with his eyes closed.

"That's good news," resounded a voice from behind Cunningham.

Cunningham turned around and gazed at the fearful sight of virtual being, Mandeville, standing in his full military attire. Cunningham's jaw dropped silently.

"A sight for sore eyes, Cunningham," said Mandeville, steeped in self-righteousness. "Yes, I'm my, younger, self again. It's time to go home; go back to the presidential retreat and assume command. God! Can you imagine the faces of Lieutenant General Burrows and Major General Anderson?"

Cunningham remained silent.

"Lost for words, Cunningham?" spouted Mandeville. "Still, understandably so." Mandeville looked at his encased human self on the throne. "Serve me well, my human form," he ordered.

The Mandeville's human form nodded slowly.

"Now," said the virtual Mandeville abruptly towards virtual Cunningham, "show me to the terminal occupied by the human, Mark."

"This way, General G. Mandeville," instructed Cunningham, regaining his virtual senses.

Mandeville followed, marching with expectancy.

Mandeville and Cunningham entered an escalator, which began its descent to the vaults after a voice command from Cunningham. Soon the escalator smoothly came to a halt. "Vault area," sounded a calming female voice. The doors opened, revealing a vast space populated by uncountable computer terminal places occupied by human forms equipped with an array of wires and plugs leading to the terminals.

Mandeville exited the escalator. "It's nice to hear the voice of a former mistress, Cunningham. Don't you think so?"

"Whatever turns you on, General."

"Get over it, Cunningham," demanded Mandeville. "Be gracious in defeat."

"Sure!" exclaimed Cunningham. "It's just dandy being your servant."

"Humour will do, I suppose," remarked Mandeville, and he moved forward with extended arms. "Ah, my children, my comrades, who control the past and present. A sight to behold, a sight to be proud of, which oozes confidence for my military dictatorship. Mandeville relaxed his arms and turned his head to face Cunningham. "Where is he? Where is my creator?"

"Where you requested, General," replied Cunningham. "At the head of all the terminals, smack bang in the middle, at the Oval Table as you call it."

"Excellent," said Mandeville, returning his gaze ahead. "Leave us, Cunningham. And instruct the human Mandeville to prepare for my energising."

"Yes, sir," said Cunningham, saluting and then boarding the escalator to return to the bridge.

Mandeville made his way to the Oval Table where he stood tall, close to the human, Mark. Mandeville allowed himself a gratifying laugh. "I played you like a 'finely tuned fiddle', Mark," he gloated. "Remember? I think I've quoted that correctly. Just nod if you understand me. A virtual being has the same language. But, of course, you know that." Mandeville looked Mark directly in the face. "Well, I'm waiting."

Mark managed a brief nod, uncomfortable with his surroundings.

"Good," said Mandeville, satisfied. "As with your nod, I'll keep this brief - a brief briefing, you might say." Mandeville laughed again. "Sorry, you can't," he added, and then he paused to gather his composure. Eventually he continued, "So here we are, Mark, my creator. You should have stopped when you had the chance - you know, back in the Oval Office - and killed me off for good. Curiosity is a weakness, Mark, so you wanted more to write about. Are you keeping up with me?"

Mark proffered another strained nod.

"You gave me a second chance, for which I'm very grateful. And so should you be, wanting to know what is going to happen. Is that why it was easy to get you here? Too easy, on reflection. One could be suspicious, Mark. Nevertheless, I can't imagine that you deliberately allowed yourself to be killed off. Who knows? One will just have to wait and see. At least we know the story so far. Are you with me still?"

Mark gave a much more detectable nod.

"Ah! I see you're getting the hang of it. These surroundings will become more comfortable the more you bed in. So, where do we go from here? Well,

I'm off to my rightful place down there. I imagine you know what I mean. To get my house in order, as well as yours. Our timing is perfect, Mark. Christmas is a perfect time to expect a Second Coming on Earth. Should I thank you for that? Still, it's all a game, Mark, and the next level will be the downfall of your government with the help of the one who stole your soul. Not that she knows it yet ..."

Mark emitted a sigh of frustration.

"Hit a chord, didn't she? She was my ace, the one I knew would get to you. Anyway, coming back to the future, I also have to clear up the Middle East, or had you forgotten? Burrows has made a mess of the place. Oh, and of course Hope and Glory, which is aptly named, as mine will be the glory."

Mark's eyes fixed a stare on Mandeville.

"That's right, Mark. Mine will be the glory now that I have my creator under my control. And, to put your mind at rest, your virtuality is doing so well back home." Mandeville guffawed. "It's a win, win, win situation. Don't you agree? I'm free to continue my own imagination that leads to reality."

Mark kept his stare focused on Mandeville and winked.

"Um ..." pondered Mandeville. "Well, that's my brief for now. I could ... chat? Yes, that's what you lot say. I could stay and chat forever, Mark, but needs must. See you around, buddy."

Mark's gaze followed Mandeville closely until he disappeared from view. The bedding-in process began to accelerate, which allowed Mark to concentrate on his first thought: one day, Mandeville, now that I'm here, as one with my terminal and in control of my virtual being.

Epilogue

"Hello, Mark," said Kevin, observing Mark swiping his clocking-on card from behind the counter. "Did you have a good holiday over Christmas?"

"Yes," replied Mark. "Managed to get things done, and finish my book."

"Glad to hear it," replied Kevin, looking up from his paperwork. I'm sorry about the mix-up. Computers, you know. Wrong information."

"Well, it's all cleared up now," interrupted Mark diplomatically. "I was in such a state that I totally forgot I was on holiday. And as for my wife, I even told her that I had a publishing contract to cover up. Still, everything is explained, controlled and hunky-dory."

"I imagine you have," suggested Kevin.

"Have what?"

"A contract," confirmed Kevin, smiling. "Erm, Network Publishing?"

Mark looked through the protective window directly at Kevin. "Well, I'll be damned! You were - are - white-eyed ..."

"You needed a push."

Mark thought about the day he was given the elbow from work and what he now knew. "You had no ..."

"Shush," interrupted Kevin, while a colleague passed behind him.

"No glasses," continued Mark, observing the colleague out of earshot.

Kevin smiled again. "How the fuck would you know? That was the whole point. The beginning of Mandeville's scheme. I was fucking ..."

"I see you haven't lost your charm," commented Mark, interrupting the outpouring of further obscenities. "Maybe you should be reprogrammed."

"I was," continued Kevin, "so that I could roll the eyes white. I was one of the first."

Mark remained silent. He's one of his spies, he thought. God! Suspicious bastard! Mark stared at Kevin, knowing he had to reciprocate.

"So, how's the new book coming on?" probed Kevin.

"I've imagined the start for it," answered Mark nonchalantly. "I just need to get my mind in order. Bed in, you might say." Mark continued focusing his stare on Kevin, smiled and rolled his eyes, which appeared white. "However, that will be another story, Kevin."

226

"Good!" exclaimed Kevin. "I look forward to it. Glad you escaped the red-eyed: wouldn't have suited you."

Mark grinned, unimpressed, and reverted back to his normal eye colour of blue.

"So," deduced Kevin, "you'll be wanting more time off work?"

"How about permanently?"

"No fucking chance, arsehole," answered Kevin. "You need this job for cover."

"I imagine I will, Kevin," goaded Mark, tired of the conversation. "See you later: I imagine I've got a bus to catch."